Murder on the Silver Screen

A Clara Fitzgerald Mystery

Evelyn James

Red Raven Publications 2025
www.sophie-jackson.com

Contents

Chapter One	1
Chapter Two	10
Chapter Three	19
Chapter Four	25
Chapter Five	35
Chapter Six	44
Chapter Seven	53
Chapter Eight	62
Chapter Nine	71
Chapter Ten	81
Chapter Eleven	90
Chapter Twelve	99
Chapter Thirteen	107
Chapter Fourteen	116
Chapter Fifteen	125
Chapter Sixteen	134
Chapter Seventeen	143
Chapter Eighteen	152

Chapter Nineteen	161
Chapter Twenty	170
Chapter Twenty-One	180
Chapter Twenty-Two	188
Chapter Twenty-Three	197
Chapter Twenty-Four	206
Chapter Twenty-Five	216
Chapter Twenty-Six	224
Chapter Twenty-Seven	231
Chapter Twenty-Eight	240
Enjoyed this Book?	251
The Clara Fitzgerald Series	252
The Gentleman Detective	255
About the Author	257
Copyright	258

Chapter One

T he movies had come to Brighton.

It was early spring 1925, and everybody in town was talking about the fact that the movie company Silverlight Screen Sensations had descended to Brighton to film their latest silent film. The working title was 'Love and Despair,' and the rumour around town was that it was a movie about espionage, and that the main stars were double agents working against each other without realising it. Excitement was over boiling in the area, as people wondered whether they might be able to get roles either in front of the camera or behind the scenes. They had heard stories about movies needing extras, surely there would be scenes where it be helpful to have locals milling around just like they would on a regular day?

Big lorries arrived in Brighton on a Sunday. It proved to be one of the better Sundays of that spring, with the sunshine glossing the town with its orange light, and the skies for once not overcast and grey. There was just the slightest hint of summer on that day, and the promise of better times to come.

The lorries drove through town, heading towards the large green at the far end where normally the fairs would be held. Now, instead of merry-go-rounds, and coconut shies, there was now a baffling array of props, backdrops and people milling backwards and forwards, doing all manner of inexplicable tasks.

For instance, there was a fellow who was creating dummies made out of straw and cloth, which seemed to represent a body. This observation lead to immense speculation among the populace as to what they were for.

There were enormous camera units, which looked like oversized machine guns with their giant lenses. Then there was a strange crane device with a seat on it, which no one could quite explain the purpose of. Why would anybody wish to be lifted up on such a device unless it was like one of the fairground rides with which they were more familiar?

In this tumult of change, anybody who had the slightest knowledge about how movies worked, no matter how vague or incomplete, was doted upon like they were an oracle. Anyone who could sound authoritative about what was going on, was bought pints in the pub, fawned over in the street, and generally became the centre of attention. This led to a few strange stories circulating around, such as that the cameras ran on steam power, and the whole filming process would be done using a series of still photographs such as you found in a Magic Lantern, which would then be spliced together to create a moving picture.

Despite these errors, the excitement in the town was palpable, and the closer people could get to those in charge of making the movie, the happier they became. The local baker beamed at everybody who came in his shop and proudly told them how he had a regular order for pastries to be taken to the film set every day.

Several of the local hairdressers found themselves being called in to assist with getting the cast's hair to look as was desired. While Miss Mavis at the library bragged that she had the film director walk into the building and had ask her if he could use the premises for one of the scenes. This swiftly led to other rumours about similar places that were going to be used by the movie company to film the latest production.

Anywhere the director of the film, or any of his team, wandered, people watched them and speculated on whether they were choosing a new setting. Whether they happened to walk into the local pharmacy, or into the local church, everybody began to talk about how there must be a scene in the film where such a place was necessary. Before filming had even begun, there was a running theory in town of exactly how it would play out scene by scene.

As for the movie team themselves, they tried to keep things as under wraps as possible about what they were doing. They arrived a full week ahead of the cast to set up their equipment. The director and the producer were among them, priming people about where they were going to go on which day. There was a strict schedule that they had to follow to ensure that the film was produced on time. They did their best to ignore the curious locals.

None of this commotion particularly disturbed Clara O'Harris (*nee* Fitzgerald); her life was busy enough without worrying about a movie being made in the town. She was part of the committee for the preservation of the Brighton Pavilion, and they had been asked if they would allow filming to occur within the confines of that particular historic building. Clara had been outvoted in the subsequent proceedings, and the committee had agreed that this would be not only delightful, but practical. They would be paid a small fee for allowing the premises to be used, and afterwards the pavilion would appear on screen, and with any luck, people might see it and choose to come and visit. The pavilion depended upon visitors making donations to keep it afloat, and it was always eating up money. The plaster work was peeling, the ceilings sagging, and the overly ornate and fanciful décor was, in general, falling into decay. The elaborate structure had not been built to last, and that was now becoming apparent.

Clara's objections to having the movie makers use the property were based on her prior experiences with renting out the premises. People, in her opinion, could be appallingly negligent when it came to causing damage in historic places. The usual visitors were bad enough, (putting out cigarettes on the banisters, shaking wet umbrellas over hand painted wallpaper) but she had a hunch film makers would be much worse. While she had no working knowledge of how movies were made, she had briefly gone past the large green on her way to the committee meeting, and had witnessed the amount of cumbersome machinery waiting there to be used. The large cameras, bulbous lights, cranes, pulleys, and other devices, all looked capable of knocking off plaster, tearing wallpaper and scratching the wooden floorboards.

Besides, they had only recently had a discussion with a conservation expert on textiles, who said that it would be best if the wallpaper and soft furnishings in the pavilion were not exposed to bright light, to save them from fading even further than they already had. What would he say about those vast lights with their great big bulbs that must spew out immense illumination and heat?

While Clara was feeling aggrieved by the presence of the movie makers, and feared what they might do to her beloved pavilion, her brother, Tommy, was over the moon to see them in town. Something of a movie buff himself, he regularly went to the pictures and liked to see all the newest releases. He not only recognised the names of the main cast who were coming to Brighton, but also the names of the director, producer, and the writer. If people had really wanted accurate information about how movies worked, and the people involved, they would have been best off to speak to him. He could have told them that the man crafting dummies out of straw and cloth was clearly making inanimate stunt doubles for the stars. There must be a scene in the film where someone had to fall from a great distance, and they would throw a dummy rather than an actual person. He would have told them that the crane arm with its seat on the end was for the director, so he could get high above the scene being filmed when he needed to. And he would have explained that the cameras ran on electricity and required their operators to turn the handles of the machine at a set speed to correctly film the process. A skilled task, which was not to be dismissed as simply mundane manual labour, for only a steady consistent speed would produce a film of the quality that was to be expected.

But no one asked Tommy Fitzgerald about what was going on, and he was largely distracted from offering his opinion by the condition of his wife, Annie.

Annie Fitzgerald was pregnant, and in the early months of that pregnancy. As she would happily say to anyone who would listen to her, she was perfectly capable of carrying on as she had always done, but Tommy would not hear of it. If he caught her scrubbing the front step, he made her get up and sit down in the drawing room while he went back and did the scrubbing himself. If he found her bent over the washing tub, rubbing hard at his shirts, he again moved her out of the way and took up the task himself. In fact, any hard labour that he caught her at, he would shuffle her away, make her sit down, and fuss around her with cups of tea. The end result was that he was driving Annie slightly crazy, but he refused to change. He felt she wasn't taking her pregnancy seriously enough and just wanted her to be a little bit more careful.

The Sunday afternoon following the first arrival of the big lorries, Annie was debating the situation she found herself in with Clara, at the Home for Convalescing Ex-servicemen that Captain O'Harris, Clara's husband, ran. Clara listened with a sympathetic ear as they ate fish paste sandwiches and drank tea.

"I can't stand all this fussing," Annie informed her old friend.

Clara and Annie had known each other for years. They had met in the hospital during the war; Annie had been a patient there, having just survived an unfortunate Zeppelin raid that had resulted in the deaths of her parents and the complete destruction of her home. Clara had been working as a nurse, though her effectiveness was often placed into question due to a violent aversion to blood. She was prone to fainting at the sight of a bleeding wound. She had mastered the shortcoming now, but at the time it was both inconvenient and embarrassing.

She had volunteered to become an auxiliary nurse at the hospital, to give her something to do while Tommy was away serving his country, and also to feel as though she was playing her part. Her own parents had been killed in London in another Zeppelin raid, and she was feeling truly alone. Working at the hospital was a welcome distraction.

That was how they had met, Annie and Clara realising they could both be useful to each other. Annie needed a place to live, and a reason to keep going. After her tragic loss she had fallen into a state of depression, which had brought her close to taking her own life. Clara was anticipating the return of her older brother, who was being invalided out of France after taking a bullet that had stripped him of his ability to walk.

MURDER ON THE SILVER SCREEN

Between their shared tragedies they found common ground, and Clara invited Annie to join her at home and to help her take care of Tommy. Annie was in essence to be a nursemaid to the young man, seeing as Clara would need to continue to do something to supply the household with an income and could not be at home all day. It did not take long, however, for Annie to become their housekeeper and devoted friend to the Fitzgeralds.

Now Annie was married to Tommy and would soon be a mother. Clara was contemplating what it would be like to be an auntie, finding the notion both alarming and delightful.

She had married Captain O'Harris the previous year and no longer lived in the same home with Annie and Tommy, but that did not stop them from spending considerable amounts of time with each other. Clara foresaw that once the baby arrived, they would spend even more time together.

"He is driving me up the wall," Annie explained to her friend and sister-in-law.

"He is simply worrying about you, and the baby," Clara replied.

Only she knew how deep the anxiety in her brother truly ran. He had been worried for the longest time that he was incapable of having children, developing a deep fear that something about the war wound he had suffered would mean he was now essentially sterile. The news of Annie being pregnant seemed to him some sort of miracle, and that made him all the more intent on fussing around her.

"Try to be patient with him," Clara suggested.

Annie pulled a face at her.

"He is disrupting my routine," she said folding her arms across her chest, in a manner that said more about her feelings on the subject than the words themselves.

"That is not his intention, Annie, he just wants you to be well."

"I *am* well," Annie huffed. "He treats me like I'm made of bone China and could break at any moment. Even the doctor has told me to keep going about my usual routine, and that I don't have to change anything."

"Try to just enjoy the peace and quiet of it all," Clara suggested. "Once the baby comes you will be too busy to sit down and have a cup of tea."

"You say that as if I make a habit of sitting around drinking tea," Annie said now looking at Clara sternly. "You know full well that I am a busy person, and I don't just sit still, I can't think of anything worse or more boring."

Clara had a feeling she wasn't going to win her over, and suspected she would need to have a quiet word with her brother and explain that he was doing more harm than good with his attentions to his wife. When it came to compromises, Tommy was likely to be more amenable than Annie, especially when it came to his wife being allowed to do as she pleased in the kitchen.

She was offering Annie another sandwich, when they heard footsteps outside the door, and someone knocked hard. Clara called for the person to enter, and Private Peterson appeared around the door.

"Some fancy cars just turned up in the town centre," he told them eagerly. "I was cycling back from the paper shop, and I saw them all arrive. They are the fanciest cars you have ever seen, even fancier than the ones Captain O'Harris has in his garages. One is a brilliant silver colour with a hood ornament in the shape of a woman with robes flying all around her. I think it could be that the cast of the movie have finally arrived. I am telling everybody."

He departed from the door as swiftly as he had arrived.

Peterson was one of the men recuperating at O'Harris' home but, more recently, he had taken up a role where he assisted new arrivals with their own recuperation and recovery. By welcoming new men into the house, and making sure they had all they needed, along with being an informal shoulder to cry on, he was helping others while also continuing his own recovery. Peterson had been one of the hardest patients O'Harris had had to deal with. When he first arrived, the home was his last hope for improvement. He was doing better, but he wasn't quite ready to break ties with the home. He was now living in a small house a few streets away, to give him a modicum of independence, but he returned to the home every day to assist there. It was a compromise that seemed to be working, and which gave hope that, ultimately, Peterson would be able to live a fully independent life.

"I am not sure about all this movie business in town," Annie gave a derisive snort at the news that Peterson had brought them. "It just seems to disrupt regular life."

"It's a little bit of excitement for the town," Clara shrugged at her. "I suppose I shall get myself involved in it sooner rather than later when they turn up at the pavilion to film."

"You would be best to stay out of it," Annie said firmly. "This whole movie business, these famous stars, it'll all end in tears you know. The only thing they will bring to this town is trouble and disrepute."

Chapter Two

Tommy Fitzgerald did not share his wife's opinion on the movie makers in the town. He was excited about their presence, and he had been fortunate to be walking the dogs when he saw the expensive luxury cars that heralded the arrival of the main cast members. Immediately changing the direction he was walking, he hastened to follow them, desperate to see who would appear from the cars when they arrived at their destination.

The cars were heading to the *Grand Hotel*, one of the nicest hotels along the seafront, and also one of the most expensive. With Pip and Bramble, Tommy's Labrador, and miniature poodle, eagerly anticipating that they would get a run on the beach now they had come in this direction, Tommy hastened to follow the cars. They were not driving fast, which was lucky for him because these days his running abilities were not what they once were. His war wound meant that though he could jog along, he quickly felt the pull in his hip, and in the uncertain months of early spring the dampness tended to make him stiff. He would be better when the summer months came, and he would even be quite competent when he got back to playing on the cricket team in the warmer parts of the year, but hurrying along the seafront when there was a chill breeze blowing off the ocean was not the easiest for him.

The cars stopped, one behind the other, alongside the pavement outside the hotel. It seemed that they had been expected; the porter at the front door was wearing his long dark coat, and fancy hat with gold trim, as he calmly walked down the front steps to open the door of the first car. A woman emerged from the back seat wrapped in a long fur coat, which she pulled slightly tighter around her neck as she felt the chill from the sea blowing across her.

She cast her eyes around, first at the hotel facade, then back towards the sea which was looking at its grey and murky best on that particular day. Unlike the Sunday when the lorries had turned up, this one felt more like the usual seaside spring day. The clouds were laden with rain, the air felt damp, and there was a strong possibility that anyone out without an umbrella would shortly be drenched to the skin.

Giving a dainty shudder, the woman turned her blonde curled head back towards the hotel and accepted the arm of the porter as he escorted her up to the front door. Tommy recognised her as Violet Starling, an aspiring actress who had already appeared in several prominent films. The usual magazines were touting that her career would be both spectacular and extensive, and there were rumours that she had walked out on the arms of a number of her leading men. She was still only in her early twenties but was both wealthy and respected within the film community. She was even said to have dabbled in a little bit of directing.

Tommy was a little starstruck by her appearance. Only last winter he had watched her latest flick, where she had been the heroine trying to escape from an evil scientist who was attempting to reproduce the experiments of Dr Frankenstein, though on this occasion his interests were in producing his own woman rather than a monster. Scenes from that movie now tumbled through Tommy's head as he watched Violet enter the hotel and he gave a slight sigh to himself. Who would have thought he would be standing there, looking upon the woman who had beamed out at him from that silver screen?

The driver of the first car now carefully moved it along the pavement to enable the second car to pull up directly in front of the hotel. With Violet through the doors, and presumably being attended to by the hotel manager, the porter now returned to open the passenger door of the second car. This car was a glossy silver colour, chrome from head to foot, and Tommy cringed at the thought of what one tiny scratch could do to that impressive body work. He had no doubt it was an expensive vehicle to begin with, and with the addition of such a finish, it made it even more luxurious and extravagant.

When the porter opened the back door, he allowed a man to step out who Tommy recognised immediately as Joshua Mackenzie, another famous film star and a popular leading man. Mackenzie had featured in all the best films of the period; it was said if you wanted your picture to be a success, you employed Mackenzie. People would go to the pictures to see it just because he was in it. He was smoking a pipe as he stood on the pavement and turning up the collar of his long black coat. Unlike Violet, he made no attempt to look around his surroundings, merely tucked himself deeper into his coat, hands going into his pockets, as he clenched his pipe between his teeth, and followed the porter as quickly as he could up the steps. With his passenger gone, the driver of the exquisite silver car drove off as well; where it was intended to park these two luxury vehicles Tommy didn't know, but he was certain it must be somewhere where they would be both safe and well sheltered from the elements.

Tommy loitered on the pavement for a while longer to see if anybody reappeared, then splatters of rain convinced him that it was probably time to go home. The dogs were not impressed with this decision and Pip pulled pointedly towards the beach just beyond the seafront. Reluctantly, because Tommy was already feeling the spits of rain going through his coat, he decided to indulge the dogs and clipped off their leads so they could scamper across the sand. By the time they had finished with their antics on the beach, they were all soaked through, and Tommy wandered home looking forward to getting before the fire in the parlour and warming himself.

That evening, an emergency meeting was called at the *Brighton Gazette* headquarters. The arrival of the movie stars was news that couldn't wait to be dealt with the following morning, and a late-night edition was planned to avoid being overtaken by any of the national newspapers. The editor of the *Gazette* was well aware that newspapermen from all the main publications had descended on the town to keep their eyes on events; if he wanted to be ahead of the game, he needed to have his people working night and day to cover everything that happened.

Among those he had summoned was Gilbert McMillan, one of his top journalists, at least according to Gilbert. Gilbert was also one of the sneakiest and most underhand of the men who worked at the paper. If anybody could get the best gossip about the stars who had arrived in Brighton, it would surely be him. He was taken to one side by the editor while the first run of the late-night edition was quickly put together.

"McMillan, we need to be on the ball with this one," the editor said firmly. "You need to be ahead of everyone else, if one of those stars sneezes, I want to know about it before anybody in London does. I won't lie, this is going to be a difficult task, and I am quite prepared for you to play dirty to get us the scoop we want."

Another man might have been uneasy about this suggestion, but Gilbert McMillan didn't even blink.

"Don't worry about it boss, I will make sure you have all the news first off. I'm sure I can find plenty of ways to get the other fellows distracted and running in different directions to the way they should be going. I have the nose for this sort of news."

Gilbert tapped the side of his rather large nose. He was a fairly ugly fellow, with ears that jutted out from the sides of his head and nicotine-stained teeth. You couldn't imagine him being anything other than perhaps a fence for criminals or a newspaperman. He didn't seem to have the face for a respectable job. But, right then, he was exactly the man his editor needed.

"Go to it, Gilbert, and don't come back until you've got some decent news for me."

With a pat on the back from his editor, Gilbert departed from the offices of the *Brighton Gazette* and headed straight for the *Grand Hotel*. There he would find himself a means to get inside and ferret out the latest news ahead of everyone else. He happened to know one of the young men who worked in the hotel, and was hopeful that he would assist him.

Not expecting to return to his own bed for some time, he would have to make the best of things, camping out somewhere in the bowels of the hotel, in the service areas where he could disappear from any prying eyes. Gilbert was excited about the possibility of what he was doing, he felt just like a spy in one of the movies Joshua Mackenzie had featured in. It all seemed like something of a game to him, and he couldn't wait for that game to begin.

That night a storm raged around Brighton. It was more than a mere spring squall and seemed to have stirred straight out of the winter as it rattled the windowpanes. Clara was wrenched from her sleep by the howling of the wind around the chimneys and sat up in bed. Captain O'Harris was lying beside her, oblivious to the tempest that was raging in his garden. Clara felt a strange sense of unease as she watched the rain hammering down outside the window, the curtains not being fully drawn. Clara liked the dawn sunlight to filter in through them in the mornings.

She wondered how all the great big tents that had been set up on the green would be holding up in this storm. With no suitable location in the town to store all their vast equipment, the tents had been erected as a means of sheltering everything and everyone. She could imagine those canvas walls pulling at the pegs that held them into the ground, and the concern of the men in charge of them that the wind might simply whip away the tents and fling them into the sea. She was glad she was in a house and not outside on a night like that.

Feeling quite wide awake, Clara decided to head downstairs and make herself a hot drink rather than attempt to go back to sleep just yet. She would only lay there and listen to the storm outside. Being careful not to disturb her husband, she found her dressing gown and her slippers and inched her way quietly down the staircase. She was just passing the nook beneath the stairs, which had been set up to house the telephone, when the object in question started to ring unexpectedly.

The tinny ringing of the telephone's bell seemed to echo around the front hall, and Clara froze at the sound of it. She half expected other people to start appearing, assuming there was some calamity to explain why the phone was ringing at such an hour, but no one else appeared. Now feeling slightly uneasy, she lifted up the receiver of the telephone and put it to her ear. Her jaw tense, because she assumed the worst and feared that she might hear either Tommy or Annie's voice on the other end of the line, she spoke into the mouthpiece.

"Hello?"

"Thank goodness, that would be Mrs O'Harris, would it?"

"Speaking," Clara said wondering who would be seeking her out at this time of night.

"I apologise about the late hour, but this is the first moment I've had to myself to be able to contact you. Look, I can't go into too much detail over the telephone, but I am deeply concerned about my well-being."

"You have my attention," Clara said. "Might I enquire who I am speaking to?"

"I would prefer not to state my name over the phone either. Do you know how easy it is for people to overhear conversations on the telephone? I've learned that the hard way. But I would like to meet you, if that would be possible?"

It was not the first time Clara had someone speak to her in such a surreptitious manner and wish to seek her out secretly. All she could tell from the voice on the other end of the telephone line, was that it was female, and from the tremble in it, it did suggest that whoever was speaking was truly worried. Clara never backed away from a call for help, and she immediately made-up her mind that she would assist whoever it was who had called her in the dead of night.

"I am quite prepared to meet you, do you have a time and place in mind?"

"I was hoping you could suggest somewhere private, somewhere that no one would be able to see us speaking? It's important that no one recognises me."

"Then, perhaps the best thing would be for you to come to my office," Clara suggested. "It's very private, and easy to find."

"No, I can't do that, if someone saw me go into your office, they would know what I was up to. I have to assume that the people who are after me are fully aware that you are a private detective and that I might seek you out. I have to be more careful than that."

"You perhaps give your pursuers too much credit, only people in Brighton who have sought out my services actually know where my office is. But if you are truly opposed to that idea, might I suggest that we meet somewhere where it is both public, but we can also be private? That way we can see if anyone is pursuing you."

"Where would that be?" The woman asked her voice virtually dropped to a whisper.

"Why not come to the pier? There is a teashop near the end, it opened up quite recently. If you walk along the new pier, you'll be able to see if anyone is following you because there's nowhere for anybody to hide. However, the teashop at this time of year is pretty quiet, and we can find a table in the corner, next to the windows, and speak there privately. What do you say?"

There was silence on the line and Clara half wondered if her enquirer had put down the phone, then the voice came back in a strangled whisper, barely audible.

"I have to go now, but I will take you up on your suggestion. I will meet you at the teashop on the end of the pier, would 9 o'clock be too early?"

"If 9 o'clock suits you I shall be there," Clara promised her.

The woman gave out a long sigh, it was difficult to say if it was a sigh of relief, or of despair. Clara wondered just who was on the other end of the line, and why they supposed their life was in such peril. The speaker didn't sound all that old, and it was a terrible thing to consider that such a young person would believe themselves to be hunted.

"Until tomorrow," the woman spoke and then she put down the receiver.

Clara put her own telephone receiver down and considered what had just happened. Who had just spoken to her, seeking her out in the dead of night? Only time would tell, and she anticipated the morning meeting keenly. But there would be several hours of darkness before it was time to head to the pier, and Clara would have to do something to while them away. Now too wide awake to even consider sleep, she headed to the kitchen nonetheless to make herself a hot milk drink.

What new mystery would she find herself engaged in tomorrow? And just how accurate was her midnight caller's fears that she was being hunted?

Chapter Three

The following morning, bright and early, Clara set off for the pier. She had mentioned nothing to Captain O'Harris about her plans, other than that she was meeting with a friend. Something about the telephone conversation the night before caused her to feel the need to be circumspect with what she said, even to her husband.

There was a part of her that even wondered if it had been some sort of weird dream, induced by the strange storm and her wandering about in the dark. Might she have briefly dozed off and imagined the entire thing? If so, she did not want anyone to know about it.

The other thought that troubled her was that the person contacting her was the one who was hallucinating. The woman had sounded sane on the telephone, other than being in a severe state of nerves due to her anxiety, but could Clara be certain she was not actually someone who was paranoid and delusional?

Clara did not normally question her client's motives in such a manner, but the oddness of her summons, coupled with the lack of any clear proof the woman was in danger made her doubt herself.

The only thing to do was head to the pier and see who turned up.

Brighton's newest pier was only a handful of years old and had been built to replace the one that had been lost in the war. A combination of severe storms, war damage and a fear that the old pier could be used as a landing point by the enemy, had resulted in the structure being partly demolished and then allowed to succumb to the ocean. But a seaside town without a pier is like a church without a pulpit – fundamentally lacking. The new pier had been built with high ambitions and stretched out gracefully into the waves. Some had questioned the integrity of the design, and whether it would survive a severe storm with its ornate and whimsical ironwork and wooden posts, but in terms of popularity it was drawing in the visitors in droves.

Boasting entertainments such as novelty penny games and viewing machines, a souvenir shop, brass binoculars on fixed posts to admire the view and, of course, the teashop, it was proving a success and was in use even on a cold, drizzly spring morning.

Clara headed along the wooden boards of the pier, dodging small children and dogs who were being ignored by their respective guardians. That neither child nor canine had yet fallen off the edge of the pier was more to do with the carefully designed side panels than the awareness of the adults who had brought them there. Clara decided that, should she ever be required to bring her future niece or nephew to the pier, she would make sure to lash them to her with some sort of long leash to avoid such a calamity. Not that Clara would be so negligent in the first place, she promised herself.

The teashop had only just opened; a girl was in the process of switching the sign on the door from closed to open as Clara appeared. The first spots of rain were slicing through the sky, and Clara was glad to duck into the shop and avoid being drenched. The building had been designed to make the most of the view and had large glass windows on three sides. Clara picked a table in a corner where the windows met and formed a right-angled nook. She had a perfect view of the ocean to her left and the front of the teashop to her right.

Settling in to await her client, Clara ordered tea and toast from the waitress who came over. As the only person in the teashop at that moment in time, she had the girl's undivided attention, and it was not long before her breakfast arrived. Clara carefully poured milk and tea into a thick white cup, while listening to the rhythmic ebb and flow of the sea, and the squawking of low flying seagulls. Before she had started on her toast, the rain was falling and pattering hard on the glass windows.

For a time, Clara sat alone, watching the world go by. An elderly couple joined her around quarter past nine. The man was flapping water off his umbrella as he stepped in the door, and the woman was patting at her neatly arranged hair. Neither looked like someone who was in fear of their life or prone to ringing people at ungodly hours of the night. They found a table close to the service counter and fell into quiet conversation. Their appearance seemed to spark further arrivals, with several people now darting into the tearooms out of the rain. A young mother with a child in a pram battled with the door, the wheels of her infant's carriage proving reluctant to hop over the step until the elderly gentleman assisted her. Clara waited to see if this might be her client, she was the right age from the tone of the voice she had heard over the telephone last night. But the woman merely ordered tea and crumpets, then settled herself at a table near the door which offered room for the pram.

Two women next entered, both deep in conversation and hastening to a table diagonally opposite Clara but far enough away she could not hear what they said. Their buzzing conversation filled the room with its rumbling undertone, even though only snatches of words could be made out.

Clara checked her watch; it was now nearly half nine and it seemed she had been brought out on a wild goose chase. Her tea and toast consumed, she decided it was time to leave, though the weather outside did not tempt her out the door at once. Perhaps another pot of tea while she waited for the rain to ease?

She was disappointed no one had appeared, though it was not the first time such a thing had occurred, for some reason it had seemed especially important that the woman who had spoken to her so frantically the night before should be here. Maybe, as Clara had feared, it had been all a dream. A very vivid one for sure, but a dream, nonetheless.

She changed her mind on a second pot of tea; the greyness of the sky convinced her the rain was not going to stop anytime soon. She rose and went to the counter to pay her bill. Her back was to the door, as it swirled open once again, bringing in a draught of damp air that blew over the baby in the pram and set the infant crying.

Clara turned around, about to leave herself, when she found her way blocked by a beautiful woman in a fur coat. Clara was not one to assess her own sex in terms of ugliness or beauty, she believed there was more to a person than what their appearance might suggest, but she could not help but be instantly dazzled by the creature who had just stepped out of the rain.

She was younger than Clara, in her early twenties, with blonde curls that bounced around her shoulders and, even damp from the rain, had a glossy, well-tended appearance. Her face was the quintessential classical beauty, high cheekbones, blue eyes, neat but full mouth and straight nose. Any artist would have fallen at her feet to have her as his muse and model.

But it was the aura that came with her that seemed to truly make her wondrous, it was as if a little bit of magic had followed her into the shop. You could almost imagine she glowed, which was nonsense, but it summed up the power of her presence.

None of that beauty, however, could mask the deep distress on her face and the haunted look in her eyes. That this vulnerability seemed to make her more attractive was counterintuitive, but true, nonetheless.

Clara was convinced at once that she had found her client.

The woman cast her eyes around the teashop as if she was not really taking in anything she saw, then she caught sight of Clara right before her and almost jumped.

"Y...you must be Clara O'Harris?"

The woman stepped towards Clara, raindrops shedding from the folds of her fur coat.

"I am," Clara replied, standing to offer her a hand to shake.

The woman blinked, as if not sure how to react. In the end, she ignored the offered hand.

"I am sorry I am late. I couldn't slip away unseen."

She was trembling despite the fur coat. Clara suspected it was not the result of the cold weather.

"Why don't you take a seat over in that corner and I will order you some tea?" Clara suggested, motioning to the table she had just vacated.

"I would prefer coffee," the woman replied, moving around the wailing infant's pram, and heading to the table.

She moved with poise and grace, despite her clear unease.

Clara was turning to the counter to order her client a cup of coffee when she heard the old man speaking to his wife. Their table was not far from where Clara stood, and it was easy to overhear them.

"Did you see that?"

"I saw only that woman bringing in a terrible draught, people ought to be more considerate," the old woman responded to her husband.

"No, no, did you not recognise her?"

There was a short silence in which the woman must have indicated her ignorance.

"That was Violet Starling, the movie actress!"

"Well, how would I recognise her. I never go to the pictures."

"She was in the newspaper recently. That scandal with an MP, don't you remember?"

The man's wife muttered that she had better things to do than spend time reading about young women cavorting with married men who should know better. That brought the discussion to a swift ending.

Clara glanced over in the direction of the young woman, now seated at the table in the window. She was attracting looks from the pair of older women who had been busily debating the price of wool a few moments before. Clara saw no reason to doubt the old man's statement that the woman who had summoned her for help was none other than the starlet, Violet Starling. The aura of the woman was enough to convince her that the young lady was something unique, something, might one dare say it, special.

She collected the cup of coffee she had ordered and, at the last moment, also purchased two of the jam pastries that were sitting on the counter. Violet looked like she could do with something sweet, and Clara fancied that before her talk with the movie star was over, so would she.

Chapter Four

Violet Starling delicately removed her hat, drawing out the many pins that had kept it on her head in the blustery weather Brighton was currently enduring. She placed the hat on the table and fluffed out her hair across her shoulders, casting a few loose golden strands upon the floor.

Her cheeks were flushed from the chill outside, the only colour that was currently upon her face, otherwise she would have looked deathly pale. Clara placed the coffee before her, along with the sweet pastry. Violet immediately took a cube of sugar from a sugar bowl and dropped it in the cup.

"Thank you for waiting this long. I expected to find you already gone."

"I was close to leaving," Clara replied. "I was beginning to think I had dreamed our conversation last night."

"If only it were a dream!" Violet gave a miserable laugh. "I would be so much happier if all this was just the fiction of a nightmare, but sadly that is not the case."

"Perhaps you could explain everything to me in full?"

Violet took a deep breath.

"I assume you know who I am?"

"I didn't until the man at the table by the door mentioned your name to his wife. You are Violet Starling."

Violet smiled.

"It is hard to go anywhere without being recognised by someone."

Clara refrained from saying that Violet had hardly come to their meeting incognito. Even if no one knew her name, the expensive nature of her clothes and her glorious hair would have marked her out as someone who had wealth and was probably important.

"If it is any consolation, I did not recognise you," Clara smiled at her. "But then, I do not go to the pictures often."

"Would you laugh if said I am the same? I am so very busy all the time that if I have an evening free from any engagement all I care to do is go to bed early!"

Violet took her coffee with trembling fingers.

"If you do not know who I am, then I suppose you do not know the scandal that has recently dogged me?"

Clara decided not to repeat the information she had heard while stood at the counter. She would rather hear it from Violet's own lips.

"I am afraid I don't."

Violet sipped her coffee then returned the cup to its saucer.

"My name has been unfortunately associated with a Conservative MP. A married one, for that matter. It made all the papers and produced quite the scandal. It paints me in a pretty grim light."

"Is there truth in the story?"

Violet stiffened a fraction.

"I see you are not one to allow a girl a little smidgeon of discretion."

"Not if this scandal could in any way relate to what is happening to you now. You are the one who summoned me here and said you feared your life was in danger."

Violet nodded her head as she accepted this statement.

"Very well, I suppose if anyone deserves the truth it is the person I hope will save me from myself. Mrs O'Harris, I did indeed have a brief affair with that particular politician. It was a foolish enterprise, and I regret it wholeheartedly, but there was no reason for the newspapers to print pictures of us together."

"It is what the newspapers do," Clara pointed out.

Violet pulled a face.

"But that was months ago, and I do not think it relates to what is happening now."

"What is happening now?" Clara pressed her.

"I told you over the telephone that I fear for my wellbeing. For the last couple of weeks, I have felt uneasy, as if someone is watching me. Of course, I could blame that on the newspapermen who have been chasing me since the scandal broke, but this has felt *different*."

"Different, how?"

"Threatening. That is the only way to describe it. Not just someone watching me to find all my secrets, but something darker than that."

"Have you had any threats made against you?"

Violet shook her head.

"Nothing like that, if I had I would have told the studio, and they would have made sure I had extra security at once. No, this is all just a hunch on my part, but it makes it no less real to me."

Violet sounded desperate, as if she expected Clara to tell her she was imagining things and should not worry. Clara hastened to reassure her.

"I believe you," she said quickly. "Something has unsettled you, I can see that plainly. Aside from feeling watched, has anything occurred that could make you question your safety?"

"Silly things have happened. Things that any other time I would not have given a consideration to," Violet looked a touch embarrassed at her statement. "There was a particular incident at the studio when I was filming my last moving picture. The picture was about the famous scientist Nikolaus Tesla and in the final scene my character was to storm into his laboratory and pull apart his latest experiment. I was meant to be in love with the man, but he was too wrapped up in his work to acknowledge my existence."

"I didn't realise there was a love story associated with Nikolaus Tesla," Clara remarked, though she would be the first to confess her knowledge of the gentleman's life was limited.

Violet merely shrugged.

"I couldn't tell you if there is any accuracy to the plot, that is not my concern. My point is I was meant to march in and pull these cables out of the machine he was working on. They would spark harmlessly as if I were disconnecting them. It is the sort of special effect they do in movies all the time; it's a bit like the tiny explosions they have on stage during a theatrical performance. They look good, but they are not dangerous."

"I feel I can guess where you are going with this."

Violet pulled a face.

"I wish I could have guessed. I stormed in as I was supposed to and crossed to the machine. I pulled on the cables as I was told and didn't give it a thought after that, probably because the cable I grabbed was electrified and I was knocked unconscious instantly."

Violet had begun to tremble even more violently. She pulled off the glove from her right hand and presented the palm to Clara. There was plainly visible a partly healed burn mark.

"I was lucky not to have died," she said solemnly.

Clara took her hand and studied the injury. Knowing how serious electrocution could be, she had to agree with Violet that she had been extremely lucky.

"What did the studio say?"

"An unfortunate accident," Violet muttered, aggrieved that her near death disaster had been written off so blithely. "There was a mix up with which cable was meant to be electrified for the sake of the machine and the dummy one I should have pulled at."

"But didn't the cables have a rubber casing to protect those handling them?"

"The cable I pulled at did not have a casing. I was told expressly to pull on that wire."

Clara had to agree with Violet that this seemed more than an unfortunate accident.

"Has anything else happened like this?"

"My car brakes malfunctioned," Violet replied. "Fortunately, my driver realised before we were going at speed and was able to bring us to a safe halt. He inspected the vehicle and told me the brakes had been tampered with, but when I told the studio they laughed it off. They think I am being paranoid."

"How soon after the electrocution incident did the brake tampering occur?"

"That happened a few weeks after my misadventure with electricity," Violet sniffed, holding back tears as she told her story. "There has been one other thing, but I am a little embarrassed to mention it."

"You can tell me anything," Clara promised her.

Violet dabbed daintily at her eye with the ball of her hand, doing a remarkable job of avoiding smearing her mascara.

"I have trouble sleeping," she said. "Especially in strange hotels. My doctor has prescribed sleeping powders. I take one each night and then I am out like a light. One night, about a week ago, I took my usual sleeping powder and went to sleep. I awoke suddenly the next morning in hospital, riddled with belly pain and feeling like I had been incredibly ill. It turned out the hospital had pumped my stomach. I couldn't fathom what had occurred, until they said I had tried to overdose on sleeping powders.

"Mrs O'Harris, I must impress upon you that I did no such thing. I took a single dose of my sleeping powders. Yet, somehow, I had consumed too much. I survived because the studio unexpectedly sent someone up to my room with rewrites of the script. She was meant to enter my room and wake me so I could read them. When she arrived, she found me unresponsive. She raised the alarm."

"That was extremely fortunate for you," Clara agreed. "Had she not brought those script revisions..."

"You need not say it aloud, I would have been dead," Violet cringed and bit at her lip as she considered the situation. "My point is, I never took an overdose. I do not know how I came to have more sleeping powder in my system than I should have, but I swear it was not deliberate."

Clara believed her. Violet's adamant denial had the ring of truth to it.

"The only other possibility is that someone tampered with your sleeping powder, either increasing the dose or adding something to it that would be harmful to you."

"That is the only conclusion I can come to," Violet concurred. "But the studio does not believe me. When I explained myself, they thought I was trying to cover up what I had done. It is awful, Mrs O'Harris, to be disbelieved over such a thing. I might add that I was raised a Catholic and suicide is abhorrent to me. I would never shame my family or risk my soul in that way."

"I believe you, Miss Starling," Clara promised her. "You have convinced me that someone seems to be striving to cause you harm. Why that would be, I cannot state at this juncture, but I will gladly take on your case and investigate further."

Violet breathed out a sigh of relief.

"Thank you, Mrs O'Harris. You do not know how much that means to me."

"The first thing I need to do is find a motive for these accidents. Knowing why someone might wish you hurt will make it easier to prevent further incidents and get to the bottom of the mystery."

"In that regard, I can offer you nothing," Violet shook her head. "I have gone over and over what could possibly cause someone to wish me ill, and nothing springs to mind."

"What about your affair with the MP?"

"It is over and done with. Why would he wish to hurt me?"

"Maybe not him, per se, but what about his wife?"

Violet considered the statement.

"Honestly, I do not believe the woman would care enough. In any case, I would surely notice her about the studio? I know her face well enough."

"Do you have any rivals within the studio?" Clara tried next. "Perhaps another actress who would care for your roles?"

"I know they say acting is a cutthroat business but that is rather extreme!" Violet said in astonishment.

"Nonetheless, jealousy can cause people to do some pretty terrible things."

Violet paused to allow this statement to sink in.

"I have rivals, of course I do. There are other women who would love my roles. I could offer you a few names, but I really do not believe they would stoop to something like this."

Clara took the names, nonetheless, even with her limited knowledge of movies, she recognised a couple.

"Now, let us discuss how to keep you safe over the next few days while I investigate this matter," Clara continued. "I recommend you allow me to assign someone to guard you at all times."

"A bodyguard?" Violet looked aghast.

"It would be prudent. My brother has done such things before and is very discreet."

Violet pursed her lips.

"I am not sure what the studio will say. They are very particular about people being on the sets of the movies they make. They are always worried about information being leaked or newspapermen getting to see something behind the scenes."

"We shall just have to persuade them. This is for your safety, Violet, nothing is more important than that."

Violet hesitated for a moment more before finally agreeing. Relieved that they had come to this agreement, Clara suggested that Violet remain with her for the rest of the day, so that she might be introduced to Tommy, her new watchdog.

"We do not have any filming today," Violet admitted. "Just a rehearsal this afternoon. I would like to remain with you, your company is consoling. I feel safer already."

Clara was glad to hear this.

"May I ask, do you think you were followed here?"

Violet shook her head.

"That is why I was late. I took my time waiting for the right moment to slip away. I went out via the service entrance of the hotel. No one saw me."

Clara was not sure if that was true, but she did not want to place doubts or further worries in Violet's mind.

"Then let us head for my house. Look, the rain has eased a fraction, so we should not get too wet."

Violet glanced out of the window, saw that Clara was correct and a fragile sun was trying to shimmer through the clouds, and smiled.

"I feel this is a good sign," she said.

She took her time replacing her hat and putting the pins into place. Clara noted she had barely touched her coffee, and her pastry had been ignored (though Clara had consumed hers). Clara wrapped the uneaten pastry in a paper napkin to take home with her. No doubt, Captain O'Harris would eat it, and she did not care to waste it.

They headed out onto the pier, Violet receiving similar looks from the customers in the teashop that she had when she arrived. Despite her confidence she had slipped away from the hotel unnoticed, Clara suspected it would be easy work for anyone determined enough to track her down. All they had to do was ask people if they had seen the actress passing by. Violet clearly did not know what the word 'incognito' meant.

"I am so glad I found the courage to call you last night," Violet remarked as they headed back along the pier. "I nearly didn't. I had almost convinced myself I was being paranoid. When everyone keeps telling you, you are jumping at shadows and being foolish, you start to believe it."

"I am glad you came to me," Clara responded. "I believe you have a genuine reason to be concerned, and I shall do everything I can to find the culprit swiftly."

"Thank you, your understanding and belief in my worries is so refreshing!"

Violet smiled to herself, her first genuine sign of happiness since they had met. Talking to Clara had lifted a weight from her, and she now beamed brightly, looking like the young woman she really was.

Her laughter, however, brought more eyes in their direction, and many of them recognised the source of the sound.

"Violet, we really need to talk about your appearance."

"What's wrong with it?" Violet asked in horror.

"Nothing," Clara sighed back to her. "That is part of the problem."

Violet looked confused. Clara hastened her along with an arm through hers. There would be time to discuss how Violet might walk around town without being noticed once they were safely away from prying eyes.

Chapter Five

Tommy had been planning on taking another walk down to the seafront, in the hopes he might catch a further glimpse of Violet Starling and Joshua Mackenzie. He was all set to make the trip, with coat and hat donned, and the dogs on their leads, when the knock came at the front door.

As he was stood in the hallway of the house, it was no effort for him to reach over and open it.

"That must be Jenny, come for her weekly cooking lesson," Annie had popped her head around the kitchen door.

Jenny was a young girl who lived a few houses down the road and was desperate to get a position in a household as a cook. Annie had taken her under her wing, and the weekly lessons generally consisted of cooking, tea drinking, and a great deal of gossip. The girl was a dab hand at pastry according to Annie – which was high praise indeed, Annie rarely considered anyone as competent a cook as she was.

Anticipating the sight of a scrawny teenage girl with an unfortunate turn in one eye, Tommy was completely unprepared for the sight that actually greeted him when he opened the door.

"Violet Starling!"

Tommy completely missed his sister, who was in fact stood in front of Violet and had been the one who had knocked, as his gaze fell unerringly on the movie star before him. Captivated immediately by her aura and energy, he simply fell silent and stared in astonishment.

"Don't just stand there, Tommy, let Jenny in," Annie was heading down the hallway to see what the fuss was about.

"It isn't Jenny..." Tommy managed to mumble as he stood starstruck.

He was not someone to usually be cowed by the sight of a celebrity before him, but there was something about Violet Starling that had held him in awe since the first moment he had seen her on the screen. He couldn't say what it was that caused him to go into a stupor at the sight of her, probably some silly infatuation, but if ever there was a woman to leave him speechless it proved to be her.

Of course, he had never anticipated ever meeting the object of his innocent adoration, which had made it all the easier to indulge his idle feelings, knowing they were nothing more than a daydream.

Except, now Violet Starling was on his doorstep.

"Who is this?" Annie demanded of Clara, shoving her husband aside so she could better see what was going on.

"Annie, please meet Violet Starling, who is having a difficult time and has requested our help."

"Delighted to meet you," Violet bobbed her head at Annie. "Mrs O'Harris has been telling me all about you. I am sorry to disturb you on a day when clearly you are busy."

"We are not busy," Tommy squeaked, suddenly finding his voice. "You ought to come into the parlour and... sit by the fire. Its cold out there."

"Cold and wet," Violet chuckled lightly, her voice to Tommy like a trickling stream.

An analogy he had never understood until that moment. He

gulped.

"I best make you all a cup of tea," Annie headed back to the kitchen, oblivious to her husband's distress. "And something warm to eat too. It is a bit early for crumpets, but I think I have some muffins to toast."

"This way, Violet," Clara nudged her brother out of the way and escorted her new client to the parlour.

Clara found it slightly odd returning to the home she had lived in all her life now she was no longer a resident there. She had grown used to waking up at the convalescence home and descending its great staircase to the vast rooms below. Even O'Harris' private study was larger than her former parlour. Stepping back into her old home brought on complicated feelings, not least because she was suddenly aware of how small it was, when all her days she had considered it quite spacious.

Violet made no comment on the size of the parlour as she was shown in and offered a seat. She was just relieved to get out of the public gaze. The whole walk to the house they had had people gasping and pointing at them. A handful had even stopped Violet and asked for her autograph. It had reminded Clara how obvious the woman was, and the likelihood she had not been followed by her mystery assailant seemed all the more remote.

Well, Clara was glad if they *had* seen her in Violet's company. Let them know that she was on the case and would be protecting the starlet from now on.

"Clara!" Tommy called his sister from the doorway of the parlour and motioned for her to come across the hall to the dining room opposite, where they could speak privately.

Clara joined him in the opposite room, where at least he could regain some use of his tongue.

"That is Violet Starling!" he declared in a fraught whisper.

"It is indeed," Clara smiled at him.

"You don't have any idea who she is, do you?"

Clara considered lying, but decided now was not the time to try to avoid professing her ignorance.

"I have more of an idea who she is now, than I did earlier this morning before I met her," she countered.

"Violet Starling is the leading lady of the age! She has been in more movies than any other British actress to date, and most of them have been big titles, which have played for weeks and weeks. Her name is synonymous with great romance and adventure pictures."

"She certainly has a presence about her," Clara concurred mildly. "A bit too much presence. It was inconvenient coming here with everyone fawning over her."

Tommy recalled his own reaction at her arrival on the doorstep and felt embarrassed.

"What is she doing here?"

"She believes her life is in danger and, after discussing the matter with her, I feel I must concur. Someone is intent on causing her harm, and has come very close to succeeding in killing her more than once."

Tommy's silence was no longer due to being starstruck; now he was appalled to know the young woman sitting in his parlour was the subject of an assassin's attentions.

"I asked her to come here, as I felt it was somewhat more private than my office, and I also wanted her to meet you. I was hoping you would agree to act as Violet's bodyguard while she is in Brighton?"

"Her bodyguard?"

"We need to do something to protect her while I try to discover who is behind these attacks. I appreciate this is an awkward situation and, if you do not feel you can spare the time from Annie, I will understand."

Tommy felt suddenly torn; his pregnant wife had been the focus of his attention for the last few weeks, and he had not been away from the house for any length of time since Annie had told him the news. Acting as bodyguard to Violet would mean spending considerable hours away from home, perhaps even days at a time. He was not sure he could do that, or that Annie would appreciate his absence.

Clara, on the other hand, thought that Annie would probably welcome the chance to be able to get on with her chores without Tommy's ever watchful eye.

"I don't know," Tommy hesitated.

"Why don't we discuss it with Annie?" Clara suggested.

She headed for the kitchen as she spoke, leaving Violet comfortably alone in the parlour. A quick glance through the door revealed the actress was drying her hair before the fire while softly humming to herself. The sight of her luminous golden hair brought a fresh panic to Tommy.

The thought of looking after this goddess, and ensuring her safety for the next few weeks, while tempting, also filled him with a sort of dread. A man was not meant to meet his idol – at least not a man like Tommy.

Annie was arranging teacups on a tray as they entered the kitchen.

"I found some muffins," she informed them. "They are from the bakery rather than my own, but I hope they will not be too disappointing."

The fact Annie had deemed the bakery's muffins suitable to purchase in the first place indicated they were probably rather exceptional in their quality. Annie only bought baked goods when she considered them equal to her own.

"Annie, the woman who is in the parlour is Violet Starling," Clara began.

"I know," Annie replied. "I have seen her picture often enough in my magazines. I have to say, she has quite a presence when you meet her in the flesh. Something that cannot be captured by a photograph."

"You noticed it too?" Tommy said, relieved that he was not alone.

"Yes, there is something so tragic about her," Annie sighed. "One of those people who you have an awful feeling is going to die young. It is as if there is a wistfulness about them that tells you their fate will not be a happy one."

That was not what either Tommy or Clara wanted to hear.

"Annie, Violet's life is in danger, and I would like Tommy to keep an eye on her, while I try to get to the bottom of who wishes her harm."

Annie paused from the tea tray arrangements at Clara's statement.

"I said she had a tragic aura. There was a girl at my school who was just the same. Beautiful, the sort of person everyone wanted to be around, but you just knew there would not be a happy ending for her. Rather like a butterfly that has such vibrancy and beauty because it will only exist for the shortest of times."

"I am not sure timespan has anything to do with the evolution of butterflies coloured patterns," Clara frowned, beginning to find all this talk frustrating.

"What happened to the girl at your school?" Tommy asked with a hint of fear in his tone.

"Oh, she got married and had three children before she was twenty-two," Annie said. "Lost her figure completely and now works in her husband's shop along the seafront selling confectionary to the tourists."

"How is that tragic?" Clara challenged.

"Well, it isn't. But that isn't to say the tragic thing isn't still to come."

Clara made a dismissive cluck at the back of her throat.

"Everyone has tragic things happen to them in their lifetime. We lost our parents unexpectedly, but no one ever said either me, or

Tommy, had a tragic aura about us."

Annie waved a hand at her.

"I stand by what I said. Some people seem to have this fragility to them, and Violet Starling is one of them."

"In any case," Clara decided to get the discussion back on track, "Violet Starling needs someone to protect her. Would you be opposed to Tommy keeping an eye on her? It would mean he would have to be out of the house a great deal."

Annie's shoulders tensed at this statement.

"Honestly, Annie, you are entitled to say no," Tommy hastened to add. "I don't want to leave you in a bad situation. You are my priority and keeping an eye to make sure you are not overdoing things is my main focus at the moment."

"Yes," Annie said thoughtfully. "I had noticed."

"If Tommy is not available, perhaps I shall ask O'Harris," Clara mused. "Or possibly Private Peterson. I am sure both would agree, but they are not as observant as you, Tommy, and I would like to have eyes and ears on Violet that will pick up on anything suspicious."

"I understand, but really my place is here," Tommy said staunchly. "I am sure Annie has more use for me than Violet does.

Clara was pretty certain only she saw Annie's eyes go wide in alarm at this statement.

"Tommy," Annie turned to her husband, "I will not hear of it. I cannot be selfish. This poor woman has come to Clara for help and is clearly in a desperate situation. What right do I have to deny her that help? You will be of greater use to Violet than you will be to me. I am perfectly capable of taking care of myself, and this is clearly a vital task you are being asked to attend to."

Tommy started to protest.

"I will not hear of it," Annie put up her hand to stop him. "I will be beside myself if something were to happen to Violet because I denied her your protection. Clara is correct, you are a good detective as well as a gentleman, you will see things that neither O'Harris nor Peterson would. I therefore must insist you help this young lady."

Tommy wasn't sure what to say. He glanced at his sister who quickly masked the smile that had been forming on her lips.

"You will really be all right without me?"

"Tommy, I shall be absolutely fine," Annie assured him.

"But what if you need someone to lift something heavy?" Tommy protested.

Annie nearly groaned impatiently.

"I am sure I can find someone to assist me. Jenny, for instance, would gladly come over more regularly."

Tommy finally had no protests left and agreed that he would look after Violet. Annie became almost cheerful at the news, saying she had changed her mind, and crumpets ought to also be included on the tea tray.

"She seems very happy I am going to act as bodyguard to Violet," Tommy said in confusion.

"We are both happy. It takes a weight off our minds to know you will be looking out for her, and preventing any further harm coming her way," Clara assured him.

Tommy was not entirely convinced, but since he could not fathom any other reason for Annie being so happy about him being away from the house for such a length of time, he had no option but to nod his head and agree.

"Let's tell Violet the good news!" Annie said gleefully, going to pick up the tea tray.

Before she could, Tommy darted in front of her.

"Let me."

"The tea tray is hardly heavy!"

"Even so," Tommy would hear no argument, and gathered up the tea tray to take through to the parlour.

Annie caught Clara's eye as Tommy headed off down the hallway.

"Did you arrange this on purpose?" she asked.

"No, it is just a coincidence," Clara smiled.

"Then God *has* been listening to my prayers!" Annie groaned.

Chapter Six

Warmed through, and full of muffins and jam, Violet set out with Tommy to head back to the *Grand Hotel*. She had rehearsals in an hour and would need to make arrangements with the movie director about Tommy's presence. He departed with her, still looking somewhat dazed by his new arrangement, and with an uneasy backward glance at Annie.

Jenny had now arrived and was learning how to make perfect dumplings. Annie, catching a glimpse of her husband as she moved past the kitchen doorway to fetch more flour, waved him away as if he were one of the dogs interfering with her cooking.

Tommy felt a touch hurt, but he departed, nonetheless, with promises to Clara that he would keep a close watch on Violet, and report back anything that seemed suspicious.

Clara, meanwhile, had her own tasks to perform. Violet had been less than helpful when it came to suggesting suspects, so Clara was going to have to speak to everyone who had been with Violet over the last few weeks to try to find some clue to the culprit.

Violet had provided a list of people who had been around her at each of the incidents, as best as she could remember. Clara hoped it would be sufficient to make a start.

Her first step was to speak to everyone who was closest to Violet, from her driver to her manager. One of them might have something to say about the attempts on her life.

She first headed to the green where the film crew had set up their tents, to speak to the director of the film. Violet had made it plain that he was the person in charge of everything that was going on while the movie was in production, unless someone from the studio happened to come down to the set. He even had sway over the producer, who she explained was just the money man, and a rather quiet individual at that. Whatever the director said, the producer agreed to because he did not dare disagree.

The director's name was Norris Manx, of distant Polish extraction, though he had spent considerable time in America and, when he was attempting to impress people, he had a habit of adopting what he considered a Hollywood accent. He was a short man with a round belly, and a nose that seemed to take up the majority of his face. He also had a voice loud enough to yell across a film set with little need for the megaphone with which he was provided.

Norris was seated on a canvas folding chair within one of the tents, looking over some script alterations he had asked for, while a variety of people rushed back and forth around him, some briefly stopping to speak to him or deliver something to him.

A young man in a dark green sweater lurked just at his shoulder, waiting for instructions from Norris. He proved to be the director's assistant, who would perform whatever task or errand Manx needed done, whether that be fetching him coffee or running down an absent actor. He spotted Clara first as she walked through the open doorway of the tent.

There had been no security at the entrance to the green, Clara had waltzed in without anyone giving her a glance. She might have said something about this lack of interest in a stranger wandering about the tents, except it served her purpose not to be noticed. She had found the tent that housed the director by the simple method of asking the nearest person to hand where it was.

As she had expected, the storm from the night before had left a path of damage in its wake, and a lot of the set workers were busy restoring the tents; hammering in the pegs that held ropes and repairing some of the larger backdrops and props, which had been unfortunately damaged when the tent they were sheltered in had collapsed. This was creating something of a delay to Manx's filming schedule, which had put him in a particularly vile temper that morning.

Movie making was always run on a tight timeframe, and delays caused by damaged props and backdrops was an inconvenience Manx could not afford. It looked likely they would lose a whole day of filming if the items could not be restored in time, which meant he was already examining the script to see what scenes he might be able to cut out, if push came to shove.

Manx's assistant saw Clara coming and was filled with immediate panic. He did not recognise her, and seeing that she had her sights set on his boss, he knew that trouble was coming his way. The last thing he needed was for Norris to have his work further disrupted.

The young man jumped forward to intercept Clara. She stepped past him without breaking stride, so he grabbed her arm. Clara turned on him her most fearsome glare and he immediately let her go, holding his hands up in surrender, but at least now he had her attention.

"Mr Manx is very busy and cannot be disturbed. I don't know who you are, or why you have wandered in here, but must I advise you that these tents are for film crew only."

Clara took a good look at the assistant, sizing him up. He did not intimidate her in the slightest.

"I have urgent business with Mr Manx," she declared, turning aside to head towards the director once again.

Gritting his teeth, knowing the likely consequence of his actions all too well, the assistant grabbed her arm once again. This time, Clara spun around and slapped his hand away.

"You will unhand me, sir!"

Her righteous indignation was impressive, and the assistant would have backed off if he were not more afraid of his employer than he was of Clara.

"Mr Manx must not be disturbed."

"I have to speak to him at once. This is essential, as I think Mr Manx would be most put out if his leading lady were to be prevented from appearing in his picture."

Since Clara was only a few feet from Norris, she succeeded in attracting his attention. His head shot up and he narrowed his eyes at her.

"Edwin, step away!"

"Yes, Mr Manx," Edwin obeyed with a dip of his head, and shuffled away to the far side of the folding wooden table Mr Manx was using as a desk.

"What is this about Violet? She hasn't done something stupid again?" Manx demanded of Clara.

"Violet is perfectly well, and it is my intention to keep her that way," Clara assured him. "Your leading lady has been the focus of some unpleasant attentions, which I do not believe the studio is taking seriously enough."

"It will be all that business of accidents Violet has been muttering about," Edwin whispered to his boss, though it was a stage whisper and perfectly audible.

Clara saw on his face the intense distaste he clearly felt for Violet as he spoke and made note of it.

"Accidents that Violet believes were deliberately staged to cause her harm, and I think she is correct," Clara interjected.

"Look, miss...."

"Mrs O'Harris, private detective."

Norris waved off Clara's statement, too caught up in his own affairs to be interested in who she was.

"Violet is an actress, and actresses tend to be dramatic about these sorts of things. They prick their finger on an overlooked pin in one of their costumes and assume the entire wardrobe department is out for their blood."

"I hardly think that is a fair comparison," Clara countered. "Violet has been electrocuted, had her brakes cut and, most recently, been poisoned."

"The sleeping powder overdose was her own doing," Edwin said snidely. "She might regret it now and be trying to pretend it was someone else's work to cover up her own intentions, but it is as plain as day what she was doing."

"It is not as 'plain as day' to me," Clara informed him. "Violet has stated to me she only took one of her sleeping draughts and I have no reason to doubt her."

"She has caught you up in her web," Norris chuckled at Clara, amused that she was taking this all so seriously. "Violet is over dramatic about everything. Actresses are like that. Please, do not take any of this to be truth. Each of those incidents was investigated to the satisfaction of the studio."

"But not to my satisfaction," Clara informed him. "I suspect I have higher standards in that regard. In any case, Violet has hired me to look after her, and to find out who is responsible for these mishaps, and that is precisely what I shall do. I have already assigned her a bodyguard..."

"Oh, for heaven's sake!" Manx slapped the table and threw back his head. "Can't you see this is all about publicity for her? Honestly, you people are so naïve!"

Clara was close to losing her temper, but she managed to rein herself in. She was not going to be dismissed as an emotional woman. She had seen the very real fear in Violet's eyes, and she believed every word she said.

"You seem to have very little regard for the wellbeing of your leading lady, surely you should take a greater interest in this considering the time and money it would cost you if anything were to happen to her."

"Are you threatening me?" Manx demanded.

"No, merely making a point," Clara responded. "I shall be loitering around, looking into this affair until I have answers. I had hoped you would be able to offer me more information, something I could use to go on, but now I understand why Violet is so desperate for fresh eyes on this matter."

"Edwin, get rid of this woman!" Manx snapped, going back to the script before him. "And when you are done, we will have words about why you let her bother me in the first place!"

Edwin pulled a face, then headed towards Clara, flapping his hands at her to get her to move away. Clara recalled how Annie had shooed Tommy out of the house like she would her chickens and found herself indignantly suffering the same fate. She left the tent without protest, however, for she could see no point in trying to get anything further from Mr Manx.

"Do not come back," Edwin informed her as he shuffled her outside.

Clara was not yet done with him.

"You do not like Violet?"

Edwin sighed at the distraction.

"I do not dislike her, as such, she is simply a silly girl who does not appreciate the opportunities she has been given and makes such a fuss all the time. Honestly, all actresses are the same."

"What about actors?"

Edwin shrugged.

"I suppose they can have their moments too. They should all thank their lucky stars."

"Would you like to be an actor?" Clara asked him.

Edwin's mouth dropped in a feigned look of outrage.

"What a thing to say? Are you suggesting I am not satisfied with my role as Mr Manx's assistant? He is a great man and being in his shadow will surely lead me to great things."

His denial told Clara everything she needed to know.

"Were you and Mr Manx around at each of the accidents involving Violet?"

"Now you interrogate me?" Edwin huffed.

"Interrogate is a harsh word, I was merely enquiring."

"As it happens, I was witness to the electrocution incident, which was all the girl's own fault. She pulled at the wrong cable. You can't help people if they will be stupid."

"Violet claims she was told very plainly to pull a particular cable."

"And I say she pulled the wrong one. We all saw her do it. I remember Mr Manx nearly screaming at her as she reached for a live cable instead of the correct dummy one. It was not as if we hadn't made it as obvious as possible for her to avoid mistakes. There was a red piece of string tied around the cable she was to pull."

"Violet was told to pull on the cable with the red cord around it?"

"Yes!" Edwin was becoming frustrated at her slowness. "Stupid woman ignored the instruction. There is no mystery to the accident."

"What about her brakes being tampered with?"

"That is what she says happened, but cars malfunction all the time. They are unreliable things, which is why I prefer to take the bus or walk when I can. Surely, you know how frequently the contraptions break down?"

"Her driver told Violet there were signs the brakes had been tampered with," Clara added.

"Are you sure about that?" Edwin raised a haughty eyebrow at her. "Have you asked him yourself?"

Clara did not want to admit she had not, as that would imply she was relying on Violet's word alone, and Edwin would have a field day. Despite his denials, she was not going to be shaken in her belief of her client. Violet was neither stupid nor delusional, as far as Clara could tell in the brief time they had spoken together, she seemed a grounded person who was very troubled by the events in her life.

"Dismissing Violet's concerns is a lot easier than actually looking into them, isn't it?" Clara remarked.

Edwin tsked.

"Women are all the same. I am not surprised she has you on her side. You all band together, don't you? Things don't go your way, and you claim there is someone out to get you and turn to the first woman you can find who will back you up and make it seem as if the world is against you."

"I cannot recall ever doing that," Clara responded. "Perhaps that is how *you* behave, but I follow the truth wherever it leads me. I should add that I have defended both male and female clients, and found my culprits among both men and women, so do not suggest I am biased."

"Just because you do not see it, does not mean it is not true," Edwin said, delivering his parting words with a flick of his head as he spun on his heel and stormed back into the tent.

Clara would have liked to pursue him and insist he was wrong, but that would not be very productive, she had better things to do. It was not she who was blinkered, but those around Violet who dismissed her as a silly woman who did not know reality from fiction.

Clara was all the more determined to help Violet and make things right, whatever it took. She would not be fobbed off by men like Mr Manx and Edwin; a woman's life was in danger, and she was going to do all in her power to prevent a murder occurring.

Chapter Seven

Tommy was beginning to overcome his initial nerves about being in the company of Violet Starling. Admittedly, he still found it hard to answer a direct question from her, and to make polite conversation, but he was able to obey whatever she directed him to do without stumbling over his feet. He was also enjoying the deflected attention he was getting from the residents of Brighton as he walked beside the movie actress.

He had already spied a couple of people who knew him and were surprised to see him in the company of someone so famous, when they happened upon Oliver Bankes, the local photographer.

Oliver's presence at the *Grand Hotel* was not a coincidence. He had been sent by the editor of the *Brighton Gazette,* (for which he worked on a freelance basis) to take photographs of Violet Starling and Joshua MacKenzie for the newspaper. The arrangement had been given the director's consent and was one of the few occasions when a newspaperman was actually welcome at the place, or at least, Oliver was welcome.

He was in the foyer of the hotel, talking with Joshua as if he had always known him and casually remarking on the weather, when Tommy and Violet walked in. Immediately, a gaggle of people descended on Violet, demanding to know where she had been. The most voracious in this interrogation was a gentleman with a severe parting to his oiled hair and a pencil line moustache. He narrowed his eyes at Violet and grabbed her arm the second he saw her in a possessive manner Tommy didn't care for.

"Where have you been?"

Violet stuttered, her words falling in broken sentences from her mouth in the face of this intimidation. Tommy hastily inserted himself into the situation.

"A gentleman never grabs a lady in such a manner," Tommy had a presence about him when he wanted, the sort which implied that as affable as he appeared, he would throw the first punch if a fight erupted.

The man who had hold of Violet was somewhat startled by Tommy's sudden appearance and the way he placed himself in front of the starlet, before extracting her from the man's grasp.

"Who are you?"

"Thomas Fitzgerald," Tommy grinned at him, offering a hand to shake. "Miss Starling's bodyguard."

His opponent glared at Tommy in a manner that was intended to be intimidating, and no doubt on another person very well might have succeeded, but Tommy had served in a war and had met one too many criminals over the course of his time helping Clara to be easily scared. He merely broadened his grin and tried to shove his hand nearer to the man. The fellow refused to shake it.

"Well, I am Mr Stevenson, Miss Starling's manager, and I have not authorised her to have a bodyguard, so you can clear off!"

"Please, Bobby, let him stay!" Violet found her voice and begged. "I really am frightened and having someone to keep an eye on me would make such a difference."

"You have nothing to be scared of, other than me," 'Bobby' Stevenson growled at her. "You were meant to be here for this photo shoot twenty minutes ago."

"I forgot," Violet said meekly.

"That's your problem! Always forgetting! Get over there now and see the make-up girl. This might only be the local newspaper, but it is all publicity!"

"You don't have to do as he says," Tommy interjected, ready to stand up for Violet.

She shook her head at him in a gesture of surrender.

"Yes, I do, Tommy. Thank you, anyway."

She slipped past him and, much to Tommy's amazement, suddenly managed to have a bright smile on her face, as if she had not been on the cusp of tears a moment before.

"Remarkable," Tommy mumbled to himself.

"As for you," Stevenson poked a hard finger into Tommy's chest. "You can clear off!"

"Miss Starling asked for protection, and I have undertaken that role," Tommy countered.

"And I say Violet is perfectly all right, and any 'bodyguard' has to be approved by me, and I know I did not approve you!"

"Then you are looking into providing her with some protection?" Tommy pushed.

"Of course not! The girl has a screw loose, all actresses do. Thinks she has someone out for her blood, trust me, they get a little bit of fame, and it all goes to their heads."

"I have seen her fear."

"And you just saw her go from misery to beaming joy! She's an actress, and I say this without hesitation, a damn good one. That's why I represent her, but you cannot take a word she says seriously. These movie folk are always being overdramatic and putting on their parts. Half the time I suspect they don't know what they are truly feeling anymore."

"I think you are exaggerating."

"And I think you have never been around actresses and actors before, am I right?"

Tommy went to correct him, then found his words faltering. He *didn't* have experience working with movie stars; the closest he had come was meeting some pantomime performers and the amateur actors in the local drama society.

"Look, I am just going to keep an eye on Violet. No harm in that."

"I say who goes near Violet, and you are not approved!" Stevenson snarled at him, displaying yellow teeth.

"I don't recall needing your approval," Tommy huffed, determined to defy the bully.

"Anyone who comes near Violet needs *my* approval," Stevenson said with a sneer. "And she already has people looking out for her. You have a choice, leave of your own volition or I get the hotel staff to escort you out."

"Look, we don't need to be enemies..."

Stevenson was not going to play nice, he spun around sharply and waved at the hotel manager who was loitering nearby. The manager came over hastily.

"This fellow isn't welcome. He needs to leave and be kept out!" Stevenson commanded the man.

"Hey, that's out of order!" Tommy responded, but his protests carried no weight when they came up against Stevenson's authority.

Before he knew what was happening, Tommy was being escorted out of the doors of the *Grand Hotel* by two of the burlier staff. He spun around on the top step, ready to say his piece to the manager who had followed them.

"I am Violet Starling's bodyguard! Ask her!"

"Sir, you have been instructed to leave by Mr Stevenson, and I suggest you do not make a greater scene than is necessary."

"Please, just ask Miss Starling," Tommy tried to cajole him into helpfulness, but to no avail.

The hotel manager had his men escort Tommy down the front steps.

"Do not return, or I shall summon the police," the manager called out as Tommy was being shoved into the crowd of people loitering just outside the hotel.

The majority of the crowd were newspapermen trying to catch a glimpse of the movie stars and they gave derogatory laughs at the sight of Tommy being ejected from the hotel.

"Trying to beat us to it, huh?" one jeered at him. "Well, find a spot here like the rest of us and stop trying to be clever!"

He was now given a shove by one of the irate reporters, who thought he was trying to encroach on their territory. Not expecting the push, Tommy was caught off guard and fell into another man, who pushed him back with a roar of indignation. In the slight scuffle that ensued, Tommy lost his footing and ended up on his backside on the wet pavement, puffing hard and furious at the entire situation.

"Hey now! Hey!"

Someone was pushing through the newspapermen towards him. He heard a bumping, jangling noise of something wooden and, the next moment, Oliver Bankes was stood over him, tripod in one hand, camera in the other.

The newspapermen, recognising the local photographer and knowing he was one of the few to have actual permission to go near the movie stars, backed off to give him room. Oliver was not the likeliest of saviours, with his slightly bumbling nature, perpetual clumsiness, and his mild manner, but on this occasion, he was a welcome sight. Putting down his camera tripod, he offered a hand to Tommy.

"Thanks," Tommy said, accepting the hand.

He had gone down hard on his bad leg, the one that still ached from the injuries he had suffered in the war, and he was in pain, a sharp, nagging sensation echoing up his spine. He had been taking his time about getting up, as he was not sure he could do so without his weaker leg crumpling beneath him.

Tommy hated giving in to his war wounds; he especially hated appearing weak before others.

"What was that all about?" Oliver asked as he hauled Tommy to his feet. "I saw you being forced out of the hotel and came to see if everything was all right."

Tommy's trousers were soaked through where he had landed on the pavement, and he suspected he might have torn them.

"I was trying to help Violet Starling and her manager took offence."

"Robert Stevenson?" Oliver asked. "Stage name, you know, after the famous writer. Wanted to be an actor himself but didn't have the talent so instead he now manages others."

"And he isn't doing a very good job at it," Tommy snorted, moodily.

He limped away from the crowd of newspapermen, not wanting to give them any fodder for their publications. Oliver followed.

"Miss Starling is concerned about her safety after some odd accidents have recently befallen her," Tommy explained as they moved away towards the seafront.

The crowd had thinned out here, with only a handful of locals who had come to try their luck in catching a glimpse of the stars.

"Concerned about her safety?" Oliver repeated. "She seemed

perfectly fine just now."

"She is an actress," Tommy shrugged, then he winced as his back twinged.

Despite the cold and wet, he opted to sit on the top of the sea wall that divided the road from the promenade and beach beyond. He was already damp, what did it matter if he got a little wetter?

"What will happen now?" Oliver asked, glancing back to the hotel.

"You mean, concerning Violet's safety?" Tommy frowned. "I don't know. I don't think Stevenson will let me back into her company readily, no matter how I try to persuade him. I sense he is the possessive sort."

"He does have that sort of manner about him," Oliver nodded. "Do you think Violet will be safe without you watching over her?"

"I couldn't say for sure Oliver," Tommy shrugged. "The whole reason she came to see Clara today is because she is fearful for her life, and I was supposed to be providing her with security and protecting her. That hasn't exactly gone to plan."

Oliver glanced back at the hotel, chewing on his lower lip.

"Look, if we can't get you in there to watch over her, there might be another option."

Tommy was surprised to hear Oliver making a suggestion, but he was quite prepared to listen.

"You mustn't tell anyone, but Gilbert McMillan has managed to install himself among the staff at the hotel. He is acting as a general dogsbody, but with his eyes and ears open for anything that might be occurring."

"Gilbert is inside the hotel right now?"

"That he is, and if we speak to him about your concerns, I am sure he will keep a close eye on Violet."

Tommy hesitated to go along with the plan. Gilbert was many

things, but generally he was not considered either a hero or someone who was deemed discreet. To reveal Violet's story to Gilbert was to risk it becoming fodder for his next newspaper article. On the other hand, unable to enter the hotel himself, it might be the only way that Tommy could help Violet.

After debating the matter for a while, he agreed to Oliver's idea, and followed him around the back of the hotel. They were not noticed as just at that moment Joshua MacKenzie made an appearance on the steps of the hotel. It was clearly a staged performance to give the newspapermen something to report. More publicity, Tommy thought to himself grumpily, still stinging from being outmanoeuvred by Stevenson.

In the yard at the back of the hotel, where the bins were kept and deliveries were made, Oliver asked him to wait with his camera while he headed inside to locate Gilbert. Tommy was annoyed at being forced to stand in the cold yet again, especially as the sky was threatening further rain, but he appreciated that Oliver was trying to be clandestine and avoid ruining Gilbert's undercover operation.

He hummed to himself, trying to forget the pain in his hip and back, along with the chill of his body which was now making him shiver, while waiting impatiently.

Oliver returned within five minutes with Gilbert, who was looking as disreputable as usual, except now he was doing so while in the uniform of the one of the hotel's many workers.

"Oliver has given me a quick outline of your concerns," Gilbert said, glancing back over his shoulder at the service entrance to the hotel. "I can't speak to you for long, in case someone sees me."

"I am impressed you have been able to convince anyone you work at the hotel," Tommy said.

"Is that sarcasm?"

"Just a little," Tommy grinned at him, his humour returning. "Doesn't everyone know your face by now, Gilbert?"

"You would be surprised at how anonymous I can be when I want to," Gilbert said with an air of pride. "In any case, I have friends within the staff prepared to help me. I just have to stay out of the sight of the manager. Now, hurry up, we don't have long before I need to be back inside."

Tommy wasted no more time and elaborated on the situation to Gilbert. The journalist nodded his head as he listened attentively, a frown furrowing his already rather ugly brow. When Tommy was done, he considered the situation carefully.

"An actress in peril is quite the story."

"This is not about the newspaper, Gilbert, it is about keeping Violet safe," Tommy reminded him.

Gilbert wafted a hand at him in a gesture that said he understood.

"I will keep an eye out for her, don't worry. Maybe I will even catch her assailant and give myself my own scoop!"

"I would rather you just watch and take note of anyone acting suspiciously," Tommy countered. "The police will need to do the rest."

"Don't worry, Tommy, I am on it," Gilbert promised with a cheerful grin.

Then he saw a maid coming out of the service doors and scuttled away before anyone noticed him talking to Tommy.

"I know it is not ideal, but it is better than nothing," Oliver said once he was gone.

"But is it enough?" Tommy said, a nagging doubt at the back of his mind.

He didn't like leaving such a role up to Gilbert, but what else could he do?

Chapter Eight

Clara's efforts with Norris Manx had come to nothing, but she was far from finished. After being ejected from his presence, she headed over to where a group of workmen were re-pegging a large tent that had clearly taken a pounding during the recent storm. She hoped that one of them might be able to tell her more about the incident involving the live cable that had electrocuted Violet.

The men were looking harassed and initially did not respond to Clara when she spoke to them. They were too busy, and under too much pressure, to stop work to pay attention to a random woman.

Unfortunately for them, Clara was both persistent and interfering, and she did not care to be ignored. She moved among them until she was in a position that made it difficult for them to continue working without her being in the way.

"You are standing where we want to hammer in our pegs!" an older man with a grey beard bellowed at her.

"Oh, sorry," Clara responded without moving an inch. "Did any of you work on the last movie that Violet Starling was in?"

"Oh, for crying out loud!" the bearded man stormed towards her, looking as though he might grab her and fling her out of the way.

Before he was upon her, Clara had produced one of her business cards from her handbag and was holding it in front of his face.

"Clara O'Harris, private detective. I am sorry to delay your work, but if you will kindly speak to me for just a few moments, I shall get out of your way and leave you alone. This matter is rather urgent."

The older workman did not take her card, just glared at it as if it were something offensive.

"We have no need of a private detective, especially one who is a *woman*," he managed to place a great deal of venom into his voice and make the word 'woman' sound like a curse word.

His comrades chuckled and sniggered under their breath. Clara was unmoved.

"I take it you are the foreman of this group?" Clara addressed their spokesman.

"I am, and I have a lot of work to do right now. So, if you don't get out of my way…"

"Yes, yes, you will make me," Clara shrugged at him indifferently. "I am assisting Violet Starling, who is concerned that someone is determined to cause her harm. I want to ask if any of you were present on her last movie when she was electrocuted." Clara's words had the effect she had hoped they would on her audience. They all fell into stunned silence, even the bearded foreman lost some of his belligerence.

"Someone wants to hurt Violet?" he asked, anger mingling with fear on his face and creating a strange contortion of his features.

"I fear that may be the case, but no one is taking the matter seriously. Should anything happen to Violet, it will be a dark mark against all those who dismissed her concerns as the nonsense of a young woman. I hope you and your men will not be amongst those who would treat her fears with such chauvinistic disdain?"

The foreman did not understand all the words Clara had just said, but he did understand the implication. He no longer tried to shove the annoying woman away from his work site, instead indicating that his men should pause for the time being.

"What do you want to ask us?" the foreman crossed his arms and became amenable.

"You will speak to me freely?"

"Violet has always been nice to us," the foreman explained. "Nicer than the others. She never yells or badgers us, and she treats us like people. She is a kind young lady, and I wouldn't want to see hurt come to her. So, yes, I will speak to you freely, and I suggest everyone here do the same." At his words there was a murmur of agreement from the other workmen. Clara was relieved that at last she had found some people who seemed to care about Violet and were not going to fob her off with nonsense about the starlet being over dramatic.

"What is your name?" Clara asked the foreman.

"Mr Ferguson," the bearded man replied. "I am in charge of the props and sets for the movie studio where Violet works. I typically follow Mr Manx and work on anything he is doing. Not a lot of the other fellows at the studio have the patience for him."

"I have met him," Clara nodded. "I think I understand."

"He has high priorities, that's all," Mr Ferguson shrugged. "But we were talking about Violet?"

"Yes," Clara was pleased to get back on topic, and spent a few minutes elaborating to the workmen on Violet's fears for her safety. When she was done, Mr Ferguson scratched at his ear.

"We knew about the electric cable incident and the car brakes, but we hadn't been told about the sleeping powders," he said, a look of deep distress crossing his face. "You are certain that was not simply a mistake?"

"Violet swears she did not take an overdose and, coupled with the other incidents, it makes for a disturbing pattern."

Ferguson considered this for a moment and nodded his head.

"The electrocution business was nasty," he scratched at his beard. "We all saw it happen and could do nothing. She reached for the wrong cable. There was no time to stop her."

"Violet claims she reached for the cable she was told to touch," Clara reminded him. "Who gave her instructions on which cable was safe to handle?"

"I did," Ferguson said anxiously. "I was responsible for that scene because it was potentially dangerous. I told Violet she was to reach for the cable I had marked with a small piece of red yarn. I tied the yarn in place myself, on the cable that was inactive and would have been fine to handle. It wasn't even near the live cable. But when the scene came, she reached straight for the wrong one. I was too far away to do anything. It was horrible, as I knew what was going to happen, but all I could do was watch."

Clara could imagine the man's horror as he saw the actress reaching for the wrong cable.

"She was lucky not to die," Clara said sombrely.

"Very lucky. I yelled for the power to be cut as I saw her reaching for the wrong cable, so she only received a small jolt compared to what would have happened if I had not reacted so fast."

"What happened immediately after she was electrocuted?" Clara asked.

"Pandemonium," Mr Ferguson replied with a humourless laugh. "Everyone was rushing about, someone called out the nurse who we have on set during filming for emergencies. Violet was carried away; I could not see if she was conscious or not. I was waiting for Mr Manx to lay into me, tell me I had done something wrong, but when he finally walked away from the set towards me, he was very calm. 'She pulled the wrong cable,' he said to me. It was like he was in a trance as he said. Just kept repeating the sentence over and over.

"After they took Violet to the hospital, I left the set. I was so shaken up, I could not bring myself to look at the cables for a couple of days. When I went back, the power was off, so I could handle the cables. I checked them all over, looking for any breaks or faults, but they were exactly as they had been. Finally, I looked for the piece of red yarn and there it was, on the safe cable. I tell you, she just reached for the wrong one."

Mr Ferguson shook his head.

"I think the world of Violet, but she is a little bit daft. She does all manner of peculiar stuff, and I assumed she had misunderstood my instructions."

"That is possible," Clara nodded without committing herself to saying anything further. "What about the motor car incident?"

"We don't know much about that. You would have to ask Violet's driver. We just heard that her brakes had failed, and it had nearly caused an accident."

"How long after the electrocution incident did that occur?" Clara pressed him.

Ferguson glanced at his men, clearly unsure of the answer. Someone mumbled something to him, and he nodded his head after a moment.

"Yes, that's right, it was around a month after, maybe only three weeks. We heard about it after it had happened."

"Who told you?"

"Violet's driver, Mario," Ferguson responded. "When we are at the studio, the garages where they keep the cars for the stars are next to where we keep all the props and scenery. We see Mario quite often. He was working on the car one day and came over to share a mug of tea with us, that was when he told us about the brakes."

"Did he say they had been tampered with?"

"No, just that they hadn't worked when he was driving the car, and it had given Violet a scare. She was reluctant to get back into the car unless he first tested the brakes in front of her after that."

Clara could not blame Violet for her caution. She had already suffered a terrible accident on the set, only to be followed by another mechanical failure that could have led to her death. She must have wondered what would happen next.

"I shall have to speak to Mario."

"You know everything we do now, miss, and we have to get everything prepared before filming starts," Ferguson responded. "Which is meant to be Monday, but we have props to repair and this tent to secure."

He pointedly looked at Clara. His concern for Violet had finally run out, and now he was thinking about his job, and avoiding getting into trouble with Mr Manx. Clara thanked him for speaking to her and moved out of his way. She had received from Ferguson everything she felt he could offer her and now it was time to move on. A picture was forming of the events that had scared Violet, but she had more questions for the girl.

Clara checked the time and decided to head for home for some lunch before considering her next move. As her old home was on her way back towards the *Grand Hotel* and speaking to Violet, she opted to head there rather than go out of her way across town to her new residence.

When she arrived at the house, she was warmly greeted by the dogs, who were delighted to see her for the second time that day. Annie was saying goodbye to Jenny in the hallway as Clara made her appearance. She glanced up at her and smiled.

"Just like old times, you popping in for luncheon," Annie

chuckled.

Jenny donned her hat and wished Clara farewell as she departed, the dogs following her as far as the garden gate before they ran back into the house and Annie closed the door.

"I thought I would drop in before I headed to the *Grand Hotel*. I hope I am not imposing on you," Clara said, feeling slightly abashed that she might be taking her sister-in-law's hospitality for granted.

Annie made a dismissive noise.

"Whenever did I complain about having you drop in for a bite to eat? Besides, you best go into the parlour and speak to your brother."

"He is here?"

"And feeling sorry for himself. He was kicked out of the *Grand Hotel* by Miss Starling's manager," there was a slight sparkle in Annie's eye, as if she were enjoying Tommy's discomfort.

It occurred to Clara, that her sister-in-law had not been so oblivious to Tommy's starstruck manner around Violet as she had first supposed.

"Oh dear, I had hoped he would be keeping an eye on her," Clara sighed as she headed to the parlour.

Tommy was sitting in an armchair with his legs propped up on a foot stool. He looked sorry for himself as Clara entered.

"What happened?"

"Violet's manager refused to let me stay," Tommy replied. "He had me thrown out, and then there was a minor scuffle with some of the newspapermen outside. I fell and hurt my back."

Clara decided now was not the time to berate him for failing to win over Violet's manager. She would go over herself this afternoon, and demand that he allow Tommy to carry out his work.

"It's not all bad," Tommy added, seeing Clara's thoughtful expression. "Gilbert is installed at the hotel in secret. He has agreed to keep an eye on Violet."

"You told Gilbert about Violet's situation?"

"I didn't really have a choice," Tommy grimaced. "At least she has someone on the inside watching out for her."

Clara was not convinced anyone would want Gilbert McMillan looking out for them, but she had to agree it was better than nothing. Gilbert had a good nose for trouble and was quick to pick up on anything being out of place or odd.

"Well, I cannot say my day went any better. I met Mr Manx, the director of the movie, and he was disinterested in everything I had to say. He is of the opinion that either Violet did these things to herself, somehow, or is making something out of nothing."

"That was the response I received from Mr Stevenson, her manager," Tommy concurred. "They don't take any of her worries seriously."

"Which makes *me* worried," Clara frowned. "We shall have to do our best from the outside. As yet, I have no idea about who might wish to hurt Violet. Those people willing to speak to me say she is a nice young woman, and they like her a lot."

"Maybe it isn't a personal vendetta?" Tommy suggested. "You read about professional rivalries all the time in the film world."

"Maybe," Clara wasn't sure they could speculate on motive without more information. "Whatever the case, we need to get one of us back into that hotel to watch over her. I am sure I can find a way around Stevenson when I go there this afternoon."

"You haven't met him," Tommy said bitterly, shuffling in his seat and feeling the accompanying twinge in his back that reminded him of the man.

"Everyone has their weak point, you just have to find it and manipulate it," Clara said with a confidence that she didn't feel.

Tommy gave her a dismal look.

"I hope you know what you are doing."

Chapter Nine

Clara arrived at the *Grand Hotel* a little after two. She was not surprised to see there remained a gaggle of newspapermen outside, each intent on getting a story about the stars ahead of their rivals.

If only they knew what she did, Clara mused to herself, they would be itching to get the full details.

Clara walked past them without making eye contact, (she had learned the hard way that making eye contact with a newspaperman often led to getting tangled up in their business, as they assumed you had something to say) and slipped into the hotel.

The *Grand* was currently in its 'off-season' state, which meant that it was quieter than usual, with only a handful of guests, but plenty of workmen wandering around getting on with maintenance jobs they could not complete when the place was busy.

Clara found the front desk was currently unmanned. She peered behind it to the small office beyond, which was essentially a wooden booth with glass windows on all sides to allow the person within to see the comings and goings in the foyer. There was no one there either.

Clara was not a person graced with a great deal of patience, and she wanted to get matters resolved with Mr Stevenson sooner rather than later. She was therefore on the cusp of making her own way upstairs to locate his room by herself, using a process of trial and error, or perhaps by asking one of the maids flitting around, when she heard someone making odd noises to her right.

The person was making the classic percussive hiss that everyone knows is the way you get someone's attention, at least when you are watching a play. It was far less appropriate in an everyday setting. Clara glanced over to her right, and spied Gilbert McMillan lurking in the shadows of one of the ornamental pillars that decorated the foyer of the *Grand*. She recognised him mainly from the shape of his distinctive ears, which even in the shadows that silhouetted him were noticeable.

Clara gave a quick glance around her to see if anyone was watching, then headed over to the journalist, sighing to herself. Gilbert was one of those people who, while often useful, was also rather odious and frequently a nuisance. He liked to suppose he was friends with Clara, but she preferred to keep him at arm's length under the heading of 'an acquaintance.'

"Clara, good to see you! How is married life treating you?"

"It is very enjoyable," Clara assured him. "What about you? Is life with your lady friend going smoothly?"

"Nah, she ditched me," Gilbert said without losing the grin on his face. "Said I kept odd hours, and she could not see a future for us. Personally, I think that was her mother talking, but what can you do? The hunt for a good story will always be my first love, and if she was not prepared to accept that, nothing I could do about it."

Clara was not sure the correct response to this information. Gilbert did not seem particularly distressed, so making consoling statements seemed inappropriate, then again, agreeing with him that his young lady had not been worth as much consideration as his journalism seemed even harsher.

She opted for ignoring the information as the safest option.

"You summoned me over?"

"Straight to business, Clara, as always. That is why we get along so well, we understand that our work has to come first," Gilbert said cheerfully.

Clara refrained from disagreeing, though she would have liked to, because she knew that would lead to extending the conversation longer than she cared for.

"I have been lurking at this hotel for nearly a day now," Gilbert said proudly. "I have seen a fair few interesting things, but I was unaware of the drama relating to Miss Starling until your brother informed me of the matter."

"He explained he had met with you and asked you to keep your eyes on her."

"Which I am endeavouring to do, but her suite is like a fortress. Her manager has the room right next to hers, and he keeps someone outside in the hallway at all times to prevent anyone reaching Violet without his permission."

"As extreme as that sounds, it might be for the best under the circumstances. At least if Violet is being so closely watched no one can slip into her room and cause her harm," Clara thought about what Gilbert had said. If Tommy had been allowed to take up his role as protector to the starlet, he would have been doing something very similar.

"It means I can't get close to her!" Gilbert grumbled.

"Some things *are* more important than your story, such as Violet's safety," Clara pointed out.

Gilbert gave her a look.

"We shall have to disagree on that. In any case, while she is at the hotel I am having trouble getting close enough to know what is going on. I thought I should let you know."

"Thank you, Gilbert," Clara said, though she had a hunch that Gilbert had really told her because he hoped she would come up with an idea as to how they could get around Mr Stevenson's guards. "Can you tell me anything about the people who are watching over Violet?"

"They all work for Stevenson," Gilbert shrugged. "One is a driver, another seems to be employed purely to look mean and keep people away from those Stevenson represents."

"Tommy mentioned Stevenson seemed rather possessive of Violet."

"She is currently the only actress he has on his books, and she is the most successful girl he has ever represented. There are plenty of other agencies and managers out there who would like to take her off his hands given half a chance. Last year, Violet was nearly poached from him by the Manticore Theatrical Agency. They are one of the biggest in the business, and Violet would have been a real win for them. I dare say they would have done wonders for her career too. Stevenson fended them off, somehow, but the suspicion is they are not finished trying."

"Violet is quite the asset then?"

"She has been the star of more British movies this year than any other leading lady in England, and most of them have been huge successes at the pictures. Some people will tell you Violet can sell any movie, and make it a success, just by having her name attached to it."

"Impressive," Clara agreed. "But Violet is more than merely a money-making asset. She deserves to have autonomy over her life and to choose who represents her."

"That isn't how these things work," Gilbert snorted at Clara's naivety. "The studios get their stars to sign contracts, having them work for them for so many films before they can look at going to another studio. All the young stars sign such agreements, as it gives the studios a hold over them if they prove to be good at what they do. There are lots of aspiring actors and actresses out there, and the studio likes to hedge its bets as to who might be the next best thing and hold onto them."

"Sounds awful," Clara shook her head.

Gilbert shrugged.

"It's how things work, that's all. Anyway, it wouldn't surprise me if Stevenson thought Tommy was someone from another agency trying to sneak his way in to poach Violet. That's why he reacted so fiercely."

"Then I shall just have to convince him that is not the case," Clara replied, bracing herself for the potential battle to come. "Where do I find Mr Stevenson?"

"Wait, you are going to confront him now?"

"Why would I delay? I am deeply concerned for Violet's wellbeing. She is a person to me, not just a useful asset, and I intend to keep her safe."

Gilbert considered this for a moment.

"I am going to help you."

"Oh dear, must you?"

Gilbert did not grasp the despair in her tone for what it was.

"Don't worry, I shan't compromise my position here. I will show you to Mr Stevenson's room and point out who is on duty blocking the path to Violet's suite. You know, if you want, I will gladly act as a bodyguard to Violet. Save Tommy having to keep coming here."

"If only you were saying that for purely altruistic reasons," Clara sighed at him. "Gilbert, how could I recommend you as a bodyguard to Violet, when I know you will be hunting for secrets about her the whole time you are supposed to be protecting her?"

"Why do the two things have to be mutually exclusive?"

Clara glared at him sternly.

"Even you must see that as a conflict of interest, and an affront to Violet's privacy. I would be betraying her trust."

Gilbert shuffled his feet, reluctant to admit he did see her point.

"Fine," he grumbled at last. "But put in a good word with me with Stevenson. Say I am reliable and trustworthy, then maybe I will be asked to run errands for them?"

"I think I can find my way to Violet's suite alone."

Clara turned away and headed for the stairs.

"No, wait! You can't go without me!"

Gilbert was hurrying behind her when they both heard the loud report of a gun being fired. It had not come from above them, but from a room to their left.

"That sounded like it came from the ballroom!" Gilbert was scurrying off without another word.

Clara did not even hesitate to follow him. All she could think about as she ran was that she had failed Violet. Someone had slipped into the hotel with a gun and shot at her. After all her promises, Clara had been unable to do anything to protect the young woman. Cursing Stevenson for preventing Tommy from doing his job, she was ready to scream at the first person who happened to get in her way.

The first person happened to be Violet, herself.

She was running from the ballroom, her hair streaming behind her, and tears rushing from her eyes. She zipped past Gilbert, who took a moment to realise what had occurred, before stumbling to a halt and spinning around to follow. Clara was just behind him and Violet ran straight into her.

Clutching at Clara tightly, she began to sob on her shoulder.

"It is terrible! Terrible!"

Clara wrapped her arms around her, feeling both elated Violet was safe and confused as to what must have just occurred. Had Violet shot someone she feared was coming for her?

"Violet, what has happened?" Clara asked, trying to get the girl to calm down through sheer force of will.

"Let go of her!"

The bellow came from further along the hallway, in the direction of the ballroom. Stevenson was heading their way at speed and clearly did not appreciate Clara being the one to console his starlet.

Gilbert, quite heroically, stepped in front of the man and was shoved so hard out of the way he fell backwards to the floor. Clara would have liked to suppose he had acted out of sympathy for Violet, but she feared it was because he was expecting Clara to wring every detail out of the girl before her manager intervened.

As it was, Clara was perfectly capable of standing up to Mr Stevenson by herself. As he stormed up to the pair, his face like thunder, she matched him with her own stare.

"I am Clara O'Harris, private detective. Violet has asked me to assist her. I think you ought to explain to me what has just occurred."

"I don't care who you are, you will release her!" Stevenson snapped, not one to be cowed.

Clara decided there was no point arguing with him, instead, she turned around with Violet and began leading her away.

"What do you think you are doing?" Stevenson demanded.

"Miss Starling needs to sit down and have a cup of tea. She is clearly distressed," Clara informed him. "I, personally, would like to know who let off that shot just now."

Clara meant that she wanted to know who had tried to take a shot at Violet, what she was not expecting was Violet to volunteer the information.

"It was *me*, Clara! I fired that horrid gun!"

Clara faltered in her stride.

"Who did you shoot at?"

"Poor Joshua!" Violet wailed. "I shot him in the shoulder! He fell down yelling in pain!"

Clara was utterly confused by this revelation, and her hesitation allowed Stevenson to catch up with them and snatch Violet away from her violently.

"Hey now!" Clara snarled at him.

"You get out before I have you kicked out!" Stevenson's temper was dangerous, and now he faced off with Clara, pushing Violet behind him.

When Gilbert later recounted the incident to his fellows at the *Gazette,* he described it as two tigers about to fight over an injured deer.

Clara drew herself up before Stevenson, her stubbornness not to be outdone by the manager's ferocity.

"I don't know who you think you are demanding people be removed from this hotel, but I have every right to be here, and I shall not simply abandon Violet. Her safety is my priority, and I shall do all in my power to protect her."

"You think her safety is not a priority to me too?"

"I think that highly unlikely, at least not for the same reasons as me. You care about her as something that makes you money, I care about her as a person."

"How dare you!"

Stevenson took a pace towards Clara and demonstrated that he was considerably taller than her. Clara was not intimidated, though anyone with common sense would have realised now was probably a good moment to back off.

Fortunately for them both, they were distracted by Violet using the opportunity to run away. She dashed down the hallway and out of sight before either could react.

"Now look what you have done!" Stevenson yelled at Clara, before giving her a hard shove that sent her sprawling back against the wall before he ran off in pursuit of his starlet.

Clara regained her balance as quickly as she could, and with Gilbert at her elbow, started to follow. They dashed back to the foyer of the hotel, only to realise there was a commotion occurring out the front.

"She dashed outside!" Gilbert said in alarm, realising his story of the year had just run out into a crowd of rival newspapermen.

They hastened to follow, but all they saw outside was a swirling crowd of people. Violet had briefly been intercepted by the newspapermen, but then Stevenson had charged out of the hotel like a raging bull. He had thrown himself among the journalists and started laying punches on whoever came to hand. In the confusion, Violet had escaped once again and had now disappeared. Stevenson, on the other hand, was being held in place by three newspapermen, while another two were rolling on the ground holding various body parts he had damaged as he flailed into the group.

The newspapermen were furious, but they also saw a good story in the making. Nothing better for the newspapers than describing how their own reporters had been assaulted by Violet Starling's manager, from whom it appeared she was fleeing.

Gilbert and Clara stood on the steps of the hotel watching the scene before them.

"I wish he had punched me," Gilbert sighed, deflated he was not the one now brawling with the manager.

Clara gave him a disbelieving look, then her attention was back on the street.

Where had Violet run to?

Clara's fears for the starlet's safety now grew – if she had been in peril when she had Stevenson and his goons watching over her, how much worse would it be now that she was out there alone, with her potential killer free to do as he or she pleased?

Chapter Ten

Inspector Park-Coombs was summoned to the *Grand* by the hotel manager, who was deeply alarmed by what had happened. He had guests threatening to leave after they had heard the gunshot, glimpsed Mr MacKenzie being taken away by an ambulance, and then witnessed the scuffle outside the hotel involving the newspapermen and Stevenson.

The arrival of the police did not help matters, but it did at least look as though the hotel manager was attempting to restore order to proceedings.

Park-Coombs strode in wearing his long, light brown overcoat and trilby hat. He looked around the foyer, his eyes briefly landing on Stevenson, then moving onto a newspaperman who was holding a bloodied handkerchief to his nose. Park-Coombs had brought a handful of constables with him when he heard the extent of the trouble that had occurred that morning. They were fanned out behind him as he took in the scene.

"Good afternoon, Inspector."

Park-Coombs glanced to his right and saw Clara leaning against the front desk in the foyer. He nodded at her with a twinkle in his eyes.

"Should have known you would be here."

"It has been quite the afternoon so far," Clara sighed to him. "I am deeply concerned about Violet Starling and where she has disappeared to. Might I ask you to send some constables out to look for her? She could be in danger."

Park-Coombs twitched his thick moustache as he heard this information.

"Violet Starling, the movie actress?"

"The one and the same. She ran off after the incident with Joshua MacKenzie, and it is paramount she is found swiftly."

The inspector turned back to his constables, who had overheard this conversation and were now looking keenly at him, all hoping to be picked to find the missing actress. Park-Coombs motioned randomly at two of them, disappointing the rest, and sent them off to try to locate Violet.

"I don't expect she has gone far," Park-Coombs said confidently. "Probably just needed some air."

Clara was less convinced about Violet remaining nearby; she had seen the panic on the girl's face. For all they knew, she had already caught a train, and was heading to any number of places, though Clara was fairly certain she had not left the hotel with any money, which would certainly limit her options.

"Now, what precisely has gone on here?" Park-Coombs flicked his attention to the group of individuals before him.

They consisted of twelve newspapermen – all those who had been outside at the time Stevenson had caused chaos – three of which were sporting injuries, including the fellow with the broken nose. Stevenson was sat on a chair amongst them, arms folded across his chest, barely containing his fury. The only reason he was not moving was because he had twelve watchdogs determined to see him pay for assaulting some of their number.

Then there was the hotel manager, who was flitting around in the background, trying to keep any guests away from the drama, and two men in long dark coats who worked for Mr Stevenson. One was the driver who chauffeured Miss Starling around, the other was a fellow who acted as a general dogsbody for the manager, and also as a bit of muscle. Both looked surly, and made Park-Coombs want to arrest them on the spot simply for making his policeman's instincts twitch.

Among those who remained, was Mr MacKenzie's manager and his secretary - both were agitated they had not been able to follow the actor to the hospital – and lastly there was Clara and Gilbert.

Park-Coombs quickly assessed the situation before him and decided to start his investigation by asking Clara what she knew.

"There was a gunshot from the ballroom. Gilbert and I went running to see what had happened," Clara explained to him. "I feared someone had taken a shot at Violet. She has hired me because she is scared that someone is out to kill her. As it happens, Violet was the one who shot the gun at Mr MacKenzie. The bullet hit him in the shoulder and lodged there."

"Anyone know why she shot Mr MacKenzie?" Park-Coombs asked aloud.

MacKenzie's manager, Mr Hershel, put up his hand and replied.

"They were rehearsing a scene for the movie. As part of the scene, Violet pointed the gun at Joshua and shot him. Only, the gun is supposed to only ever contain blanks, and during rehearsals it is meant to be unloaded."

"Then Miss Starling believed the gun was empty?" Park-Coombs clarified.

"If you are suggesting Violet would deliberately shoot Joshua you are a bigger fool than you look!" Stevenson could not help himself.

Insulting a police inspector was hardly a wise move, but Stevenson was not renowned for his wisdom when his temper was up.

"You should be less concerned about what happened here, and more concerned about finding my actress!"

"I think I shall determine how I divide my manpower," Park-Coombs said to him politely. "After all, it is not a crime to run off, but it is a crime to shoot a man."

"It was an accident, I am sure of it," Mr Hershel insisted. "Violet was distraught after the gun went off and Joshua collapsed."

"Where did this gun come from?" Park-Coombs enquired.

"We brought it from the props department," Hershel explained. "Miss Jamieson collected the items we desired for the rehearsal last night."

Miss Jamieson was Mr Hershel's secretary, an older, plump woman who looked terrified in the face of being interrogated by a policeman. The colour had completely drained from her face, and only her years of professionalism were enabling her to keep from descending into shock over recent events.

"You collected the box of props?" Park-Coombs prompted her.

"Yes, I did," Miss Jamieson voice came out as a squeak. "I fetched them last night in Mr Hershel's car. There were not many items to bring over. I had them all in the same box on the back seat of the car."

"Who gave you the box of props?"

"The head of the props department, Mr Ferguson."

Park-Coombs made a note of this.

"Between you bringing the props back to the hotel, and the time of the rehearsal, where were they kept?"

"In the car. I only fetched them out when it was time to use them."

"Was the car locked?"

Miss Jamieson nodded her head.

"I had no reason to suppose anyone could tamper with them. How could I know someone would load the gun?"

Mr Hershel patted her hand, which finally broke her resolve, and she started to cry.

Park-Coombs turned his attention to Mr Stevenson.

"Who instructed Violet to fire the gun?"

"What?" Stevenson spluttered.

"Who told Violet to pull the trigger? As it was a rehearsal, I wondered why it was necessary for her to actually fire the gun?"

"For realism," Stevenson threw up his arms as if this ought to be obvious. "We try to make the rehearsals as realistic as possible; it helps with the performance. Violet was not in the right frame of mind this morning, and her acting lacked her usual flare, so I told her to pull the trigger and make the gun click, rather than just go 'bang, bang' when she pretended to fire it. I was trying to get her spark back!"

"So, you told her to shoot Mr MacKenzie?"

"Hang on!" Stevenson shot to his feet, but the newspapermen were ready for him and bunched closer. Stevenson glowered but sat back down. "It was a prop gun! I told her to pull the trigger as if it was real to get her into the role. She was lacklustre and the rehearsal was drab. Do you really think I would have told her to pull the trigger of a loaded gun when it was aimed at Joshua MacKenzie?"

Park-Coombs refrained from supplying him with an answer, but he made another note.

"Mr Stevenson, I shall have to arrest you for common assault."

"There is no cause..."

Park-Coombs pointed his pencil at the fellow with the broken nose, then the two others with injuries, to silence Mr Stevenson.

"You have committed a crime against these gentlemen. Constable, arrest him," Park-Coombs now wagged his pencil at one of the policemen who had accompanied him that morning.

Stevenson protested but had the sense not to fight as he was escorted away to the police station.

"I shall need to arrest Miss Starling too when she shows up. Even if this was an accident, she did shoot Mr MacKenzie," Park-Coombs continued. "Can anyone tell me how he is doing?"

"They took him to hospital to remove the bullet," Mr Hershel responded. "He was in a lot of pain but was otherwise in good spirits. Not the first time Joshua has been shot – he served in the war."

"I take it Miss Starling ran away because she was distressed by what she had done?" the inspector asked.

"Actually, I think she was trying to get away from her manager," Clara interjected. "She did flee the ballroom in tears after the accident, but she was with me, and showed no sign of departing until Stevenson came after her. I believe she is afraid of that man."

"Mr Stevenson is a bully," Mr Hershel added. "The poor girl is under his complete control. I feel for her, I really do. I would like to see something done to release her from her contract to him. She deserves better."

"Could she not just leave him?" Park-Coombs frowned.

"You don't understand how these contracts work," Hershel shook his head sadly. "Violet's career is wrapped up with Stevenson's. He is responsible for negotiating with the studios on her behalf, if she were to leave him, it could infringe on her contract with the studio, unless he agreed to the arrangement. Even a successful film star like Violet could find herself out of work if Stevenson wishes it to be so. There are plenty of aspiring actresses who would fill her shoes in an instant if they could."

Park-Coombs frowned at this information, thinking it was a terrible world they lived in where a girl was beholden to a bully out of fear for her career.

"Inspector, might I have a word?" Clara moved towards him.

Gilbert was at her side immediately; she looked at him pointedly.

"In private."

Gilbert gave her a nonchalant shrug, as if he didn't care. Clara did not put it past him to eavesdrop on any conversation she had with the inspector.

"I need to see the ballroom, why don't we talk there?" Park-Coombs suggested.

Clara concurred, and they headed to the scene of Joshua's shooting. There was a puddle of blood on the floor where the actor had fallen, it was staining the wooden parquet tiles. Park-Coombs glanced at it as they entered.

"What do you want to discuss with me?"

Behind him, Clara pulled the ballroom doors closed and moved the inspector towards the windows on the far side, hopeful that this would prevent them from being overheard.

"Violet Starling came to me yesterday saying she believed someone was trying to kill her," Clara got to the point at once. "There have been a series of accidents involving her, any of which could have proven fatal. She believes they were not accidents at all."

"And you have been looking into the matter," Park-Coombs nodded. "And then this happens."

"Exactly. I am not sure how this shooting fits in with the rest, but I cannot help but think it was meant to be another attempt on Violet's life. Possibly the assassin thought the prop gun was to be aimed at her during the rehearsal of this scene."

"It is suspicious that the gun was loaded with real bullets. A good prop department manager would never allow such an oversight, unless it was done secretly."

Park-Coombs caught Clara's look as he revealed this unexpected knowledge.

"My cousin's son is fascinated by the moving pictures. He sometimes comes over to our house and brings his movie magazines with him. He is a veritable treasure trove of information about how the whole thing works. He is coming down to visit this weekend, so we can take a trip to see them filming this new picture."

"Let us hope there is still a movie being made, as it seems to me, we have someone out to cause genuine harm to Violet and, so far, only luck has saved her from danger."

"What were the other accidents?"

"She was electrocuted on set. The brakes of her car were tampered with, and someone overdosed her on sleeping powders, though I am not sure how they managed that as yet."

Park-Coombs rubbed at his chin thoughtfully.

"Nasty business. We best find Miss Starling as quickly as we can. Do you have any suspects in mind?"

"Not as yet, Violet has not offered me a motive for someone wanting her dead, though if anyone was to act so callously, I could well imagine it being Mr Stevenson."

"The manager wanting to shoot his own star, why?"

"Jealousy that she might be stolen from him? Possessive people are not always rational about these things. Maybe he feels that if he cannot have her, no one can, but that does not really fit the facts, as Violet is tied to him by her contract."

"No doubt she makes the gentleman a lot of money," Park-Coombs nodded. "He sounds more like a pimp than a manager."

"Not so far from the truth, I fear, especially when it comes to young actresses. They are so desperate for roles and afraid of being overlooked."

Park-Coombs could think of nothing to say to that. He promised

Clara he would do all he could to find Violet swiftly. She thanked him and let him get on with his work.

Clara remained a few moments more in the ballroom, lost in her thoughts, then a maid entered to start cleaning up the blood puddle, and Clara decided it was time to head home.

Chapter Eleven

"I was beginning to think I would have to send out a search party to look for you."

Captain O'Harris gave his wife a broad grin as she entered the hallway of the Home for Convalescing Veterans of the Great War. He had his arms full with a large box that he was transporting from his office to the drawing room across the hall.

"I answered a plea for help that became somewhat more involved than I had anticipated," Clara explained.

O'Harris' grin faded as he saw her sadness.

"What happened?"

"Tell me what's in that box first," Clara said, forcing a smile. "Should you not put it down where you intended it to go? It looks heavy."

"It is heavy," O'Harris conceded, heading onwards to the drawing room. "It contains a film projector, one of the newest models, and I also have a selection of film reels to fill it."

"A film projector?"

"I thought it would be a good addition to the range of activities we offer the men," O'Harris explained. "Not all of them are comfortable going to the pictures. They can find the theatres cramped or be afraid the darkness and noise will initiate a relapse."

"It is a grand idea," Clara said, watching as he placed the heavy box on a sofa in the room.

The sofa creaked quietly in protest.

"I shall need to create a proper 'movie theatre' for it eventually, but for the time being I thought I would use this drawing room. We can pull the drapes, put the screen up over the window, and bring in further seating." O'Harris surveyed the room, which at one time had been his study. It was north facing and generally dark, even in the summer, which made it ideal for projecting movies.

"I am looking forward to the first viewing," Clara informed him.

O'Harris was brought back to the moment and glanced at his wife with a softly enquiring expression.

"Well, what's wrong?"

Clara sighed and flopped down on the sofa beside the boxed projector.

"I went out today to meet with Violet Starling."

"The film diva!"

Clara gave him a look.

"Why would you call her a diva?"

"She looks like she would cut you dead in the street in her films," O'Harris shrugged. "And if you ever read any of the gossip about her, she is quite demanding and somewhat unreasonable. I think in one production she refused to use the dressing room they had arranged for her until they provided her with fresh lilies in it every morning."

"That sounds like the sort of thing magazines like to make up, and is nothing like the woman I met today," Clara promised him. "Violet is a sweet, shy person, and she is mortally terrified for her life."

"Someone wants to hurt Violet Starling!" O'Harris was astounded.

He sat down in the armchair opposite Clara and leaned forward attentively. Clara proceeded to describe to him her eventful day and the troubles Violet was experiencing. When she was done, O'Harris' face had crumpled into a look of concern.

"This Stevenson fellow sounds like a dog."

"I completely agree," Clara grumbled. "He had the nerve to shove me into a wall."

"What!" O'Harris leapt up. "How dare he? I shall give him a piece of my mind!"

Clara was always amused at how protective O'Harris became around her; on the whole, most of the men in her life let her get on with protecting herself and would only intervene if there was a real risk of her being seriously hurt. Tommy would have asked her if she had shoved Stevenson back, for instance.

O'Harris, however, always became righteously indignant whenever he heard that someone had threatened Clara. He regularly forgot that his wife was very capable of defending herself.

"I am perfectly fine, John. It was Gilbert who took a proper tumble at Stevenson's hands, and you should see the mess he made of some of the newspapermen who were waiting outside the hotel. In any case, he is in the hands of the police now."

"That horrid journalist, Gilbert, was there?" O'Harris was calming down, restored to equilibrium by the knowledge Stevenson was in police custody.

"Gilbert is always where there is a story occurring," Clara said ironically. "At this precise moment in time, he is pretending to be a staff member at the *Grand Hotel* in an effort to secure a scoop on either Violet or her co-star, Joshua MacKenzie."

"The one she shot today?" O'Harris shook his head. "I know they always say the movies are a cutthroat business, but I didn't think that was what they meant."

"I am really worried about Violet," Clara groaned and rubbed at her temples, feeling exhausted by the day she had just had. "I was meant to be protecting her, but all my plans came to nothing. Stevenson refused to allow Tommy to be her bodyguard, and now she has run off."

"I am sure if I asked the fellows here, we could arrange a search party for her," O'Harris replied, meaning the men at his home.

Clara almost refused, then she considered the idea. As much as she had faith in Inspector Park-Coombs, she also knew he had limited resources to expend on chasing down Violet. The couple of constables he had sent to look for her would be summoned back to their regular duty soon enough, and the hunt for the missing actress would be aborted until they had further information.

The inspector was probably hoping Violet would simply turn up once the evening came on and she realised how cold and uncomfortable it was away from the hotel. Clara was not so nonchalant; she had seen the real terror in Violet's eyes as she had fled. Maybe a search party would be a good idea? The men at the Home would certainly agree as it would give them something different to do, and they liked to feel useful. They could fall back on the skills they had to learn during the war to search for the missing actress, and what gentleman would refuse to go looking for a damsel in distress who also happened to be the famous Violet Starling?

"It's worth a try," Clara nodded to her husband. "If we find her, we should bring her back here. I don't trust her around Stevenson, and no matter what he says I shall not be deterred from protecting her."

O'Harris smiled to himself, pleased to see the return of her determination. Clara was like a warrior going to battle when it came to defending someone who asked for her help, and it was a trait he greatly admired. It was one of the reasons he loved her so much – her stoic persistence in trying to put right the wrongs of the world.

"I shall get onto things straight away," he rose from his seat. "How far could she have gone from the hotel?"

"I dare say, not far. I didn't see her with a handbag, so my original thought that she could have boarded a train is unlikely. She had no coat or hat either, so she must be cold. It is possible she has already returned to the hotel. Perhaps I should make a telephone call to determine…"

As she spoke, the telephone in the hall began to ring. There was something about its tone, (which was exactly the same as it always was, but somehow in the moment seemed more intense and urgent) that filled her with a sense of dread. Clara rose to her feet and rushed past O'Harris before he could respond to the summons.

Clara grabbed up the receiver, her heart pounding furiously in her chest.

"Hello?"

"Clara, it is Park-Coombs."

"Inspector," Clara's feeling of dread skyrocketed, and her stomach churned unhappily. "You have news?"

"I do Clara. We found Violet Starling."

He did not sound elated by this news. Clara braced herself.

"Is she all right?"

"Clara, Violet went to the train station to try to return to London, but she did not have enough money for a ticket. She went and stood on the platform, people say she was agitated and crying. When the next train pulled in, she…"

"Don't say it, Inspector, I refuse to believe she deliberately threw herself in front of the train," Clara's voice was tense with tears.

"Nonetheless, she ended up on the rails," Park-Coombs concluded. "Dr Deáth has retrieved the body, but the cause of her demise is rather obvious. I have witnesses who heard her scream, and realised she was on the track, but it was too late to do anything."

Clara felt as though the blood was draining from her body. A sensation of intense cold crept over her, starting at her legs and working upwards.

She had failed.

Clara O'Harris had been asked to protect a woman from her assassins, and she had failed.

"Clara?"

"Inspector, this was not a suicide," Clara insisted to him, determined that at least something would come from the tragedy, and the person behind Violet's death would be found.

"She had tried once before. I was talking to Stevenson..."

"Do not listen to a word he says! Violet was afraid for her life, but she was not afraid of herself! She did not throw herself beneath that train!"

Behind her, Clara heard O'Harris gasp.

"Clara, I know this is upsetting, but the evidence points to Violet being overcome. You know what these movie actresses are like. They take life a little too seriously." Clara clenched her teeth, wanting to scream at the inspector for his patronising tone.

"All day people have been dismissing Violet's concerns as her being overdramatic. No one would take her seriously and now look at what has occurred! I refuse to be like them. I believed Violet when she said she feared for her life. I shall never forgive myself for failing her."

"Don't be so harsh on yourself, Clara, you couldn't have known she would do this."

Clara was tired of his attempts to dismiss the matter as a suicide. Why was it every man in Violet's life had been so keen to make her out to be flighty, and her own worst enemy? No one had really cared about her; all they cared about was her ability to make them money.

Now she was gone, and Park-Coombs was reacting just the way her killer no doubt intended – writing her off as another over-emotional woman who could not handle the pressure and fame of stardom.

"Clara?"

"Inspector, I intend to prove Violet's death was not a suicide, and in doing so I shall find her killer."

Park-Coombs gave a familiar groan.

"You can do as you please, Clara, but I think you are wasting your time."

"It is my time to waste," Clara informed him. "Good evening, Inspector."

She put the telephone receiver down with a fierceness that surprised herself. Warm tears were pricking at her eyes. She was furious with all those who had refused to believe Violet, but she was especially furious with herself for not trying harder.

Why had she not attempted to seek her out when she left the hotel? Instead, she had hung around to hear what Stevenson had to say, thinking she could be useful there, and then – *then!* – she had simply gone home!

She clenched her fists so hard she felt her nails digging into her palms.

A tender hand on her shoulder reminded her that O'Harris was just behind her. His quiet understanding was all it took to unleash the tears of fury, guilt and grief that now ran down Clara's cheeks. She spun around and leaned against him.

"I have been so stupid!"

"No, you have not. You did your best, as you always do."

"My best was not good enough today," Clara pressed her head into his shoulder.

The tears flowed but she did not sob. Clara was not one for crying and found it very hard to release her emotions that way. She shook with emotion, nonetheless, and was grateful for feeling O'Harris' strong arms curling around her and holding her close. For a long time, she said nothing, just leaned against him, berating herself mentally.

Then Clara pulled herself together. Crying over spilt milk did not put the milk back into the bottle. She had a job to do.

Violet had asked her to find the person threatening her life, and Clara would do that. She might have failed to protect the actress, but she would not fail to find her some justice. She would prove Violet did not simply throw herself beneath a train out of despair. There had been a concerted effort made against the actress to destroy her, for a reason Violet could not fathom. Well, Clara *would* fathom it, and when she was done, she would make the person who did this to Violet pay for their actions.

She moved back from O'Harris, wiping at her eyes.

"I suggest supper before we get back to work, it is going to be a long night."

Clara looked up at her husband and his gentle smile. He understood her completely. He wasn't going to try to convince her to stop blaming herself, instead he was going to help her make things right.

"I need to telephone Tommy and tell him the news, then we should summon everyone here to begin our investigation," she said, still trembling a fraction from her intense emotions.

"Everyone?"

"Tommy, of course, but also Oliver, as he has been around the hotel a lot recently taking photographs, and he may have seen something that he didn't realise was important at the time. And I'm afraid, we shall have to summon Gilbert. As disagreeable as he is, he was in the hotel and might have information, also he is a direct contact with the other newspapermen who were stalking Violet and he might be able to get something from them that I cannot."

O'Harris pulled a face, but didn't argue with her logic.

"What about the inspector? Is he invited."

"He made it plain he thinks there is no case here," Clara said, her anger flaring again. "So, we shall let him continue in that delusion until we have information to disprove his assumption."

O'Harris nodded in understanding.

"I shall tell cook to prepare a large and hearty supper for our guests."

"And I shall begin making telephone calls."

Feeling she had a purpose again, Clara turned back to the telephone as O'Harris headed down the hallway. As he slipped past her, Clara spoke.

"Thank you, John."

O'Harris turned around, his smile lighting up his handsome face.

"Don't mention it, Clara, you know I am always here to fight your corner."

"Thank you for trusting me," Clara added.

O'Harris snorted with laughter.

"Oh, that is easy! You have a knack for never being wrong!"

Chapter Twelve

By seven o'clock they were all gathered around the small table in O'Harris' private study eating supper and discussing their plans for the evening. Annie had decided to accompany Tommy after hearing from him how upset Clara had been over the tragic death of Violet. She fancied that Clara would appreciate having another woman around the table. Men could be so dense when it came to female emotions, (or male emotions, for that matter) and it was best to not leave these things entirely up to them.

As it happened, by the time they had all arrived, Clara had regained her composure and, though still angry at her failure, was able to see it in context. After all, she could hardly protect Violet when *she* had been the one to run away from *her*. Perhaps she should have tried searching for her, and maybe she ought to have gone immediately to the train station, as it *had* occurred to her that Violet may board a train, but she had been distracted by other events, and guilt was not going to bring Violet back.

Besides, the police had gone searching for Violet, and if they could not locate her, why would Clara have had any more luck?

She would run the matter over and over in head for many nights and would perhaps always doubt what she had done, and question herself over the matter, but ultimately nothing would be changed, and she had to focus on what she could do now.

Tommy was as distressed as Clara by the news that Violet had perished. His guilt was just as strong, knowing he had been cast out by Stevenson, and had consented rather readily to giving up on the notion of being Violet's bodyguard. But in his case, he *had* been of the opinion that Violet was probably over-reacting. He had fallen into the trap of thinking that actresses, and young women in general, had a tendency to be too quick to see threat and danger in a given situation.

He had never really supposed someone was out to hurt Violet. He was trying very hard not to dwell on that, especially as he had cursed Violet's name after he had taken his tumble at the hotel and hurt his back. He was still sore and stiff, and he had thought some rather unkind things about the starlet as a result.

Gilbert and Oliver did not share in the guilt. Oliver was somewhat bemused at the events of the day, and as to why he had been asked to attend the supper, but then bemusement was Oliver's regular state of being.

Gilbert was just excited that Clara had included him. He had heard about Violet's demise ahead of anyone else, which meant *he* had heard about it ahead of any other newspaperman. His excitement that he had a scoop was only tempered by the knowledge he might have an even bigger one if Clara proved to be correct, and someone had murdered Violet.

As they sat and ate, Clara outlined her plan of action.

"The news will be out tomorrow that Violet is dead. I imagine you will make sure your editor has the story, Gilbert, ahead of the national press?"

Gilbert beamed broadly to indicate she was correct.

"In any case, the movie studio will issue a statement at some point explaining what has happened. In the meantime, we need to use our knowledge to our advantage while trying to determine who murdered her. Only a handful of people at the studio will have been informed of the tragedy. If anyone else knows about her death, then we will have to question how they came across that information."

"Oh, that might mean they are the killer?" Oliver interjected, catching up with what she was saying.

"Exactly," Clara smiled at him. "I have a few ideas of where to begin, but it will require us to be somewhat underhanded in our actions."

Gilbert's grin managed to get bigger.

"Tonight, I intend to sneak up to Violet's suite and search it from top to bottom for any clue as to who might have held a grudge against her. In the meantime, Gilbert will be searching Mr Stevenson's room."

Gilbert tilted his head, looking hurt.

"Why do I have to search the manager's room?"

"Because it would be uncouth for a man to search Violet's bedroom," Clara answered him without hesitation.

"May I remind you, the lady is dead," Gilbert huffed.

"If you are nervous about searching Mr Stevenson's room, then Tommy can do it instead," Clara pretended to misunderstand.

"I am not nervous!"

"Stevenson is at the police station, under arrest for assault, and I doubt he will be allowed to go free for a while. You should be safe to search his room, Tommy."

"Hey!" Gilbert nearly shouted. "*I* am searching his room! Gilbert McMillan fears no man in his search for the truth!"

"What about a woman?" O'Harris said under his breath, so only Clara heard.

She managed to keep the smirk off her lips.

"Good, then, Gilbert, that is arranged. You have the means to get me into the hotel and can gain access to the keys for the suite."

"You shouldn't go alone, Clara," Annie interrupted. "You already told us how nasty Mr Stevenson was to you, and his staff will surely be no better."

"Never fear, Annie, I have already considered having a lookout to keep watch and make sure we are not disturbed or come to any harm. O'Harris volunteered as soon as I mentioned it."

"I shall be watching the corridor for anyone approaching," he promised Annie. "If Stevenson returns unexpectedly, or one of his people wanders in that direction, I shall alert the searchers while distracting whoever approaches."

"What can I do?" Tommy asked, a little disappointed that he was not going to be involved with the search of the hotel. It sounded like it could prove quite interesting, and he fancied having another round with Stevenson, if they were wrong and he had escaped the clutches of the police.

"You cannot be near the hotel because you will be recognised," Clara explained to her brother, understanding his disappointment. "However, I need you to head to the movie encampment on the green and do some nosing around. Talk to people and see who knows about Violet's death without revealing it. I also want to know more about how that gun ended up being loaded with real bullets. I thought you could take Oliver. We may need photographs of anything suspicious."

That was rather unlikely, but Clara had asked Oliver to attend to see what he knew about Violet's stay at the hotel – it had turned out he had not known much – and he had then indicated he wanted to help. Sending him home seemed unkind, even though Oliver was not renowned for his abilities as a detective.

She was relieved Tommy said nothing about the absurdity of having Oliver tag along to take photographs at night. He seemed to appreciate what she was doing.

"That pretty much covers everything we can do tonight. I would like to go to the train station and find out exactly what people saw, but I think that would be better done during the day. Tonight is about acting as surreptitiously as possible. Are we all agreed?"

Everyone was nodding their heads when Annie spoke up.

"What about me?"

Clara hesitated. She had anticipated Annie would go home and had not considered her having a role in their investigation. Now she wondered where best to send Annie.

"It's too cold for you to be bumbling around with us on the green," Tommy said with a look of concern.

"It is not all that cold, and I have a coat," Annie grumbled at him, then she glared around the table. "I am tired of people treating me as if I am made of glass. I am perfectly capable of accompanying any of you on this errand, and you need to appreciate that."

"Well said, Annie," Gilbert cheered her on.

Annie glowered in his direction which quickly quelled his enthusiasm.

"I am sorry I have been so neglectful of your feelings, Annie," Clara apologised. "I truthfully did not think you would want to be involved, but I would very much appreciate your assistance in searching Violet's suite. I imagine it is quite big, and a second pair of eyes would be useful."

Gilbert made a murmur about *him* being a perfect second pair of eyes, but he caught the stern look O'Harris cast in his direction and hastily fell silent.

"You are not just saying that to appease me?" Annie demanded.

Clara did not falter for a moment.

"Of course not! Had I known you would be interested in helping,

I would have suggested the arrangement earlier. But I know you are very busy Annie and prefer to spend your evenings at home. I would not like to impose on your routine."

"You are not imposing," Annie said primly. "I am quite ahead with my chores, what with having Jenny assisting me."

Having soothed Annie's ego, Clara relaxed.

"If we are all agreed, I suggest we finish our supper and head off at once. Time is now of the essence."

Half an hour later, they were bundling into two cars provided by O'Harris. The first, carrying himself, Clara, Annie, and Gilbert would head to the *Grand Hotel*, while the second car, being driven by Jones, the O'Harrises' chauffeur, would take Tommy and Oliver to the movie makers' temporary encampment on the green. With a handful of parting words and wishes of good luck in their endeavours, the two parties separated and headed for their respective destinations.

Gilbert was elated to be part of the main search. He would have preferred to be rooting around in the late Miss Starling's rooms, of course, but he would settle for those of her manager. He was ahead of the game and that was all that mattered.

He instructed O'Harris how to find the back road to the hotel, and where he could park the car out of sight, then they all headed through the yard, and in through the service doors.

The hotel was quiet, except for the night staff doing things such as the laundry and cleaning the main downstairs rooms. With the hotel virtually empty, there was not much for them to do, and they were going about their tasks in an idle fashion. The night manager would be sitting in the office behind the main desk, ready in case any of the guests required something at this late hour, but Gilbert knew how to circumvent his gaze. There was a service staircase the staff used, and he led his companions up to the fourth floor where Violet had her suite.

They met with no one. Stevenson and Violet's rooms were unguarded, there being no need to watch over them now the actress was permanently absent. Clara hoped Stevenson's two goons had gone to bed, glad to be relieved of their duties for the night.

Gilbert had swiped the master key for the floor from a row of hooks in the service area and used these to unlock the doors of both rooms.

"Good luck everyone," he gave a mock salute to O'Harris, which earned him a grumble of dislike, before he headed into Stevenson's room.

Clara exchanged her own glance with her husband, attempting to silently apologise for the necessity of involving Gilbert, then headed with Annie into Violet's suite.

"Oh heavens!" Annie came to an abrupt halt at the sight of the room when Clara turned on the lights.

Clothes and belongings were scattered everywhere; the bed was in disarray, untouched from that morning, while there was a tray of half-eaten food resting on a foot stool. The curtains were still drawn, and the air was stale.

"Has someone searched this place ahead of us?" Annie asked.

Clara could not deny that was a possibility, but the drawers and doors of all the furniture were shut and, in her experience, people in a hurry to search a room were not so careful to hide their tracks – haste overriding decorum.

"I think this might just be how Violet left it," Clara said. "I mean, why would someone searching the place throw her clothes all over the floor?"

Annie had picked up a nightdress that shimmered in the electric light.

"This is satin," she said, torn between feeling appalled or mystified as to why Violet would treat such a precious item with a complete lack of care.

Clara was heading to the wardrobe in the corner of the room. Opening it she revealed an array of outfits, all still on their hangars.

"I am surmising only her used clothes were discarded on the floor," Clara remarked. "She has plenty of others, it would seem."

It struck her then, that the woman who had purchased and worn all these wondrous items would never return to wear them again. Every now and again, she would forget that Violet was dead, then the reality would sneak up on her suddenly and catch her unawares. She felt her sadness returning as she looked at the items in the wardrobe.

Annie was puttering to herself and picking up the discarded clothes from the floor. Clara chose to ignore her, knowing Annie would not be able to settle down to searching until she had restored some sort of order to the room. Clara focused her attention on beginning her search. Considering the size of the suite, which consisted of bedroom, sitting room and bathroom, it would take time to search it thoroughly, especially with the way Violet had scattered herself about the place. But if there was a clue as to what happened to Violet, and who was responsible, Clara would find it. She owed her that much.

Closing the wardrobe doors on the clothes, which now felt like an accusation that their owner was never returning, Clara set about unravelling the mystery of Violet's life and death. She had made the actress a promise, and while she had failed to uphold one part of it, she would not fail in the other.

She would find the person who bore such a grudge against Violet they were prepared to go to any length to destroy her, and when she did find them, she would make sure they faced justice, but not until after they had faced her full, unrepentant, wrath.

Chapter Thirteen

"This is really exciting!" Oliver said as they slipped onto the green in the shadows of the night.

Their adventure happened to coincide with the moon being on the wane, it was barely a sliver in the sky, and this meant the darkness of the night was at its deepest. Tommy had brought a torch with him but was being careful where he used it. He was not sure what sort of security there might be in place around the encampment, and he didn't want to alert anyone to their presence prematurely.

They stumbled around the tents, bumping into posts they had failed to see in the dark or tripping over guide ropes. Tommy did his best not to hiss in pain every time he caught his foot and stumbled, an action that brought fresh discomfort to his tender back.

Oliver continued chattering in a low, enthusiastic whisper.

"I mean, I had hoped to come here and take pictures of the encampment for the newspaper, but the arrangement had not been approved as yet. In any case, it wouldn't have been like this, sneaking around, acting like thieves in the night."

"We are investigators, not thieves," Tommy corrected him.

"Even so, it feels as if we are doing something underhand. Is this illegal?"

Tommy hesitated over his answer.

"Possibly, though it is something of a grey area as the green is common ground so no one can technically prevent us from walking over it, but going inside the tents is going to be trespassing."

"How daring!" Oliver smiled. "I wish I had my camera."

Tommy had persuaded him to leave the cumbersome item in the car, despite Clara having mentioned him taking photographs.

"You couldn't take pictures right now, in the dark. We are going to scout out the place, see if we can find some clues, and then you can come back in daylight to take pictures."

"You think if we were here during the day then people would keep us away from anything that reveals who killed Violet?"

Tommy thought that the stupidest question Oliver could have asked – of course, the killer would want to keep them away from any clues that could reveal what had happened to Violet. Then he realised what Oliver was really trying to say. He was suggesting the scheme against Violet was wider known than simply one person with a vendetta.

Again, Tommy thought that ridiculous, why would the entire studio staff conspire in the murder of their best actress?

"I think, if the killer became aware of what we were doing, they would certainly try to stop us," Tommy politely responded.

He was trying to recall why he had been the one stuck with Oliver; was it just because he was a pretty good babysitter for the inept photographer? Tommy would have preferred to be snooping around alone, but what he preferred, and what was occurring, were two different things, and there was not much he could do about it.

"I know that is the tent where they are keeping the big scenery and props," Oliver said. "Shall we go take a look?"

"How do you know that?"

"I might have been doing my own investigating earlier in the day," Oliver shrugged bashfully. "I want photographs of this place for my archives. This is the sort of thing that it is important to make a record of because it will probably never happen again. This could be unique."

Oliver started rambling about how photography captured special moments of history for posterity, and Tommy didn't have the patience for such a lecture. He simply patted the fellow's shoulder and then gave him a gentle push towards the tent.

"Let's see what we can find out about the gun that shot Joshua MacKenzie."

It took them a few moments to find the tent flap that allowed them access to the inside of the tent, once within, Tommy switched on his torch and shone it about. There was a stack of scenery set to one side, it towered above them, ranging from eight to ten feet in height, and was painted with a variety of vistas.

"I thought they were using actual places to film?" Tommy remarked as he looked at a backdrop that appeared to be a replica of the interior of the pavilion.

"For the outside shots they will film on location as the weather permits," Oliver explained. "But the interior shots are harder to achieve due to the problems with lighting and being able to position the cameras in a suitable place. I imagine they have looked at the interiors they want to use and discovered they are not suitable, so have made painted backdrops instead."

"Clara will be pleased to hear they are not going to be filming inside the pavilion," Tommy reflected, thinking he had at least one piece of good news to report to her.

"Even filming the exterior shots in place is quite challenging, and many studios would not wish to waste the time or money on such an endeavour," Oliver elaborated. "They would rather construct entire fake streets and building frontages, than risk being delayed by bad weather or the interruptions of the general public.

"But filming 'on location,' as it is termed, creates a far more authentic feel for the finished film, and I believe it is the way things will go eventually. The people who watch the pictures are no longer simply impressed by things that look like a backdrop from a theatrical production, they want realism, and you only get realism if you film your scenes at an actual place."

"Ever thought about getting into moving pictures?" Tommy asked him, impressed by his knowledge on the subject.

Oliver smiled bashfully.

"No, my passion is for still photography. Moving pictures are much too complicated for my taste, but they fascinate me, nonetheless."

Tommy moved away from the freshly painted interior backdrops, the smell of their drying colours and the turpentine used to clean brushes strong in his nostrils. Drifting deeper into the tent, he came across an array of carefully arranged and organised props. Here was an entire section dedicated to plants and flowers, which would be used to bring some life to the flat backdrops. Here was a section filled with furniture, most of it old and worn, but which on screen would look luxurious and elegant. Here was a row of books and papers, which could be strewn across the top of a desk or placed on shelves as part of a scene where the protagonist searched for secret documents.

It was a fascinating world of theatre, a toy box for adults, with all the accoutrements needed for a person to dress up as whoever they cared to be. When he finally found the section he was looking for, Tommy was feeling a pinch of the magic of the movies and becoming lost in another world where anything was possible.

"Oliver, I have the weapons section," he hissed across the tent.

There was no response from his fellow investigator. Tommy looked up and shone his torch back the way he had come through the rows of items. He had assumed Oliver was following him, since he was the only one with a torch, but the photographer had apparently completely vanished.

"Oliver?"

"Don't move!"

There was a click to Tommy's left, which he did not need the torch to tell him was the priming of a gun. Tommy took a deep breath and slowly put his hands up in the air.

"Is that a real gun or one of the props?" Tommy asked the shadows to his left.

"Same thing. These guns are all capable of firing live bullets."

"As Violet Starling discovered earlier today."

The shadowy figure hesitated.

"How do you know that?"

"I was trying to help Violet. Unfortunately, Mr Stevenson got in the way."

"Are you something to do with the woman who visited here earlier?"

Tommy was trying to pinpoint the gun in the limited reflected glow of his torch. He thought he could just see where the metal was glinting when his assailant moved, but he was not confident.

"You must be referring to my sister, Clara O'Harris. I am Tommy Fitzgerald."

The figure in the shadows let out a breath of air, as if he were greatly relieved to hear this news. Tommy had the impression the man with the gun was more scared of the weapon than he was.

"What are you doing snooping around in the dark?"

"We came to try to discover what really happened today. We wanted to explore when no one would try to stop us. I doubt we would be welcomed here during the day, not with all that has happened," Tommy explained succinctly.

He heard another click as the safety was restored to the gun, then someone stepped closer to him, so he could see him in the glow of his torch, even though it was now pointing to the ceiling. The man who approached him was well into his middle years and had a grey beard.

"I am Mr Ferguson."

Tommy lowered his hands as cautiously as he had raised them to demonstrate he was no threat to the man before him.

"Clara told me your name. She said you would be someone to speak to about the events that have been happening here."

"She would be right about that," Ferguson nodded. "I can't tell you how upset I am about what happened today. That gun should never have had bullets in it."

"I would like to discuss this further, but perhaps you could tell me where my colleague is?"

"Oh," Ferguson looked a little shamefaced. "You best follow me."

He took Tommy back through the rows of props until they reached an area divided from the rest of the tent by some rough wooden panels. Behind the panels, was a cosy little sitting area, with a small portable stove, and a couple of wooden stools. An oil lamp was casting a soft glow where it perched on the floor.

Within the space were two men dressed in overalls and flat caps, between them, sitting on the floor and rubbing at the back of his head, was Oliver. The photographer looked quite cheerful despite being a prisoner of the two gentlemen either side of him. He was asking about the paint they used on the backdrops, and how they prevented it from glaring when lights were pointed at it.

"We caught him first," Ferguson explained, sounding apologetic. "Phillip got carried away and clonked him on the back of the head with a small sandbag."

"It's all right, it was not a hard blow," Oliver reassured Tommy. "I didn't even pass out, though it did knock me off my feet."

"We brought him here while I went to fetch a constable and have him arrested for trespassing, which was when I realised someone else was present," Ferguson added.

"Hopefully, you are now happy that we are not here to sabotage this production or steal secrets," Tommy said sternly, not as quick to forgive their assault on his friend as Oliver was.

"I have come to that conclusion," Ferguson nodded. "How about I make you lads a cup of tea in way of an apology, and we can have a chat?"

"In fairness, we *were* acting like trespassers," Oliver said brightly. "Can hardly fault them for being cautious."

Ferguson pointed a finger to the man he had named Phillip – a burly fellow who looked like he could do quite some damage when wielding a sandbag – and the man rose to make tea.

"That's Jed," he pointed at the other man present, who was the youngest of the three. "And you know who I am already. This is our break area. We have so much work to do, we are here day and night, so we made this little space as somewhere to be able to sit down for a bit and have a cup of tea."

"We also like to keep an eye on the props as anyone could wander in here, as you demonstrated," Jed added.

He rose and found a third stool, then brought over a couple of wooden packing crates for Oliver and Tommy to sit upon. They all became quite cosy in the circle of light cast by the oil lamp as Phillip made the tea.

"What do you want to know about the gun?" Ferguson began the conversation.

"I want to know everything," Tommy replied. "But, for a start, I would like to know how it ended up being loaded with real bullets."

"It was none of us," Ferguson said immediately. "Only Jed and I have access to the ammunition for the guns, which is kept locked up. Its only blanks, in any case, but that can still injure someone if fired at close range, so we keep it secure."

"You have no actual bullets here?"

Ferguson shook his head.

"None. Why would we need them? The guns are never fired properly."

"Then, who loaded the gun with live bullets?" Tommy posed the question to them all, but no one could offer him an answer.

"You should tell him," Jed cast a look at Ferguson.

Ferguson grimaced.

"Tell me what?" Tommy pressed him.

"Neither Jed nor I were the ones who handed over the prop box last night, and we didn't issue a gun either."

"The gun was not one of ours," Jed clarified. "I have been through our entire range of weapons, and all are accounted for. The one used to shoot Joshua, which the police now have, was put there by someone else."

"Then there was no accident about there being bullets in it," Tommy said. "But we all thought Violet was meant to be the intended target for whomever has been playing these games, so why was Joshua targeted this morning?"

"There was not meant to be a gun in that scene at all," Ferguson explained. "That was why we did not issue one in the prop box. I had prepared it all last night to be ready for the rehearsal. There must have been a script change I didn't know about. They do that sometimes, last minute alterations."

"But you have no idea who might have slipped that gun into the prop box?"

Ferguson shook his head.

"Nor can I say if that same person engineered the script change to include a gun or simply took advantage of the situation."

Ferguson scratched wearily at his beard.

"I am starting to believe what Violet said about the electrocution scene being not her fault. Seems someone has been tampering with the props to sabotage the performers. I owe her an apology."

"You haven't heard," Tommy said solemnly.

"Haven't heard what?"

Tommy pulled a face as he saw the alarm on Ferguson's features.

"Violet Starling is... dead."

Chapter Fourteen

Annie was doing more tidying than she was searching. Clara decided to say nothing, as it would only cause a disagreement, and she was fully capable of conducting the search alone, after all, she had intended to do exactly that before Annie had decided she was coming along.

"She had such beautiful clothes, but took such dreadful care of them," Annie clucked as she folded up a pale powder blue cardigan.

Clara did not respond. She had searched through the wardrobe and the dresser in the room, finding more clothes than she fancied she had owned in a lifetime. She had then turned her attention to the bedside cabinet, which had only contained a Bible and, slightly incongruously, a packet of cigarettes flung on top. Her next location was the writing desk in the room, hoping she might find some letters or other items that would give her a hint as to what was going on.

She found that Violet was as careless with her writing supplies as she was with everything else, and had left an ink bottle open, which Clara accidently spilt as she was rummaging. Trying to dab ink off her fingers with her handkerchief discreetly, so Annie would not see the mess she was making, (even though Annie was no longer the one who would be washing her handkerchief) she was distracted by the sound of a scuffle outside the door of the suite.

"You should go back to your room!"

That was O'Harris' voice. Clara rose from the desk and glanced at Annie, who had stopped in her mammoth task of folding Violet's assorted clothes.

"You have no right to stop me!" another male voice barked back.

Clara was fairly certain it was not Stevenson, but from the difficulty O'Harris was having in keeping the man at bay, she could surmise it was one of the big goons the manager employed to watch over Violet. Why one had come this way at this time of night she could only imagine, but from the sounds outside, he clearly was not going to let O'Harris stop him in his quest.

"They are going to get into a fight!" Annie hissed urgently.

Clara had already come to that conclusion. Neither man sounded in a mood to back down, whatever the goon was after, he was prepared to fight for it, and O'Harris would faithfully defend Clara and Annie in whatever brawl ensued. Not wishing to see her husband hurt in a scuffle, especially as she was currently coming up empty-handed in the search of Violet's room, Clara hurried to the door to intercede.

Annie was close on her heels.

"Men always have to resort to violence," she tutted disapprovingly as Clara wrenched open the door.

She found O'Harris getting the better of the other man, with him pressed against a wall while the captain had his hands around his throat. The other man was pushing back at O'Harris, and it was not clear which way the fight would have gone in the end, but both immediately halted at the appearance of the two women.

Clara folded her arms and raised an eyebrow at her husband. Annie's face was a picture of disapproval.

"That is no way to behave outside the room of a lady who has so recently left this earth," Annie puttered, giving her best scowl at the two fighters. "For shame, gentlemen."

The goon O'Harris had been throttling gave a gasp, which was probably meant to be a bashful cough of embarrassment and contrition. O'Harris let him go at once, took a pace back and adjusted his jacket. Clara looked between the pair of them, but her gaze finally settled on the stranger.

"Who might you be?"

"Who are you?" he snapped back.

"I asked first," Clara said calmly. "And I have Violet's permission to be here, bequeathed before her unfortunate…"

Clara did not finish the sentence, not just because she did not want to mention Violet's death again, but also because she felt a touch guilty about lying concerning being given permission to search Violet's rooms.

"I am Mario," the large man said, revealing he had an accent that suggested he heralded from somewhere in Eastern Europe. "I am Miss Starling's driver."

His face fell as he heard his own words.

"I was her driver."

Suddenly, Mario looked broken, his shoulders sagged, and Clara feared that any moment he might burst into tears. To see such a large and mean-looking gentleman reduced to such emotion was something of a shock.

Annie, who always had a solution for these sorts of situations, stepped forward and grabbed his arm.

"Come inside and sit down. There, there, it is a terrible tragedy, and you must be devastated."

Cajoling and comforting the grief-stricken driver, Annie escorted him into the room. After a moment, Clara exchanged a look with O'Harris, and they followed.

Mario was settled onto Violet's disordered bed – Annie had yet to get around to neatening it – and hung his head. He was not a particularly handsome fellow; his features favoured blockiness, and his eyes were a little too large and bulbous, but beneath the rugged and unappealing exterior he appeared to be a caring, if somewhat frightening, individual.

"How long have you been Violet's driver?" Clara asked him.

"Three years now," Mario responded. "I took her everywhere and always kept an eye on her. But today..."

"Try not to think about today," Annie patted his hand gently.

"Did Violet mention to you she was afraid someone was trying to hurt her?" Clara asked.

Mario nodded his head.

"The accident at the studio frightened her. But Mr Stevenson said it was just that, an accident. Then, one day we get in the car, and something doesn't feel right. We are going down a hill, when I put my foot on the brake, and nothing happen. We were lucky, we were not going fast, and I managed to veer us into a hedge, but Violet was shaken."

"You checked and found the brakes had been tampered with?" Clara pressed him.

"The hydraulic brakes system had been damaged and was leaking fluid. It looked as though someone had stabbed at it with a screwdriver. It was probably meant to slowly leak and fail when we were moving at a higher speed, but the saboteur misjudged things, and the brakes had already leaked most of the fluid before I started the car."

"Saving you from a worse accident," O'Harris nodded his head thoughtfully. "Someone had to deliberately damage those brakes, the cylinders holding the brake fluid are robust and would not be pierced by chance."

"I thought the same," Mario agreed.

"If you knew someone had sabotaged the brakes, surely that made you question what had happened with the electric cable?" Clara demanded.

Mario hefted his shoulders in a mountainous shrug, his face crumpling again.

"I didn't really think that was anything more than a mishap. And the car, well, it was Mr Stevenson's car, really, and I assumed someone was out to hurt him, not Violet. I told him about it, and he was furious, but he seemed to think he was the target too."

"Mr Stevenson has enemies willing to do him harm?" Clara asked thoughtfully.

"Plenty of them," Mario said drily. "He is not a man who goes through life peacefully."

"That I can tell," Clara mused. "Violet was the only actress he currently represents, I believe?"

"Yes," Mario responded. "He dedicated all his time and energy to her career."

"Without her, he must be pretty desperate," Clara was following a train of thought that had just occurred to her. "What will he do now?"

Mario had no reply to that.

"What about the sleeping powder incident?" Clara returned to a subject Mario might know more about.

"I wasn't here," he answered. "I had the night off. I was devastated to learn what had happened."

"Did you believe that was an accident too?"

Mario curled his fingers tightly together as he considered his response.

"No, I... I thought Violet had taken the powders on purpose."

Clara had not expected this answer. She moved closer to Mario.

"Why did you think that?"

"Violet had been acting oddly after the events at the studio and the car brakes. She was constantly on edge and flightier than usual. I thought maybe the pressure of everything had overwhelmed her. It happens more often than you think," Mario paused, his fingers now white as they wound around one another. "And look what happened today. I was right, she was in a bad frame of mind. This just proves that she did take the overdose of sleeping powders on purpose."

"It proves nothing," Clara corrected him.

Mario shot his head up to look at her. She carried on.

"I believe there has been an orchestrated string of events aiming to deprive Violet of her life. The sleeping powder overdose was just part of that scheme. Violet was lucky on that occasion because she was found in time to be saved. Three attempts were made on Violet's life, and the fourth attempt was made, and succeeded, today at the train station. I do not believe Violet jumped. I think someone pushed her."

Mario sharply rose to his feet and stood to his full height, towering several inches over Clara. O'Harris took a step forward, noticing the driver's fists were clenched, and ready to intercede, but Clara lifted her hand and motioned for him to remain where he was.

Mario was breathing hard, his chest heaving in and out, his shirt buttons perilously close to popping at the strain of his burly physique, which was trembling with outrage.

"Someone murdered her?"

"I believe so, Mario, and I intend to find that person, and bring them to justice."

"I shall wrap my hands around their throat and throttle the life out of them!" Mario declared, opening up his big fists and showing the full breadth of his hands.

Clara was impressed O'Harris had gotten the better of this man who was clearly both powerful and fully capable of using that strength to his advantage.

"I would rather the killer was brought before a court of law, so that his guilt can be demonstrated to the world, and Violet's name redeemed," Clara informed Mario. "I imagine you would desire the same, as you clearly cared deeply about her."

Mario's fury abated; the madness in his eyes faded, and he became calm.

"Violet never knew how much I loved her. I failed to protect her."

"It is hard to protect someone against a threat you do not see," Clara told him kindly. "You did your best."

"Why did you come here tonight?" Annie interjected.

Mario looked at her sheepishly.

"I couldn't sleep thinking about everything. I kept saying to myself, she is gone and soon I will have nothing of her. I wanted to have a keepsake, so I could remember her always. I came here, to her room, to take something for that purpose, before Mr Stevenson returned and refused me."

Annie understood perfectly. She glanced around the room, then went purposefully to the cardigan she had been so recently folding.

"I found something in the pocket that I think you should take."

She produced a small brooch crafted from gold with enamel decoration. It was shaped as a dark purple Violet. She handed it to Mario. The brooch sat on the palm of his hand, looking like a miniature between his fingers. Mario's lip trembled, and there was a hint of tears in his eyes.

"Thank you," he whispered, the words strained as they came out.

Then he hastened to his feet and departed the room before anyone could see him crying.

"Well, that was unexpected," O'Harris said as the man's footsteps echoed down the hallway.

"Are you hurt, John?" Clara went to her husband and placed a hand on his arm.

"Just a few bruises," he replied bravely. "I'll let you take a look at them later."

His mischievous wink convinced her he was fine and had suffered no great harm during his scuffle.

"Poor man," Annie sighed, returning to folding up clothes. "He was really lovesick for Violet, and now he has lost her."

"Lovesick or not, he was yet another of her supposed protectors who failed to believe her when she said she was being persecuted," Clara huffed. "I would like to think that were I to claim such a thing, you would all believe me and try to help me."

"Clara, the things you do and the people you meet, it would be completely feasible to suppose you were being persecuted, in fact, I am amazed nothing has happened before now," O'Harris told her lightly.

Clara gave him a look.

"Well, my point stands. If the people closest to her had spent more time believing in her, and less time assuming she was simply a flighty actress, maybe Violet would still be with us."

"Did you find anything here that was useful?" O'Harris changed the topic.

"Not really, Violet has not kindly left me a diary or some letters stating who she feared was out to get her. It was the same when I last spoke to her. She said she did not think she had any enemies, at least none she could name."

"She no doubt had acting rivals who were jealous of her success and would have liked her parts," O'Harris pointed out.

"I agree, but a rival and a murderer are two different things. I cannot believe someone who envied Violet would go to such lengths. The elaborate nature of the attempts against her, and the efforts made to make it seem that either Violet died by accident or suicide, suggest someone who is very determined, and very patient. They have spent a great deal of time and effort planning these events so as to avoid casting suspicion on themselves."

"Then what are you thinking? Who is behind this?"

"I am wondering if the key could be Stevenson himself," Clara replied. "Something Mario said intrigued me. Stevenson has a lot of enemies, and if he were to lose Violet, his career could be over, especially if he were blamed for driving her to her suicide. No one would want to work with him. Maybe whoever did this was not an enemy to Violet but saw her death as a means to destroy Stevenson."

"That's cold," O'Harris frowned, thinking how twisted a human being could be to kill an innocent person purely to hurt the actual person they hated.

"Cold, but possible," Clara replied. "I wonder how Gilbert has done in his search of Stevenson's room? Perhaps he has found something of use to us."

Clara was turning around to leave the suite and head to Stevenson's when she heard Annie's voice raised in horror.

"Clara, did you spill all that ink!"

Clara quickly made sure her handkerchief was firmly stuffed in her pocket.

"What ink?" she replied innocently.

Chapter Fifteen

Breaking the news of Violet's death had not been easy on Mr Ferguson and his men, but the result was that they were more determined than ever to help Tommy and find out who was responsible for the crimes against the girl. Over tea and the warmth of the tiny stove, with the wind howling round the tent outside, they began discussing the matter in detail.

"Let's begin with the incident involving the electric cables. Violet told us that she was instructed to only reach for the cable with a red cord tied around it," Tommy began.

"That was exactly the case," Mr Ferguson concurred. "The red cord would indicate which cable was safe for her to pull. In fairness, there was only one cable she should avoid as it was live, the rest were perfectly safe, but Mr Manx also had his opinion on which cable would look best for the camera when it was pulled, so we all agreed to mark a specific one."

"After the incident, did you look to see where the red cord was?"

Mr Ferguson nodded his head.

"When Violet recovered, she told us she had reached for the cable with the red cord, insisted on it. So, I came back to the studio and personally checked over the cables. The red cord was on the correct one, just as we had agreed."

"How long after the incident was it that you checked the cord?"

Mr Ferguson did a swift calculation in his head.

"About two days. It was the time it took for Violet to be well enough to talk to us and explain what had happened."

"Two days," Oliver already knew what Tommy was thinking. "Time enough for someone to move the red cord if they wanted to."

"Why would anyone do that?" Ferguson frowned.

"If someone deliberately placed the red cord on the wrong cable to cause Violet to be electrocuted, they had plenty of time to move it back to the correct cable and avoid anyone noticing what they had done," Tommy elaborated for him.

Ferguson looked at his two workmen, both of whom were astounded by this statement.

"You mean, someone deliberately set out to hurt Violet?" Jed asked.

"After recent events, does that not seem the most likely scenario?" Tommy pressed them. "After all I have told you, and the incident with the loaded gun this morning, does it not seem logical that all Violet's protests about someone tricking her into touching that electric cable were really true?"

It seemed that even with this evidence before them, the men were finding it hard to believe that Violet had been deliberately targeted. Either they were incredibly innocent to the ways of the world, or they were simply too horrified to believe anyone would do such a thing.

"That is just hideous," Mr Ferguson groaned. "Why would anyone do something so vile?"

"That is the question we have been trying to answer from the moment Violet approached us with her concerns," Tommy pointed out. "Can you think of anyone who was on the set that day who might have had a grudge against Violet?"

Ferguson shook his head, and his two workmen followed suit a moment later. Tommy was disappointed but not entirely surprised.

"Let's consider things a different way," he suggested. "Who would have been able to tamper with the prop cables before the filming began?"

Ferguson looked alarmed by the statement.

"It wasn't me!"

"I never said it was, Mr Ferguson."

"But I was the one who tied on the red cord in the first place!"

"Yes, but someone must have moved it afterwards. Who would have had the opportunity to remove the cord and tie it somewhere else?"

Ferguson looked too dazed by this suggestion to answer, he still seemed convinced he was going to be blamed for the crime.

"The props were set up in the morning, and we made sure the electricity was running correctly through to the main panel that had to be lit up," Jed explained, a voice of reason in the confusion. "We placed tiny smoke charges next to the cable Violet would pull out, which we would set off when she wrenched the dummy cable free, as if she had genuinely disconnected the machine. The last thing Mr Ferguson did was tie the red cord around the correct cable, then we all walked away as we had done what we needed to."

"Who came into the studio next?" Tommy asked.

"The lighting crew, who arrange all the big lamps to get the best light for the scene. Mr Manx wanted there to be moody shadows around the machine for atmosphere. They were arranging the lights for a good hour or so. I was on hand in case anything needed to be adjusted on the machine and was watching the whole time. None of the lighting crew went near the wires," Mr Ferguson said firmly.

"And after them?" Tommy asked.

"Mr Manx came on set and surveyed all our work. Then the

actors arrived. Mr Manx did not approach the machine. I would have noticed."

This was getting them nowhere, it seemed that no one had approached the prop cables after Mr Ferguson, at least as far as he could remember, which was making it look more likely that either he had deliberately tied the cord in the wrong place or, as everyone initially suspected, Violet had pulled the wrong cable by accident.

"There was someone who went near the machine, but it was only for a moment," Jed interrupted.

He seemed more alert than his colleagues to what had been going on around the studios and was trying his hardest to help Tommy.

"Edwin Cleethorpes," Jed added when everyone looked in his direction.

"Who is that?" Tommy asked, having not had the pleasure of meeting Mr Manx's assistant.

"He works for Mr Manx," Phillip said, his face pulling into a look of distaste. "He is a very unpleasant fellow. I saw him trying to butter up Violet. He wanted to take advantage of her, I should say."

"I imagine that is a problem that Miss Starling had to face on a regular basis," Oliver remarked sadly.

"It was," Ferguson concurred. "But her manager kept most at bay. He had no intention of seeing Violet begin a disastrous romantic liaison with someone and risk the consequences."

Tommy could make a good guess at just what sort of consequences Mr Stevenson was all too keen to avoid. Violet was a money-maker for him, and he would not wish either marriage or the inconvenience of an unplanned pregnancy to interrupt that.

"But he did not chase away Mr Cleethorpes?" Tommy asked.

"He didn't seem to worry about him, though probably it was because he works for Mr Manx and no one argues with Mr Manx,"

Phillip explained. "Anyway, he came over to Violet after they had run through a rehearsal of the scene with some last-minute script changes. He was leaning right against the machine for a bit while he had her go through them."

"If he did move the cord during that time, what would be his motive?" Oliver asked in his somewhat innocent fashion.

All his question received from the others in response were shrugs. Tommy felt they had reached a dead end with that line of enquiry, though he would make sure to follow up on Mr Cleethorpes.

"Why don't we consider the second incident, the tampered brakes?"

"We know nothing about that. The cars are none of our business," Ferguson assured him.

"I suppose the same would be the case for Violet's accidental overdose?" Tommy pressed him.

Ferguson nodded his head.

"We knew nothing about the sleeping powders she took until after everything had happened."

"That just leaves the gun," Oliver remarked.

He did so in such a cheerful manner that it seemed bizarre they were referring to a deadly weapon that had come close to killing a man. Tommy thought about the incident for a second, before a new question popped into his head.

"Would anyone wish to see Mr MacKenzie dead?"

Phillip roared into laughter at the statement. Tommy looked at him quizzically.

"Phillip is amused because it is not so much a question of who would want MacKenzie dead, but who wouldn't," Jed interjected to explain his colleague's amusement. "Mr MacKenzie is the sort of person who attracts enemies rather than friends."

"Even Violet hated him, and she was the sort of person who tried to see the good in everyone," Ferguson added.

"Why did she hate him?" Oliver asked.

"He was constantly trying to touch her and court her," Ferguson explained, blushing a little as he said it.

His old-fashioned words masked a great deal more than he was saying. Tommy could well imagine just what Joshua was like, and how far his attentions might go given the chance. He was disappointed to hear it, of course, he had always liked watching the star on the silver screen, but in real life people were often far from the heroes they pretended to portray.

"He is an old rogue and Violet knew it," Phillip's laughter had changed to anger. "She told Mr Stevenson, once, she never wanted to do another film with the man. I overheard them arguing about it. Stevenson would hear none of it, because MacKenzie is one of the top leading men at the studio, but he did promise Violet that the next time she starred alongside him she would never be alone with the man."

"Did Stevenson keep his promise?" Tommy wondered aloud.

None of the men could answer him, which was as he had expected.

"You seem to be making a case for Violet having good reason to want to shoot Mr MacKenzie," Oliver said innocently.

Tommy cast him a quick scowl, which the photographer completely missed. His words, however, had not eluded the attention of the other men in the room, all of whom were appalled by the statement.

"Miss Starling would never do something like that!" Phillip said immediately.

"She had no way of knowing the gun was loaded," Mr Ferguson added hastily, though he completely missed the point that if Violet were the one who supplied the mysterious gun, then she would have been completely aware of its potential killing ability.

"How would that tie in with the accidents that befell Miss Starling?" Jed spoke up.

That was a very good question, and the one thing that made Tommy believe the gun was intended for Violet, rather than MacKenzie; but if that were the case, why had she ended up being the one firing it?

"I think we have probably taken up your time for long enough," Tommy told them, putting down his now empty mug of tea.

Despite the warmth from the stove, he was beginning to feel the chilly damp creeping into his bones, and his injured back was protesting at his lengthy stay on the battered wooden crate.

"I have found the whole thing fascinating," Oliver said, in that odd little way he had.

The workmen looked at him in deep confusion.

"You find discussing how someone tried to hurt Miss Starling fascinating?" Jed asked.

"No, I meant all the things you were saying about the props and how it is all organised," Oliver smiled, unfazed by Jed's slightly outraged tone. "I always wanted to know how these things worked in the movies."

He rubbed at the back of his head as he stood up. He had a bump from the sandbag that had dazed him, and he was starting to develop a headache. He didn't stop smiling, however, and had Tommy not made the statement that it was time for them to go he probably would have remained for quite a while longer.

Tommy rose from his seat and thanked the men, handing them over a business card in case they thought of anything else.

Mr Ferguson got up to show them the way back through the maze of props to the entrance of the tent.

"I still cannot believe this has happened," he said, as he walked methodically around the props, seemingly so used to the layout he didn't have to even think about where he was going.

His path was only lit by the glow of Tommy's torch behind him, and once Tommy and Oliver left, Mr Ferguson would have to find his way back in the dark. Clearly, this did not worry him.

"I thought a lot of Miss Starling. She was always kind to us about the props. I regret now how angry I was with her over the electric cable business. I made such a fuss about it because I thought she could have been killed or seriously hurt. Now, I feel awful that I failed to listen to what she told me."

Mr Ferguson shook his head, his heart laden with guilt and sorrow.

"That young lady needed my help, and I failed her."

"Mr Ferguson, you could not have predicted what was to occur, nor were you to have supposed someone had deliberately intended her harm. To berate yourself over the matter now is unreasonable," Tommy told him gently. "It must have seemed absurd to suppose that anyone would wish to hurt her."

"I still cannot believe it. Violet was such a sweet thing. She wouldn't hurt a fly," Mr Ferguson dabbed at his eye, which was becoming teary. "Do me a favour and find out who is responsible for this."

"That is what we intend to do," Tommy reassured him.

Mr Ferguson left them at the tent flap and disappeared back into the shadows of the props. Tommy gave his back a stretch, then started walking towards the gates of the green.

"Do you think Mr Cleethorpes is responsible for the sabotage?" Oliver asked him.

"I don't know," Tommy replied. "Without a motive, we just have the coincidence that he stood next to the cables."

Oliver was thoughtful a while.

"If it was him, Mr Manx would have been furious, surely? Violet Starling was the name that would sell his movie, and her death would be a disaster for him."

"I don't suppose Cleethorpes intended for Mr Manx to ever discover he was responsible, that was the point of the accident," Tommy stared up at the stars, his mind elsewhere. "But maybe that is where we are going wrong. We are asking ourselves who would have a personal reason to attack Violet, but supposing it was instead a case of someone with a professional reason? Could there be some benefit to someone here for Violet to die before her movie contract with the studio expired?"

"I can't see how," Oliver replied. "Mr Stevenson would hardly like that, and Mr Manx would be short a star."

"Yes," Tommy said, "but remember what we were told. Everyone is replaceable and the next big movie starlet could be just waiting in the wings for her chance to shine. What if Violet was not as irreplaceable as we have been told?"

Chapter Sixteen

They knocked on the door of Stevenson's room, but there was no reply from Gilbert. Clara did not intend to waste any further time. With a quick glance at her husband to indicate he should keep watching the corridor, she turned the handle of the door and entered the room.

Gilbert was sitting cross legged on the floor in front of a chest of drawers, surrounded by a spread of papers that reminded Clara all too much of his desk at the newspaper office. He was absorbed in reading whatever he had discovered and had clearly failed to hear them knock.

"Gilbert! What a mess!" Annie declared, starting to pick up the papers nearest to her.

"Don't touch that! I have them arranged in a specific order!"

Gilbert threw out a hand to indicate Annie should come to a halt. She responded to the gesture with her most fearsome look, the one that cowed most people into behaving as she expected them to. Gilbert did not even flinch.

"Seriously, Mrs Fitzgerald, I have arranged these in a way that is intrinsically useful to me, and I would very much appreciate it if you did not move them." Annie stood up, folding her arms, and turning her indignant gaze upon Clara. Clara knew when she was expected to intervene.

"Gilbert, have you found anything that could assist us with our case concerning Violet?"

"I found her most recent contract with Mr Stevenson," Gilbert pointed to a piece of paper on the bed. "Seems Mr Stevenson travels with his paperwork, or at least that which he deems most important to him. Violet had just signed a new contract with him, making him her exclusive manager for the next five years."

Clara picked up the contract Gilbert was referring to and frowned as she flicked through the pages held together by a staple, finding Violet's signature on the last page.

"This contract was due to begin next month," Clara read through the papers. "I had hoped Violet would have had better sense than to sign such a thing."

"I imagine she felt bullied into doing so," Annie replied, peering over Clara's shoulder.

Clara was studying the paperwork, something felt off about it. Violet had acted as if the last thing in the world she wanted was to be chained to Stevenson for any longer than she already was. The other agencies were sniffing around, and she could have easily jumped ship to one of them and escaped Stevenson for good. For all his talk about having Violet tied to him through a contract, this paperwork before her clearly implied that was not the case. He was about to lose his most powerful asset. How had he managed to get her to sign this new contract if she was so close to getting what she wanted?

Clara found herself staring at the signature over and over, willing it to reveal something to her.

"What are you reading, Gilbert?" Annie had lost interest in the contract and was now peering over Gilbert's shoulder.

"You should not spy on a man while he is working," Gilbert

retorted.

"That is somewhat ironic, considering that work is also spying," Annie responded. "Do all these papers relate to Violet Starling?"

She picked up one from beside Gilbert before he could respond.

"Um... now, before you say anything..."

"This has nothing to do with Violet," Annie snapped at him. "It is a private letter Mr Stevenson wrote to his solicitor. You are reading his personal papers!"

"How am I to know which are relevant and which are not if I don't read them all?" Gilbert snapped defensively.

Clara let them argue while retrieving the paper from Annie's hand so she could read it.

"Stevenson has a lot of creditors after him," Clara observed aloud, cutting through the quarrel.

"I noticed that too," Gilbert said before Annie could start at him again. "Seems to me that if he did not have Violet, he would be a man in a lot of trouble."

"This letter is begging his solicitor to buy him more time while he tries to make arrangements to ensure his financial future," Clara glanced over at the contract on the bed. "Ensuring Violet was tied to him for another five years would surely be considered just such an arrangement?"

"Then he cannot be the person wanting to hurt Violet, as doing so would leave him in a terrible position," Annie remarked.

"A sound theory, but what if he was having trouble getting Violet to sign the contract? What if he needed to persuade her it was in her best interest to stay with him and be under his protection?"

"You mean by scaring her?" Gilbert interpreted. "It's a cruel way of doing things, but if you are right then it clearly did the trick."

"You think Mr Stevenson is behind the attacks on Violet?" Annie frowned.

"It is another theory among many," Clara remarked. "But if Violet had no obvious enemies, then what we remain with is wondering who would benefit by her being scared to death, while not actually perishing. The attacks on her life all happened within Mr Stevenson's sphere of influence. The accident on the set was while he was watching, the tampered brakes were on *his* car and were inadequately damaged to cause an accident when the car was moving at speed. The overdose also happened close to Mr Stevenson, and in a manner that enabled him to 'come to the rescue' before something serious occurred. Who else had the ability to tamper with Violet's sleeping powders so easily? And finally, the shooting happened here at the hotel, with Stevenson present and even able to suggest Violet use the gun."

"But she was the one shooting it, not being shot at," Gilbert pointed out.

"A fair point, but in her panic would Violet realise that, or would she see it as another lucky escape?"

"What if she had shot MacKenzie in the heart," Annie shuddered.

"It would have been a terrible accident, but equally a fine way for Stevenson to make his point that Violet needed to stay safely under his protection."

"Except she had already signed the new contract," Gilbert pointed out. "What would be the point of staging another accident when Stevenson already had his way? If that was the motive."

Clara had to admit that was the anomaly in her theory. The date on the contract was for yesterday, and that would have eliminated the need for another 'accident' to happen today.

"Nice theory, but it doesn't fit all the facts," Gilbert said, going back to the papers before him.

"Gilbert, we do not have the time for you to read every scrap of information from Mr Stevenson's life," Clara growled at him, mostly annoyed because he had so swiftly spotted the flaw in her suggestion. "If you have nothing there that directly relates to Violet, you need to put it back. We cannot be here all night."

Gilbert grumbled; he had fallen into a goldmine of information, and he was reluctant to let it go. Clara, however, was feeling they had overstayed their dubious welcome in the hotel, and it was about time they departed. She began picking up papers, nudging Annie into doing the same. For the sake of thoroughness, Clara did glance at the contents of each of the papers as she collected them, just in case they were relevant to Violet's death. She soon discovered Gilbert had been searching through the paperwork for absolutely anything scandalous, his journalist's nose overwhelmed by the amount of dirt he could find here on Stevenson. None of the papers Clara picked up seemed to have any link to Violet.

"Gilbert, did you even bother to try to focus on our actual case?" Clara snapped at him.

"I couldn't ignore what I was finding!" Gilbert declared. "This is a treasure trove for a man like me! Stevenson is as corrupt as they come. Take a look at these two contracts for an actress called Felicity Dublin. Both are signed but the signatures are completely different. One of these must be a fake, which means he was forging signatures on paperwork to suit his needs. There has to be a massive story here!"

Clara found herself looking back at the contract.

"If Stevenson would fake one actress' signature, what about another's?"

Gilbert jumped to his feet as he heard her say this.

"A forged signature on Violet Starling's new contract!" he declared. "How did he think he would get away with it?"

"He got away with forging Felicity's signature," Annie pointed out. "If Violet protested, who would listen to her? All Stevenson had to do was present this contract and claim she was trying to back out of it."

Clara had picked up the papers from the bed and was reading through them once again.

"There are some rather dubious clauses in this about what Violet would need to do to exit this contract ahead of the end date. She would have to pay a hefty remuneration to Mr Stevenson. I am not sure she could afford the amount."

"So, he had her trapped?" Gilbert declared. "She tries to leave, and he shows this signed contract to his solicitor, then it falls on Violet to prove she did not sign it."

"And poor Violet was not the sort of person who was good at standing up for herself, or who would know how to fight such a legal battle. Not to mention, proving the contract was forged would take a long time. Time during which Violet might lose roles or even be turned away by the other agencies she was hoping would represent her."

"What a horrid man!" Annie had balled her hands into fists. "I would like to give him a piece of my mind."

Gilbert was studying Clara rather than listening to Annie.

"Doesn't matter now, does it? What with Violet being dead," he said softly. "Something like this contract could really push a person over the edge. What with being hunted, or so she feared, and now Stevenson doing this, imagine how alone and afraid she felt."

"I refuse to believe that Violet would throw herself beneath a train because of this," Clara insisted, though she knew Gilbert had a point.

You could only push a person so far, and then they would break.

Annie was putting the loose papers from the floor back into the bureau Gilbert had removed them from. They were never going to be in the same order as he had found them, but she could not help that. She took the last few papers from Gilbert's hands, but he did not argue on this occasion. Too busy watching Clara.

When Annie was done, she went to take the contract from Clara's grasp. Clara moved away before she could do so.

"This is coming with me. It is evidence, and I don't feel it should be in the possession of Mr Stevenson anymore."

Annie made a disapproving noise and planted her hands on her hips.

"Mr Stevenson is a bad man, Annie, and I don't want him having this contract. If I can prove it is a forgery, that would at least be something. It might be the only thing I can do for Violet now."

"It is stealing," Annie reminded her.

"I do not care, Annie," Clara replied sharper than she had intended.

Annie looked hurt.

"I am sorry," Clara hastened to add. "This case has been rather upsetting."

Annie sighed but said no more. She had tidied the room so that it no longer looked like a bomb had gone off in a library, and with any luck Mr Stevenson would never realise what had occurred.

"I could write such a good piece about all this," Gilbert said cheerfully as Clara folded up the contract and shoved it in her pocket. "Big Time Movie Star Manager Scandalous Crook!"

He sounded out the headline, rather proud of it.

"You are not going to write anything until we know what Mr Stevenson has truly done," Clara responded. "I suggest you remember that we are currently trespassing in the man's room, and everything we have seen could be used against us as proof that we trespassed."

"Or stole from him," Annie pointed out.

Clara ignored her.

"You are both spoilsports," bemoaned Gilbert. "This is the best story I have ever had, and none of those others down there have even a whiff of it!"

"Hey, you lot," O'Harris opened the room door and poked his head just inside. "I think there are people coming, sounds like the evening staff doing their rounds, maybe it is time to leave?"

Clara did not need to be asked twice; she headed for the door with Annie tutting behind her and Gilbert still protesting that she was ruining his career. Outside in the corridor, O'Harris motioned for them to follow him, and they darted a short distance down the hallway before turning off down another. They were heading for the main stairs when they heard the evening cleaning ladies quietly making their way along the corridor they had just departed. The women were in the process of collecting any shoes that had been left outside the rooms to be polished, as well as dusting and sweeping in a professionally silent fashion.

They were too absorbed in their task to notice the departure of the trespassers.

Gilbert led them back downstairs to the service entrance. Clara was relieved to be outside again. It felt as if it had been ages since she had stepped out into the fresh air; she had not realised how claustrophobic it had been searching Violet's room, nor how depressing. She pulled her coat tighter around her and heard the papers she had stolen make a consoling crackling sound.

Nothing Annie could have said would have deterred her from taking them.

"I'll drive you home, Annie," O'Harris was saying, his gaze now falling on Gilbert. "What about you?"

"Oh no, I am staying here," Gilbert declared with one of his most disturbing grins.

He closed the service doors and disappeared before they could argue with him.

"He is going to go straight back up to Mr Stevenson's room and keep poking about," Annie predicted.

Clara fancied she was spot on.

"That is his decision, and we are no longer involved, so whatever befalls Gilbert befalls him on his own," she said.

Annie cast her a look, but she refused to feel bad about stealing the contract. It had to be a fake and therefore she had to prove, for Violet's benefit, just what a crook Mr Stevenson was.

Chapter Seventeen

There was nothing more to be done that night, so they all departed for their respective homes to reconvene once again in the morning.

The following day, over tea and toast, Tommy and Clara discussed their next move. Tommy detailed what he had discovered the night before, and the information given to him, albeit reluctantly, by Mr Ferguson.

"Mr Cleethorpes is certainly an odd fellow," Clara said after she had heard the story of him being the only one near to the prop machinery at the time of Violet's electrocution. "But why would he want to hurt Violet?"

"Maybe it was nothing personal, but like you thought earlier, a means to get back at Mr Stevenson?" Tommy suggested.

He had been shown the dubious contract and planned on making arrangements with a friend, who was an expert in handwriting, to deduce the authenticity of the document.

"We need to talk to more people," Clara decided. "We shall begin with Mr Cleethorpes, and end with Mr Stevenson, who no doubt will be extremely antagonistic towards us."

"If we get a word out of him, aside from him telling us to leave him alone, I will be amazed," Tommy snorted.

"We can only try," Clara reflected. "I also want to speak to Joshua MacKenzie, though at this point I do not see him as a potential suspect. I am not sure he even worked on Violet's last film."

"But for the sake of thoroughness we must interview him, just in case he knows something."

"Exactly."

They set off in one of O'Harris' cars, being chauffeured by the reliable Jones, who would take them to wherever they needed to go and – if the need arose – would serve as immediate back-up if a situation became unpleasant. Clara was already considering she may need him to help her with Mr Stevenson. There was something about Jones' quiet, unflappable demeanour that was rather intimidating to people who did not know him. Especially to people who were bullies.

They headed first to the green. The day had started with drizzle, and there was little promise that it would improve as the morning progressed. The tents on the green looked sodden, the rainwater pouring off the canvas in rivulets, and gathering in squelchy puddles on the ground.

Clara had donned her wellingtons that morning, anticipating such a situation. She ploughed through the puddles, and stomped across the wet grass, impervious to the rain, while Tommy – who had not been so forethinking – followed at a more cautious pace, doing his best to avoid drenching his shoes.

Clara headed to the tent where she had found Mr Manx the day before. She could hear someone yelling within and had a good hunch who that might be. She lifted up the flap of the tent, managing to do so with only a minimal amount of water splattering her, and stepped inside.

The tent was quiet. Normally, it was arranged as a crude office for those who required it, but today the benches and tables were empty, aside from the director sitting at his personal desk and arguing with his assistant. He had a typewriter set before him and appeared to have been writing a new script, though from the amount of crumpled paper tossed about the floor, it seemed he was not having much success.

"I thought it was the duty of the writer to make alterations to the screenplay?" Clara observed as she approached him, Tommy just a step behind.

Mr Manx shot up his head and scowled at her.

"What is she doing in here? Do we have no security working this site?"

His questioned appeared aimed at the room in general.

"From what I have seen, you have no security whatsoever," Tommy said, hands in his pockets as he sauntered around the tent taking the whole place in. "Maybe, if you did, Violet Starling would still be alive."

Mr Manx went an unhealthy beetroot red colour and Clara briefly considered they may need to call a doctor. Then he managed to calm himself down.

"Get them out of here, Edwin!"

Mr Cleethorpes hastened from behind the table and walked up to Clara as if he were about to take hold of her.

"Let us not go through that debacle again," Clara sighed at him. "I am here because I want to find out what really happened to Violet, and I am going to find a way to talk with you two, one way or another. You can either put up with me now or have me constantly hanging around as an annoyance when you could be getting on with something more important, such as finding a way to film this movie without Violet

Starling."

Edwin had not stopped his approach, and was about to grab hold of Clara's elbow, when Mr Manx intervened.

"Let her say her piece," he snarled. "I have a feeling she is the sort of person to be annoyingly dedicated to a cause and will do exactly what she says."

"Thank you," Clara said, watching as Mr Cleethorpes unhappily stepped back. "Your assistant seems a little too keen on throwing people out of your office."

"Mr Manx gets a lot of unwanted attention," Edwin said defensively.

"Especially now his star is deceased," Tommy drawled from behind Edwin.

Edwin had failed to notice that he had slipped up behind him and was only a foot from where he stood. He had also failed to notice how displeased Tommy was becoming at the way his sister was being treated. Edwin was not a man with much backbone; throwing a woman out of his employer's presence was one thing, tackling a man like Tommy, who looked like he could handle himself in a fight, was quite another.

Little did Edwin know that Tommy would be the least of his worries if he had tried to touch Clara again.

"What do you want from me?" Mr Manx demanded of them.

"I want to discuss the prior accidents that befell Miss Starling and, before you argue, I want to assure you, I now consider all of those incidents to have been direct attempts on her life. The motive behind them is unclear, but recent events have placed a new perspective on everything."

Manx glowered at his typewriter.

"Wouldn't be the first time a young actress threw her life away over nothing."

"It wouldn't be the first time someone tried to mask an act of murder as an accident or suicide," Clara countered.

Manx rattled his fingers across the tabletop, a fierce rhythm that ended with him slamming his fist onto the wood.

"Whoever did this was not just determined to ruin Violet's career. They wanted to ruin mine!"

"Surely you can simply employ another actress?" Clara asked him.

"Violet sells movies!" Manx snapped. "You put her name on a poster, and you know most of the young men who can afford a cinema ticket will show up just to gawp at her. Joshua MacKenzie is turning into an old hack, his name still brings people in, but he is playing to the housewives, and they don't have the free money for cinema tickets. Young men looking for a pretty face and with a few bob spare in their pocket are the ones we want to attract."

Clara had not realised how cynical the world of movies was. She had assumed it was about telling a story, and entertaining people. As someone who never went to the pictures herself, she had failed to understand how significant the leading actor or actress in a picture really was.

"Who would wish to do you harm through Violet?" Clara asked Manx.

"Who wouldn't?" Manx turned the question back on her. "This is an industry where everyone is trying to stab you in the back."

"Including your assistant?"

Clara was delighted to see the discord her question caused Edwin, who jumped at her statement.

"I would never..."

"Yes, even assistants," Manx interrupted his protests. "Do you know how many assistants I have had over the years? Edwin is just one among many. I have had scripts and contracts stolen from under my nose by people supposedly working for me. I tell you, everyone is out to get what they can."

"But Mr Manx..." Edwin swung around to his employer.

"You are no different to the rest, Edwin, you are just biding your time for the right opportunity," Manx waved a dismissive hand at him nonchalantly. "What do you think he has done, then?"

He addressed the question to Clara.

"Edwin was seen handing script corrections to Violet while she was stood next to the cables that would subsequently electrocute her. I have a theory that someone moved the red cord that was supposed to indicate to Violet the safe cable, thus causing her to touch a live cable instead. After she was removed to the hospital, that same person replaced the red cord on the correct cable so as to cover their tracks."

"And make it seem that it was a stupid mistake on Violet's part," Manx nodded his head. "Certainly a clever plan, and Edwin was stood by that machine for some time going over some script changes we had made that morning."

"But... but I would never do such a thing!" Edwin countered.

"If Violet had died that day, how severely would it have affected you, Mr Manx?" Clara asked.

The director leaned back in his chair and puffed out his cheeks as he considered the enormity of the question.

"If she had died, we would have had to stop production of the film and recast her role. Just like now, I would be sitting here wondering how I could find someone to fill in, knowing that without Violet's name on the poster I would probably only see half the revenue I would otherwise have got, and the studio would be furious. That's the sort of thing that could ruin a director. Ultimately, the studio would place the blame on me for allowing their star to be hurt. I would be finished.

In fact, I am probably finished now."

"I didn't do anything!" Edwin declared urgently. "I knew nothing about the red cord, I swear! I just showed Violet the script corrections and ran through them with her as I was told to! You cannot blame me for all this!"

"You are the only person the prop men remember seeing near the machine, other than Violet," Clara pointed out.

"Well, they are mistaken!" Edwin yelled back at them, growing more and more alarmed by the moment. "While I was speaking to Violet, that scoundrel she called her manager came over. He seemed to think I might be trying to seduce his starlet, the way he stalked around us. He was right behind her as I showed her the new script, and right next to those cables!"

Edwin was darting his head from one to the other of them, hoping to see a sign he was believed.

"Mr Stevenson had no motive to murder the woman who was making him his fortune," Tommy pointed out.

"Just as I had no reason to kill her off," Manx growled. "What could I possibly achieve?"

"What would I achieve?" Edwin added desperately.

"Maybe you think you can fill my shoes?" Manx said without any indication that he was upset at the statement. He seemed to consider it par for the course. "You bring evidence to the studio I was careless, and you get yourself a promotion while destroying me."

"No!" Edwin snapped. "I would never do that!"

He was trembling from head to foot as he made his statement. Now he turned on Clara, seeing her as his only hope for help.

"How could I have possibly orchestrated the other attempts on Violet's life?"

"That is a good question," Clara conceded. "Presumably, you

knew where Stevenson's car was and could have tampered with it or seen to it that someone else tampered with it. How you arranged the doctored sleeping powders is harder to explain. I assume that something harmful was added to Violet's regular dose and placed in her room for her to take without realising."

"That was a suicide attempt, I don't care what you say. When Violet was found there were several empty packets of sleeping powders by her bedside," Manx huffed. "Edwin could not have arranged that. He never had access to Violet's room when she was in it. Mr Stevenson always had someone guarding her."

"Yes, he did," Clara said, frowning at the thought.

How could someone have entered Violet's room to arrange the scene as an attempted suicide when Mr Stevenson had his watchdogs guarding her? Bribery was a possibility, of course, maybe one of her guards was not as reliable as Stevenson believed.

"Explain the shooting accident too!" Edwin now demanded. "If I was after Violet, why would I arrange for her to have a loaded gun to fire at Mr MacKenzie?"

"Maybe you were tired of trying to kill Violet and thought you would get rid of my other star?" Manx answered the question for him.

Edwin was appalled to hear his employer say this.

"No, you are wrong!" Edwin insisted. "And I was nowhere near her when she died on the railway line. I was here, with Mr Manx, trying to rearrange our filming schedule so that MacKenzie would have time to recover from his injury."

"That is true," Manx agreed with the same amount of indifference with which he had glibly stated his assistant might be out for his blood. "But I still think that last one was Violet's own doing. She finally had enough. Actresses can be so overblown when it comes to how they behave."

"If people had spent less time calling Violet 'over-dramatic' and more time considering the possibility her life was in danger, then maybe you would not now be in this situation," Clara told him, casting him a look that would have withered most men with a conscience.

Unfortunately, Manx was not one of those men.

"I was only going by what I have seen before," Manx shrugged. "Anyway, none of this makes a difference to me. Whether she killed herself or was murdered, I am still missing my main star, and the studio will have my head for it."

"I am not responsible for this, Mr Manx, I swear on my life!" Edwin bleated.

Manx ignored him.

"Do you have any more questions for me?" he asked Clara instead.

"Not for the time being, I shall leave you in peace," Clara responded.

She turned away and was joined by Tommy as they left the tent. Behind them, Edwin was now pleading with Mr Manx to believe him when he said he had not been trying to sabotage him.

Clara suspected it would take a lot more than mere words to convince the world-weary, cynical director that his latest assistant was not out for his head and his throne.

Chapter Eighteen

"Do you think Edwin Cleethorpes is a genuine suspect?" Tommy asked as they wandered away from the green.

"I don't know. Everything is so tenuous. Not to mention, everything that happened in the previous incidents is too long ago for us to make much headway with them. Why don't we focus on the most recent events instead and see if they lead us somewhere?"

It was as good a suggestion as any, and Tommy agreed to the idea, with that in mind they returned to Jones in the car and asked to be driven to the train station where Violet's final fatal accident had occurred.

"I am just going to play Devil's advocate and come out and say this," Tommy declared after they had travelled for a few minutes in silence. "Maybe Violet was pushed to such an extreme reaction by all her recent dances with death. She really did find herself beyond her limit of endurance."

Clara allowed the statement to hang in the air for a moment and gave it due thought. She had been denying Violet was suicidal ever since the sleeping powders incident, to the point she had been unable to focus on anything else, but was it possible that Violet had finally reached her breaking point?

Who wouldn't be tossed into a pit of despair by constant attempts on her life, which no one else believed were real? Violet was caught in a world where no one really cared about her, they only cared about what she could do for them, and she was a pawn in so many games. In such a world, was it unreasonable to suppose that Violet had finally reached a time when she could no longer face going on?

People all had a breaking point and the accident with Joshua MacKenzie could easily have been Violet's.

"Maybe," Clara said at last. "I would prefer to consider this yet another attempt by her assassin, one that sadly proved successful, but I cannot deny you have a valid concern. Violet may have been pushed beyond her reason."

Tommy said no more for a moment as they carried on towards the train station.

"Doesn't change that I am going to find who drove her to that extreme," Clara filled the quiet.

A smile formed on Tommy's lips.

"Never doubted that for a moment,"

They arrived at the train station a short time afterwards, Jones depositing them in the area set aside at the front for carriages and cars. He enquired if they required further assistance from him, and Clara assured him they did not. Then she headed with her brother into the station and towards the stationmaster's office.

A porter caught a glance of them as they were walking towards the door and recognised them.

"Tommy and Clara!" he waved a hand at them and cheerfully headed in their direction.

"Remind me of his name," Clara whispered to her brother before the fellow could arrive.

"Stephen Spranks. He was in school with us," Tommy whispered back.

Stephen appeared before them, a tall, gangly fellow with unassuming looks who, nonetheless, had an air about him that drew people to him.

"Are you catching the train?"

"Not exactly, Stephen," Clara said, testing out the name her brother had just told her. "We are here to ask about the sad tragedy that occurred on the platform the other day."

Stephen frowned; all his cheerfulness gone.

"Terrible thing. No one saw her about to step off, that's the worst of it. I mean, you get told people do things like that and to make sure no one ever stands too close to the edge of the platform when a train is coming in, but you never really expect it to happen."

"No one saw her?" Tommy asked, surprised by this.

"That's right. It was an outgoing train so everyone on the platform was either aboard or heading back inside. I was the only porter on duty as it was a quiet time of day, and I had just helped an elderly lady with a giant trunk to climb aboard. Then the whistle went, and the train started to pull out. Suddenly, we heard a shriek from the opposite platform, the train was already moving fast and couldn't be stopped at once. We had to let it pass before we could see what was wrong, and that was when we saw the young lady on the tracks."

"She had been crushed," Tommy winced.

"Oh no, she was not under the train. She would have had to cross the far tracks to reach it, from the opposite platform. No, she had been caught a glancing blow to the head. There was all this blood running down her face. The stationmaster called out for a doctor and luckily there was one waiting for the next train. He came over at once and declared her dead. Then we summoned the police."

"And you are sure no one witnessed her crossing the line to reach the train?"

"No one, unless a passenger saw her that was on the train. Maybe they did," Stephen shrugged his shoulders. "But how would you find out? They have all gone to wherever they were headed."

"Coming from the opposite tracks seems a little odd, doesn't it?" Tommy said.

Stephen did not seem to think this was a concern.

"Depends which direction she reached the station from. I admit, it was not the way I would expect someone to jump under a train. But people in such a terrible frame of mind are going to do rash things."

"But she gave a shriek?" Clara reminded him. "People throwing themselves under trains do not normally do that."

"But people who are being thrown or pushed do," Tommy finished her train of thought.

This information bamboozled the unfortunate Stephen, who thought for one awful moment they were suggesting someone at the station, specifically him, might have harmed Violet or caused her death.

"I didn't touch her! I would never!"

"We don't mean you, Stephen," Tommy promised him hastily, before changing the subject. "I wonder if you saw anyone else on the opposite platform at the time of the accident?"

Stephen thought for a moment, then shook his head.

"I don't recall anyone being there," he explained. "But my attention was not really on the opposite platform. We had to stop all trains entering and leaving the station while we dealt with the unfortunate lady. People were upset by the sight or wanted to complain about the delay. It was a real muddle."

"I can imagine," Clara said sympathetically. "Thank you for telling us about it. I am sure it was quite the shock."

Stephen shrugged his shoulders again.

"If I am honest, it was more of a nuisance. I know I shouldn't say that, but I was rather cross she had caused us such a problem. It is the porters like me who get everyone complaining at them when something happens."

They thanked him for assisting them, then headed back out to the car.

"I am going to change my opinion of what happened to Violet," Tommy said thoughtfully. "I think it very unlikely she decided to jump under a train from the opposite platform when it meant crossing the tracks."

"And the shriek," Clara said. "You cry out to draw attention to yourself or because you are afraid. I think someone pushed her into that train, which means she was murdered."

"Do you feel happier to have your fears she committed suicide averted?" Tommy asked her. "It makes *me* feel happier."

"Happiness is subjective. It makes me more determined to find out who was behind all this."

"Where do you want to go next?"

"I would like to talk with Mr MacKenzie and find out exactly what happened when he was shot. That is the one incident in this catalogue of disasters that fails to make sense. If someone wanted Violet dead, why arrange for MacKenzie to be shot?"

Joshua MacKenzie was currently residing at the *Grand Hotel*, recuperating from his unfortunate mishap. They were allowed to see him only after Clara had spoken with the hotel manager for several minutes, and promised she was neither from a newspaper nor a deranged admirer of the star.

Even with her assurances, the hotel manager wanted to ask MacKenzie first if he desired this unexpected guest, and he had a lengthy conversation with the actor about the woman at his front desk who claimed to be a private detective and would like to talk to him about his shooting accident.

MacKenzie proved more amenable than the hotel manager and asked that she be sent up to his room at once.

They found the ageing actor in his dressing gown, slumped on a sofa in his suite, with his arm in a sling. He had his hair slicked back and looked as if he was about to jump onto a film set. He greeted them warmly when they arrived and offered them coffee. Clara declined, not being a fan of the dark, bitter drink but Tommy gladly accepted. Getting real coffee in Brighton was something of a rarity, and since neither Annie not Clara drank it, he never had it when he was at home.

"What can I do for you, detective?" Joshua asked Clara, turning his full attention on her.

She saw through him at once; a man who was a natural charmer and thought any woman who entered his orbit would be smitten at first glance. She smiled politely back, remembering the stories of his lecherous behaviour towards Violet.

"I wanted to ask you about your accident."

"Oh yes, terrible thing," Joshua touched at his injured arm. "You can examine my arm if you like. It is all bandaged, so you cannot see any blood."

"No, thank you, I was a nurse in the war, and I know what a bullet wound looks like."

Clara didn't add that she had been a nurse in Brighton, where bullet wounds were rare, but she had seen more than one person shot during her time as a detective.

Joshua was unaffected by her refusal to touch him.

"I don't blame the girl, of course," he added. "She wasn't to know the gun was loaded. It was meant to be a prop. I heard she was dreadfully upset about it and threw herself under a train. Terrible tragedy."

Clara decided not to waste time explaining to Joshua that it was not any consideration for him that had caused Violet to take such drastic action.

"Could you tell us how the scene came about? My understanding was that originally there was not meant to be a gun?"

"No, in the original script I was supposed to get into an argument with Donna, that was the character Violet was playing. We were to shout a few things, I would grab her arms, she would slap me, the usually play acting."

"The original script did not call for you to be shot," Tommy asked.

"No, it did not. But these rehearsals take on a different hue sometimes. I think it was Stevenson who introduced the gun into the scene. He felt Violet's performance was flat and wanted to bring out some flare. She was being a bit... well, she was off-colour and her whole performance was half-hearted. I think he was trying to liven her up."

"At any point did someone suggest you point the gun at Violet?" Clara asked.

"Well, that's the funny thing about it. You see, when the gun was brought out of the prop box, Stevenson had this idea that I was to wave it at Violet instead of grabbing her arms. I was meant to be threatening her with it, and I could have sworn someone told me I could pull the trigger and pretend to shoot her if I wished. That particular scene ends with Donna apparently being killed by my character, though it is not the case, as she is the heroine, and lives to fight another day, so to speak."

Joshua was abashed by his statement as soon as it left his mouth, acutely aware of how unfortunate his choice of phrase was.

"Then how did Violet get the gun?" Clara asked him.

"It was an impromptu act from Violet. We improvise a lot during these rehearsals to see what happens, sometimes you come up with new things that are better than the original script. I was waving this gun at her, and I pretended to shoot her, just did that corny thing of going 'bang, bang,' and Violet acted as if I had winged her in her arm. Then I came closer, like I was going to finish her off, and someone shouted out that the real Donna would put up a fight. No idea who said it, but Violet took the stage direction and grabbed the gun. Took me by surprise, actually, as I was not expecting her to act so dramatically."

Joshua paused as he remembered his patronising amusement when Violet had defied him. Joshua was the sort of person who women rarely defied.

"Anyway, she turned the gun on me and pulled the trigger. As I say, no way she could have known it was loaded. Thank goodness she was aiming at my shoulder and not my heart!"

Joshua started to laugh, thinking it was all a good joke. At least this was one person who did not seem to hold any grudges against Violet.

"What happened then?" Tommy asked.

"I crumpled to the floor in agony!" Joshua laughed at the question. "What else? I lay on the floor groaning and bleeding. People were shrieking and shouting. Someone went for a doctor. I don't remember much else, aside from thinking that it was very peculiar a prop gun was loaded. It didn't occur to me until I was in the hospital how lucky I was to be alive."

Joshua had provided them with further insight into recent events, but they were still no closer to discovering who was behind all the attacks on Violet. Joshua had no idea who might have put the gun into the prop box and, as he remained thinking it had been a mistake, there was not much else they could get from him.

They left him in peace, Tommy feeling somewhat jazzed up by the coffee he had consumed. Outside in the corridor, Clara took a deep breath and looked along the hallway to the far side of the hotel.

"Clara?"

"Time to confront Stevenson, are you ready?"

"With all the coffee in me, I think I couldn't be readier."

Tommy grinned at her.

"Into the fray once again, brother," Clara remarked.

"Into the fray!"

Chapter Nineteen

Stevenson had spent nearly a whole day and night in the police cells while he was being interrogated about his involvement in the shooting of Joshua, and Violet's subsequent demise. He was fuming at how he had been treated, not least because the police had been difficult about letting him contact his solicitor to have him released. They had overstepped the mark as far as Stevenson was concerned, and he would find a way to pay them back as soon as he could.

But, for the time being, his immediate problems were getting back to his room, washing, and changing his clothes, then trying to work out what the future held with Violet deceased.

Stevenson was not a stupid man, so it did not take him long to realise someone else had been in his room, and that his papers had been moved around. After searching frantically through the drawers of the bureau, he discovered that his new contract with Violet was missing, and his temper flared.

Stevenson spent his life traipsing from hotel to hotel with Violet to fulfil her studio obligations, and thus, he had no fixed office. It had become easier to transport all his papers with him wherever he went, so he always had access to them should something come up. Never had that presented him with an issue, until that day.

He was just about to have a long talk with the hotel manager about his security arrangements when a knock came on his door. It was probably the worst time Clara could have arrived at the threshold of his room, though it might also be argued it was the best time. Stevenson was at his most vulnerable when he was angry and was not considering what he said.

Clara and Tommy's appearance at his door did not fill him with joy, and he started to slam the door in their faces the second he saw them.

"I want to talk about Violet's death," Clara said swiftly, though this did nothing to stop Stevenson from closing the door on her.

"Mr Stevenson, we really must talk!" she called through the closed door.

Tommy grimaced at her, thinking they would have more luck talking to a tortoise.

"I believe Violet was murdered!" Clara added, raising her voice.

If there had been any other guests in this part of the hotel, hearing Clara's words would have sent them to the hotel manager in terror.

"Go away!" Stevenson yelled back.

"We really must talk!" Clara insisted. "I know you and Violet had a difficult relationship, and I also know you were trying to pin her into a new fraudulent contract with you!"

The door suddenly swung open, and Stevenson loomed over Clara. Tommy was ready for a fight. Stevenson looked like he would strike Clara without hesitation.

"It was you! You took my new contract! You were in my room!"

Clara stared calmly into his eyes, not backing down an inch.

"Yes, I took that contract, but I wouldn't get too high and mighty about my crimes, when we both know the signature on that document was a forgery."

"No one knows that!" Stevenson yelled, his voice travelling down the corridor and echoing back at them.

"Actually, I have a friend who is a handwriting expert, and he is going to look at the contract and will easily prove it a fake," Tommy remarked nonchalantly.

Stevenson glowered at him.

"Violet signed that contract, fair and square."

"No, she did not," Clara retorted. "Why would she sign a contract to be bound to a monster like you again when she was on the cusp of having her freedom?"

Stevenson blinked, an easy answer not springing to mind.

"Violet was on the verge of being free from you and having the opportunity to join any number of management agencies who would treat her far better, and get her better paying work, than you ever could. She was not a stupid woman, and she was not easily intimidated. Despite her fear of you, she would not have signed a contract linking her to you in the future when all she had to do was wait and she would be free.

"The only person who benefited from that contract was *you*. You could not afford to lose Violet, so you faked her signature, knowing it would be too hard for her to prove your crime, and thinking she would simply give in and continue on as someone who made you money."

"You think you know everything," Stevenson snorted. "Violet sat in this very room and signed those papers."

"No she didn't, and you know it," Clara retorted. "We shall have the proof of the matter soon enough too."

Stevenson saw that his denials were fruitless. He stepped back from the door and threw his arms out in a sign of defeat.

"What do you want from me?" he demanded. "What does it even matter with Violet gone? I am worse off than ever, now."

"That being the case, I should imagine you would like to assist us in finding the person responsible for Violet's demise, so that we may have some sort of justice for her and, conversely, for you."

Stevenson studied Clara for a moment.

"She threw herself under a train, stupid girl."

"We have just come from the train station and we very much doubt that to be the case," Clara corrected him. "Will you talk to us for a few moments so we can get to the bottom of all this?"

"And if I refuse?" Stevenson lifted his head at them and glared down his nose in their direction.

"Then we shall leave. We will be disappointed, but nothing more."

"What about the contract?"

"What about it?"

"I want it back!" Stevenson snapped, balling his fists.

His temper had been barely in check and now it flared violently. Had Clara been alone she had no doubt he would have attempted to hurt her, but like most bullies Stevenson was cautious when he was outnumbered.

"You cannot have it back, it is evidence of a crime," Tommy replied.

"Why does it matter, anyway?" Clara frowned. "With Violet dead the contract is void and has no value."

She paused and glanced at her brother.

"Or does it?"

"You best bring that paperwork back to me pronto or I shall summon the police and accuse you of theft!" Stevenson pointed a finger first at Clara, then at Tommy. "I can make your lives hell."

Clara was not listening to him; she was thinking about his insistence on having the contract back. Was it simply because he was afraid of them giving it to the police and proving he was acting fraudulently? Even with Violet dead, the evidence of the fake contract would be a dent in his career and would probably prevent him from ever representing a big star again. Or did he think they might use it to blackmail him?

People tended to judge others by how they would act and there was no doubt Stevenson would happily blackmail a person if it served his own ends. How could he not think that Clara would do the same?

"The contract stays with us," Tommy was shouting at him, while Stevenson bellowed and postured.

"Did you set up Joshua MacKenzie to be shot?" Clara suddenly interrupted.

Stevenson fell instantly silent. The look of guilt on his face was fleeting, but it had been there for just a second.

"What nonsense!"

"You found the gun in the prop box," Clara continued. "You changed the scene so that the gun was used instead of Joshua and Violet wrestling."

"Yes, because Violet didn't want that man touching her, and I had made a promise to her she would never have to be in a scene where he did!" Stevenson snapped. "I might be many things, but I was not going to allow that vile oaf to touch my star. The gun made things easy for me, but I would have thought of something else if necessary."

"You are saying you had no idea it was loaded?"

"Don't be ridiculous! If I had known that, why would I have allowed it to be pointed at anyone? If either of the two were killed because of it, that would be my career down the drain!" Stevenson paused as he heard his own words. "As it is, my career is over. You have made that very plain. Who would ever want to be represented by a manager who allowed his only star to die? If you think I have somehow benefited from all this, you can think again! I am facing destitution!"

"Seems to me you gambled rather heavily on Violet's success and ought to have been a bit more cautious," Tommy remarked.

"Caution gets you nowhere in this game," Stevenson snorted, his temper had started to run its course. He sat down on the edge of his bed. "A girl like Violet comes along once in a lifetime, and you have to just run with it. Yes, it was a risk, but I had to give everything I had to ensure she was a success. She was good, she had such potential, but there were always a dozen other girls waiting to step into her shoes. One slip can turn a potential starlet into last week's news.

"So, I watched her like a hawk to prevent any slips. I guarded her like she was treasure. What she saw as being a prisoner, I saw as me guaranteeing her future. These girls have no idea how easy it is to go from fame to forgotten in this business. One bad decision is all it takes. She wanted freedom, but she also wanted to be the name on everyone's lips. The girl that every woman wanted to be. That comes with a price."

"It doesn't sound like an industry I would care to be in," Clara observed.

"It is a tough business, no doubt about it, and the women have it harder than the men. Fellows like Joshua MacKenzie can make all sorts of slip-ups, be named in all manner of scandals and they still get parts. A girl gets her name in the papers for the wrong reason more than once, and that is it. Her career is over."

"Why would anyone want to be an actor or actress?" Tommy asked, confused.

"Because the rewards outweigh the penalties! Get it right and you can be set up for life. Violet was just a few movies away from never having to worry about money again if she was clever. She had everything she could ever have wanted. People fawning over her, money in the bank, nice clothes and jewels she didn't have to pay for, staying in hotels like this. You know, she was poor as poor before I took her on. She could have never imagined being a maid in a hotel like this back then, let alone having a suite here!"

"For that she was to forsake her freedom?" Clara asked angrily.

"Not her freedom," Stevenson snorted. "She could do what she pleased within limits. I wasn't going to have her wrecking everything. And let me remind you that I was the one protecting her from the likes of MacKenzie! I can tell you a lesser actress would have found herself in a dire situation with him as her leading man. He has made his mark on most of the women in the industry, if you catch my meaning. I kept Violet safe!"

"By having a loaded gun pointed at her," Tommy retorted.

"I did not know... look, if you are just going to stand there accusing me, I am done with it all!" Stevenson rose from his bed and approached them again. "We've had our chat, now you can clear off. But you dare to try to blackmail me with that contract and I shall have you arrested for theft. My solicitor is as cunning as I am, and don't forget it!"

Stevenson chased them out of the room and slammed the door in their faces. They heard him stomp back across the carpeted floor and begin to swear in a range of florid and particularly offensive phrases. Then something smashed, and it seemed the man was taking out his temper on the room at the hotel's expense.

"What a ghastly fellow," Tommy said to his sister as they turned away from the room and headed back downstairs.

"Violet needed to get away from him. I wonder if she knew about the fake contract?"

"What could she have done about it if she had?" Tommy pointed out. "She had no one she could turn to, to prove it was a forgery."

"I don't suppose Violet would go down without a fight," Clara considered. "Not when her future freedom was at stake. If she knew about that contract, she would have done everything in her power to prove she had not signed it."

"Does that put us any closer to knowing who killed her?"

Clara shook her head.

"We just keep having more complications thrown at us. Who put that gun in the prop box? If we could determine that, we would know who our most likely suspect was."

"Maybe the police can trace it? Find out where it was bought and by whom?"

"Maybe," Clara agreed. "Curious, how Joshua was holding it first and pointing it at Violet. If he had pulled the trigger like he was told he could, then she would be the one dead."

"So now we know this was another attempt at a fatal accident," Tommy concurred. "We just don't know who might have been responsible."

"We have yet to find a definite motive for someone wanting Violet dead, and that is the real problem, not to mention linking that person to all the events that occurred. I wonder who was the woman who found Violet the night she overdosed and summoned help? Maybe she could offer us further insight?"

"You know, Edwin made a fair point when he said he could not have accessed Violet's room at the hotel while she was present. There can only have been a handful of people who could get close to her and stage her room to look like a suicide."

"One of them being Stevenson, another being his driver who was obsessed with Violet. Unrequited love can lead a person to do terrible things."

Tommy nodded his head.

"And what about the bodyguard we have yet to speak to?"

"If the people closest to Violet were also her most dangerous enemies, she never stood a chance," Clara sighed. "The poor woman was doomed from the start."

Chapter Twenty

Clara was growing frustrated. She had plenty of suppositions, and plenty of suspects, but no evidence to point her in the direction of the person behind these crimes. Had she died because someone had a grudge against her or was it because someone had a grudge against a person close to her?

Before leaving the *Grand Hotel,* they went in search of the second man Mr Stevenson had hired to keep people away from his starlet. Unfortunately, the man appeared to have simply vanished, nor could they find Mario the driver again. Something felt amiss.

Disappointed, Clara suggested they head home and get in touch with Tommy's friend, the handwriting expert.

Herbert Phinn had gone to school with Tommy. He had been the child who was the obvious target for the schoolyard bullies. Gawky, lacking in confidence, a little tubby and academic rather than sporting, he had swiftly marked himself out as a prime victim. That was where Tommy came in.

Tommy had always been the sort of boy to hate seeing others bullied and was physically tough enough to make even the meanest children in the playground pause at the sight of him. Already Tommy had been keeping a close eye on his little sister, once she had started at the same school, and made sure she was never in any harm, it was not much of a logical extension to take Herbert under his wing too.

Neither boy had expected to become firm friends with the other, but over the years that was exactly what happened.

They only shared a handful of interests, but one of them was cricket, and while Tommy was more a keen player than a spectator, their shared passion enabled them to form a firm friendship. Herbert had grown up to become a chemist who specialised in testing products for companies to ensure they were safe for public use. Sometimes, he was sent products that were thought to have caused people injury or illness, and would test them, to discover if there was anything in their composition that could result in a person being made unwell.

His sideline was studying handwriting, and he had become a self-taught expert on the subject – one who was regularly asked to give their opinion at court cases. He had built quite a reputation since the first time he had assisted Tommy with a case. He was rather famous in certain circles.

Herbert remained Herbert, however. A happy, bumbling fellow who went through life mostly oblivious to anything outside his field of interest. He still lived with his parents, and Tommy suspected this would likely never change. Herbert had shown occasional interest in the opposite sex, but he was so easily distracted and absorbed by his work that the likelihood of him ever establishing a lasting relationship with a woman seemed slim, at best.

Not that this troubled Herbert. As long as he had his laboratory, and work to attend to, nothing troubled him at all.

Tommy had sent him a message about the contract they suspected was fake. Herbert had responded back quickly, and suggested they pop over to his home whenever was convenient for them, and he would take a look at the document. That was what they intended to do, but there was one thing they had overlooked.

Clara was about to step into the car when the notion of what they had forgotten came flashing back into her mind.

"We don't have a sample signature for Herbert to compare the contract to!"

She said the words loudly and drew the immediate attention of every newspaperman who was lurking around the stairs. Despite Violet's untimely death, none of them had left their posts for longer than it took to report the story to their editors.

They now looked at Clara, anticipating further information, which she was certainly not going to give them. Tommy shut the car door he was holding open and joined his sister, so they could speak quietly together.

"How could we be so stupid?"

"We weren't thinking about it, that is all, but without something to compare to the signature on the contract Herbert can do nothing."

"We have to go back inside and find something with Violet's writing on it," Tommy glanced back up the stairs to the doors of the hotel. "She never gave you anything that could be useful?"

"No, I'm afraid she didn't."

They were both looking at the hotel now. It was not so much the annoyance of the delay, but the thought of having to risk going back past Stevenson's room after their recent conversation with him. Neither expected him to be in the mood to see them once again, and if he realised they were searching Violet's suite, he would be furious and probably have them banished from the hotel for good.

"It cannot be helped, we must go back upstairs and find something that will be useful to us," Clara said firmly.

Tommy was right at her side, ready to brave the lion's den with her once again.

"Don't suppose we could find Gilbert and have him give us the key to her suite?" he suggested.

Clara pulled a face.

"On the other hand, I don't believe we locked it after we last left, and as long as none of the staff have been in there, it probably remains unlocked."

The hotel had been in no rush to touch the suite and ready it for a new guest. They were still awaiting permission from the police who had advised them to leave it alone for the time being. As it was out of season, and the suite was not urgently required, the hotel manager had been prepared to leave the room as it was.

Clara and Tommy headed back upstairs, hopeful luck would be on their side and the room would be unlocked. At least there was no guard in the hallway to deter them. They walked past Stevenson's door as quietly as they could, hoping the man would not hear their footsteps on the deep carpet of the corridor. There were no sounds from his room; it seemed his rage had abated, and he had ceased destroying the hotel's property. They slipped past without seeming to rouse him and found themselves at Violet's door.

Clara crossed her fingers in a gesture of hope to her brother and tried the door handle. The handle depressed easily, and the door swung open, allowing them immediate access to Violet's room. Clara did not hide the sigh of relief she gave as she stepped safely into the apartment.

It was not much tidier than when they had entered on the first occasion, Annie's attempts to rearrange everything had made limited impact on the overall disarray of the room.

"You take the right side of the room, I shall take the left," Clara told her brother, and they set to work.

Clara headed immediately to the writing desk, which she had left in an inky mess the other night. The ink blot was visible, staining the leather writing surface of the desk's drop-down front. It was now mostly dry and would not be coming off in a hurry. Clara cringed at the sight, feeling bad that she had damaged the hotel's property, even if it had been completely unintentional and really a product of Violet's own carelessness with the ink bottle.

She fumbled around in the bureau, hoping for a letter that would bear Violet's handwriting, but as she had discovered the night before, the desk contained very little in the way of written correspondence. She did find several telegrams sent to the actress by adoring fans asking for her autograph. Clara sighed as she found herself coming to another dead end.

Behind her, Tommy was having similar luck. He had headed into the suite's sitting room to look for something there, but it seemed Violet was not the sort of person who spent her spare time writing. He looked everywhere he could think of, but not so much as a shopping list or a note could be found.

He found Clara in the bathroom, searching in vain through the medicine cabinet.

"It's no good, there is nothing here," Tommy shrugged at her.

"You would have thought there would have been one letter at least," Clara sighed. "Or a diary, even an address book."

"Yes, odd we have found nothing personal like that," Tommy frowned.

"Violet may have had those things with her when she perished, perhaps inside her handbag, but we cannot know for sure."

Clara put back the bottles of headache tablets and digestive aids she had removed from the cabinet.

"I can't see any sign of her sleeping powders."

"Are you surprised?" Tommy snorted. "Would you leave a box of those things with someone who you fancied had tried to overdose on them?"

"No, I suppose you are right, presumably Stevenson or one of his aides would bring her one at night."

Clara closed the medicine cabinet.

"This is disappointing. We may have to break into Stevenson's room again."

"What?" Tommy was alarmed.

"He must have other documents in his room with Violet's signature on them, her first contract for instance. That would enable us to have a sample of her writing to compare with the fake contract. He probably used her original signature on the first contract to fake the one on the new contract."

"Yes, I get the logic," Tommy grumbled. "I meant, what could possibly possess you to suggest we go back to his room? We barely escaped with our heads on the first time."

"He must leave it at some point," Clara was undeterred. "If that is how we get our signature, it is just the way things must be."

"I know you have a tendency to be crazy and impulsive, but really Clara, this is taking things a bit far," Tommy shook his head. "That man is a lunatic, and he was very close to punching both our lights out earlier today."

"He does not scare me," Clara said in complete honesty.

"That, I fear, is the problem," Tommy groaned. "Are you sure there was nothing in that writing bureau?"

Tommy returned to the bureau and tentatively placed his finger on the dark ink stain.

"There was nothing aside from a handful of telegrams asking for autographs," Clara responded.

Tommy's eyes lit up, he was about to say something when they heard a cry from outside, followed by the echoes of a scuffle and the shouted swear words favoured by Stevenson.

"What on earth?" Tommy was a step ahead of Clara heading to the door to see what was going on and hopefully aid whoever had seemingly fallen foul of the perpetually angry manager.

He had the door open before Clara could remind him they were not meant to be there, though it probably no longer mattered. She hastened to catch him up.

In the corridor outside, Stevenson had his hands at the collar of a man who was half fallen to the floor and turned away from them.

"You think I wouldn't realise it was you sneaking about my room, huh?" Stevenson was yelling at him. "You are working with them, aren't you? You little scumbag! I should break both your arms!"

The unfortunate fellow caught in Stevenson's grasp gave a squeak of alarm at this statement. Clara blinked as she realised who he had in his arms.

"Let go of Gilbert!"

Stevenson turned his head sharply to Clara at the same time her brother gave her a questioning look. Clara ignored the former and shrugged at the latter.

"I recognised his ears."

"Help me!" Gilbert bellowed now he heard Clara's voice.

"I knew you knew him!" Stevenson's anger had been increased rather than diminished by their arrival. "You have had him snooping about my room! I shall have you all arrested by the police."

"Come on now," Tommy said in the sort of voice you try to calm an enraged dog with. "Put the fellow down. He is harmless."

"He was in my room!" Stevenson bellowed at them, spittle flying from his lips. "He was in there just this instant, poking around!"

Gilbert made a murmur that might have been an attempt at an

apology, though it failed to calm his assailant. Clara was not about to ask what the journalist had been thinking going through Stevenson's room while the man was present – presumably, Gilbert had thought Stevenson was still at the police station – she just wanted to defuse the situation and get Gilbert to safety.

"Whatever he has done, throttling him will not help you," Tommy was the voice of reason, taking a pace forward with his hands up to show he was no threat to the fuming manager. "You will be in more trouble with the police if you hurt him."

Stevenson seemed too far gone in his outrage to appreciate what Tommy was saying. He looked as though he was quite prepared to kill Gilbert if necessary.

"Please, put him down," Tommy kept stepping forward, hoping he could get in reach of Stevenson's arms and haul him off Gilbert.

The journalist grew tired of waiting for Tommy to succeed in taming the beast and reacted in a way that was rather typical of the fellow.

He bit Stevenson's hand.

Stevenson let go in surprise, Gilbert scrambled to his feet and scarpered down the hallway. Stevenson looked astounded at the blood pouring from his injured hand, but that only lasted a second, then he was running as fast as he could after Gilbert. Clara and Tommy had no choice but to follow.

Gilbert had been in the hotel long enough to know all the back routes around it, and he was fast gaining ground on Stevenson, but there were only so many places to run in a hotel, all the corridors and staircases eventually led to the same place. Stevenson was overbrimming with fury after Gilbert's assault on him and he stomped after the man, causing a terrible ruckus, which started to bring other guests out of their rooms to see what the commotion was all about.

One of these guests was an older woman with a large Great Dane at her side. She stepped out into a corridor just in front of Gilbert, and the dog barked at him ferociously.

"You get him, Titan!" The woman declared.

Titan leapt at Gilbert, and he stumbled away, turning around only to find himself confronted by the approaching Stevenson. Gilbert panicked as Stevenson yelled furiously at him, running down the corridor as if he would not stop until he had mown the newspaperman down.

Gilbert had no choice but to cower and hope for the best, which turned out to be to his advantage because Titan lost interest in the terrified journalist, switching his attention instead to the rampaging Stevenson. With a furious growl of his own, the Great Dane sprang over Gilbert and attacked Stevenson, grabbing at his already injured arm, and bringing the man to the ground easily.

The commotion did not end there. Stevenson tried to kick Titan, which resulted in the dog digging his teeth in deeper and shaking his arm. Stevenson swore in pain, made worse as now the dog's owner came over and began hitting him with her walking stick.

"You leave Titan alone!"

The irony of the old woman defending her dog while it mauled Stevenson did not escape Tommy or Clara, and they hurried to his aid.

Gilbert had vanished, using the dog's timely appearance to cover his retreat. Tommy raced to Titan and carefully grasped the dog's collar. With gentle words of cajolement and promises that Titan had been a very good boy and could desist from killing Stevenson, he was able to detach the dog and remove him a short distance down the hallway.

Clara, meanwhile, had the older woman in charge, asking her to step back, assuring her she had done her duty and made sure a fiend, who was terrorising the hotel, had been stopped. Much in the manner

Tommy was cajoling her dog, Clara cajoled the woman and helped her back to her room.

With both dog and owner secured behind a door, the pair could finally turn their attention to Stevenson, who was now sitting up and clutching his bloodied arm.

"That's going to need stitches, old man," Tommy said, moving to help him.

"Leave me alone!" Stevenson snapped at him, though some of his venom had been shaken from him by the pain of the dog attack.

He had gone rather pale with the shock and blood loss. He looked a sorry sight as he got to his feet still refusing their help. He turned away from them and stumbled back along the corridor.

Tommy went to follow. Clara put out a hand to stop him.

"He doesn't want our help, and constantly trying to offer it won't change that."

Tommy scratched at his head.

"I suppose we better find out if Gilbert survived the encounter," he sighed. "Well, that was an unexpected ending to our morning."

Clara was quiet for a moment. Tommy glanced in her direction.

"What are you thinking?"

"I was wondering if we could do with a dog like Titan in our lives."

"Please, no!" Tommy looked at her despondently. "I would be constantly having to rescue the people you set the thing on!"

Chapter Twenty-One

Gilbert had made his way to the vast kitchen area of the hotel and was nursing his eye when they found him. He was being fussed over by a maid, who was bringing him a cup of tea and offering him a cold, wet cloth to press over his bruised socket. Clara was always amazed how Gilbert seemed to attract certain women despite his roguish appearance, disreputable character and, to put it bluntly, his rather ugly visage. There must be something about him she failed to notice.

"You two weren't much help," Gilbert grumbled at them when they appeared.

It had taken several minutes for them to thread their way through the hotel to the service area without being stopped by anyone wondering who they were. Fortunately, a number of the staff had been called away to attend to the commotion that had happened on the upper floor. Not only had the old woman reported an intruder which her dog had savaged, but Stevenson had returned to his own room and rung out for a doctor. It looked likely the staff would be very busy attending to the patient and cleaning up the mess Titan had made in the upstairs corridor.

"We were not the ones sneaking into a man's room while he was there," Tommy pointed out. "What were you thinking?"

"I didn't realise he was there," Gilbert huffed. "I was told he was still being detained by the police. I entered his room with the keys I borrowed, like before. He was in the bathroom, so I did not see him. I was rummaging through his drawers when he appeared out of the room, screaming at me."

The maid did not react to the news that Gilbert had been poking around a guest's room. Clara glanced in her direction.

"This is Helen," Gilbert caught her look and explained. "She knows I am a journalist. She helped me get the keys."

"Mr McMillan is a very clever man," Helen beamed at them. "He knows so many things, and when I heard he was here investigating a crime, I couldn't but help him."

"Not so loud, Helen," Gilbert smiled at her. "Remember, no one else must know."

"Of course," Helen mimed pinching her lips together. "Sealed!"

Clara decided not to ask any more about Gilbert's relationship with the girl. Helen was clearly infatuated with him, though she doubted it would last for long. Gilbert had a tendency to get under a person's skin, for better or worse.

"Why are you here at the hotel, anyway?" Gilbert demanded, remembering their presence.

"We needed to chat with Stevenson," Clara explained. "Then we were trying to find something in Violet's room with a signature on it, so we could compare it to the contract she signed."

Gilbert understood.

"That contract business is really on your minds, I see. What does it matter now she is dead?"

"It is the principal of the thing," Clara responded, not wanting to say it was about the only clue they had at that moment, and it probably wasn't going to lead anywhere, but it was better than sitting around doing nothing.

"Drink your tea," Helen nudged Gilbert.

"Thanks, lovely. You best get back to work before someone notices."

Helen gave him a smile and departed, humming to herself.

"You have a new friend?" Tommy observed.

"She is sweet, but she is too young for me. Not my type, anyway."

Gilbert leaned over his cup of tea seeming more dejected than usual over what had just happened. Gilbert was normally rather robust when it came to being assaulted, seeing as it happened quite frequently, and he took it as a peril of his line of work.

"Something the matter?" Clara asked, taking a chair opposite him at the table.

"Nothing," Gilbert shrugged his shoulders. "My eye hurts, that's all."

"Let me take a look," Tommy offered.

Reluctantly, Gilbert removed his hand from his eye, revealing that his eyelid was already swelling up and the skin looked a fiery red all around it.

"You are going to have a black eye," Tommy remarked.

"Thanks, I didn't need you to tell me that."

"No problem," Tommy said with a grin. "You did a pretty stupid thing, you know."

Gilbert attempted to glare at him, but the effect was spoiled by having one eye too swollen to react to the expression.

"Come on, Tommy, we have our own tasks ahead of us to attend to," Clara rose again. "Gilbert, I advise you to keep your distance from Stevenson. He is out for blood, and it could easily be yours."

Gilbert muttered something under his breath, which Clara suspected was along the lines of her stating the obvious, but she chose to ignore it. Leaving the journalist to nurse his wounds, she went with Tommy back to the car.

"What are we going to do about having a sample signature for Herbert?" Clara asked her brother as they were approaching the vehicle. "Where else could we find one?"

"Oh!" Tommy brightened up. "I remember what I was going to say right before we had to rush to Gilbert's aid. I have an idea where we can find a signature for Violet."

"Really? Where?"

"You mentioned telegrams asking for an autograph from Violet, and it reminded me that when these stars get such a request, they often send a signed picture of themselves to the person. Sometimes, these same images are published in magazines with the autograph on them, so everyone can have a facsimile of their signature."

"That's a brilliant idea, Tommy!" Clara grinned. "We find a magazine with one of these images, and we shall have our sample signature. We shall go back to the Home at once. In the library we have a large collection of movie magazines for the men to peruse, there must be Violet's autograph in one of them."

At last, they had a solution to their problem, and they instructed Jones to take them to the O'Harris residence at once. The newspapermen lurking around the steps watched them leave, wondering why Tommy appeared to have blood on his coat sleeve.

The house was lovely and warm after the chilly weather outside. Several of the houseguests were in the library enjoying the heat of the fire in the hearth and reading books. They all looked up and greeted

Clara cheerfully on her arrival.

She had slotted in well at the home and had proven a welcome addition. The men often asked about her work, and Clara was not opposed to giving them a crash course in detective skills, once in a while. There was always something happening when Clara was around, and it was usually a welcome diversion to the men's usual problems. Not to mention, every now and then, she would invite some of them to assist her.

Being around Clara was never a dull experience.

As for Tommy, most of the fellows were familiar with his face, and knew he was also a veteran of the war who had come home with his own problems, both physical and mental. He was always happy to talk about his own scenario and the journey it had taken to overcome his troubles. New guests were often pointed in his direction and advised that he would be an understanding ear to speak into. Speaking to Tommy could be easier at the start of their recovery than speaking to a doctor.

Tommy had also organised a cricket team at the Home, which would begin practicing again as soon as the weather had improved. This made him extremely popular, as he was both a good teacher and a good sport, who encouraged even the weakest of players to do their best and have fun.

"We have a task ahead of us!" Clara announced to the men in the room as she entered. "You might like to assist."

"Anything, Clara," someone called out, the sentiment echoed by the others present.

"Tommy, I think you should explain your idea," Clara stood aside to let her brother take the floor.

"We need to find the autograph of Violet Starling," Tommy explained. "We need it to compare to a signature on a contract which we believe is a fake. We are hoping there might be a reproduction of her autograph in one of the movie magazines, but it will be a job looking through them all to find it."

He needed to say no more, already the men were up and gathering the magazines from their spot on the shelves. They took them over to the round table in the library and distributed them evenly among themselves, and Tommy and Clara. For the next half an hour, they all sat together, comfortably warm, thumbing through the magazines looking for Violet's autograph.

Clara had not thought it would take so long, and she was beginning to think they would be out of luck, when one of the men announced he had something. He flipped around the magazine he was looking through to face Clara. On the right-hand page was a portrait of Violet looking wistfully to her upper left. She looked older in the picture, the lighting and the styling of her hair adding years. Clara felt a prick of emotion at seeing her image and remembering the girl was gone. She tried not to be sentimental in her line of work, but sometimes it was impossible not to be.

Blinking back tears, she looked at the bottom corner of the picture where Violet's signature was printed in black ink.

"We have it!" she said with relief.

"What will you do now?" the man who had found the picture asked.

"We will take it to a friend of mine who is an expert on handwriting," Tommy explained. "He can make a comparison between this and the forged signature and tell us if our suspicion is correct."

Clara was regaining her composure. There was much more to do as yet, and tears would help no one. Thanking the men for their assistance, and promising to keep them updated on the outcome, she headed off once more with Tommy.

"Are you all right?" Tommy asked her not long after they had left the library.

"I am fine," Clara responded.

"You don't look fine. You look like you are about to cry. I honestly thought you were going to break down into tears when you saw Violet's picture back then."

Clara paused.

"It took me by surprise, that is all," she said softly.

Tommy placed a hand on her shoulder.

"I know you won't believe me, but this was not your fault. You tried your best for her."

"My best was not good enough, Tommy, and we both know that. My best should have been finding out who was intent on hurting her and protecting her."

"You are being too hard on yourself," Tommy consoled her.

"How else I am meant to be when a young woman is dead? Her whole future wiped out?" the tears threatened again as Clara was reminded of Violet. "She asked me to save her, and I did nothing."

"You hardly did nothing, Clara."

Tommy stared at his sister a moment, aware that he was not getting through to her. Clara was going to cling to her guilt no matter what he said. After a moment, he put his arms around her and drew her close into an embrace.

Clara felt utterly dejected. She did not fail like this; she did not let people down. Yet, quite clearly on this occasion, her skills had proved wanting.

"Feeling sorry for myself is not helping Violet," she decided suddenly, forcing aside her complicated emotions on the matter. "Come along, we need to get to Herbert."

Tommy tried not to sigh as she marched away from him, once more on her mission. At some point, his sister would have to stop and allow her emotions to come out, but he supposed that was not right now. Clara was not the sort of person who could allow herself to feel things too deeply when she was on a case. She liked to maintain her focus.

He would just have to make sure, when this was all over and she could finally release the grief and guilt she was feeling, that either himself or O'Harris were around to be a shoulder to cry on.

Chapter Twenty-Two

Herbert's family home was out in the countryside, a short drive from Brighton. Once again, Jones the chauffeur was called into service and drove them there. Tommy was keen to learn how to drive but O'Harris had an almost chronic aversion to allowing anyone other than himself and Jones to drive one of his cars. Clara had been pestering him for weeks about giving her some lessons and he had repeatedly put off arranging a time and date.

Clara knew precisely what her husband was about, but on this one instance she was prepared to let matters lie. O'Harris was a generous man who would allow her anything, and would do anything for her, but he was particularly precious about the car collection he had inherited from his late uncle. She wasn't going to begrudge him that.

Tommy was less impressed at being repeatedly refused access to O'Harris' cars. He fancied, being a man himself, it should go without speaking that he be allowed to drive them and be given lessons. To be clumped into the same group of those not allowed as his sister niggled at his pride.

On the whole, Tommy never considered his sister anything other than an equal, but he was not immune to the prejudices of his day, and on this matter, he believed it was unfair O'Harris was treating him with the same unease as his sister when it came to the car.

Fortunately, Jones was always on hand to escort them somewhere. Besides, he knew that on occasion Clara got herself into scrapes that benefited from a male companion's assistance.

For that matter, sometimes Tommy got himself in scrapes where he required assistance. Jones was quite happy to be the one to offer that aid. He was extremely loyal to O'Harris and almost saw it as his duty to watch out for Clara when necessary.

Had Clara known about any of this – her brother's thinking that he should be allowed to drive O'Harris' cars when she was not, and Jones' overprotectiveness because he saw her as an extension of his employer – she would have been less than impressed, though she would take it with a smile of amusement.

Clara was quietly confident that she could get herself out of most of the pickles she dropped herself into. But it didn't hurt, on occasion, to have a little back-up, and she was grateful she had such loyal friends willing to risk themselves for her.

Though, if she knew Tommy was thinking he had more right to drive O'Harris' cars than she did, she would not have let it pass without an argument.

They reached Herbert's handsome mock Tudor home, which he shared with his parents. The place was large enough that he had his own private wing these days, with a bespoke laboratory in a workshop out the back – Herbert was a stickler for safety and was aware that a lab inside the house would be dangerous; if a serious accident occurred, it might engulf the entire property.

Herbert was known for occasionally, and always accidentally, creating explosions.

They were warmly greeted on the doorstep by the senior Mr Phinn, who had seen the car pulling up and come to the door to discover who the visitors were. A man with almost white hair and a pipe permanently clutched between his teeth, he was like an older version of his son, even down to his mannerisms.

He greeted them warmly, then showed them around the house to Herbert's laboratory. He departed at the door, wishing them a good visit and without enquiring why they were there to see his son. Such was the nature of the Phinns of this world, friendly and wholly uninterested in anyone else's business.

Tommy knocked on the workshop door just as there was a stifled explosion from within. A small yelp of alarm from Herbert had Tommy rushing inside, with Clara more calmly walking behind.

Herbert was attempting to put out a small fire on his workbench using a bucket of sand he kept nearby for the purpose. There was smoke drifting around him, and he was coughing loudly. Tommy jumped in to assist him and within moments the tiny blaze was doused.

"Turns out the chemicals in that particular face cream were flammable," Herbert turned a grin on Tommy as the fire was safely drowned in sand. "I shall be making a report on the matter."

Tommy was far more anguished over the matter than Herbert was, who found such fires an occupational hazard. Tommy was panting and still alarmed at what had just occurred, while Herbert headed to the stove in his laboratory and asked if they would care for some tea.

Clara answered for them both in the affirmative, glancing at her brother who was still astonished that no one else seemed to realise the calamity they had just averted.

"You are here about the handwriting?" Herbert said, settling a large brass kettle on the stove to boil. "I am always glad to take a look at handwriting. Such an interesting subject. People think they can get away with some dreadful attempts at imitation. It as much amuses me as brings me a touch of despair." He smiled at them and indicated they were welcome to sit on a pair of stools next to a long and well-battered table. The burn marks and stains on its surface attested to the many experiments it had been the unwilling accomplice to.

"How are you doing, Herbert?" Clara asked, thinking they ought to be polite and not simply jump straight into business.

"I am very well," Herbert beamed at them. "I find myself in the happy position of having a long-term contract with the government for the purposes of identifying potentially hazardous products being sold to the public. The government are finally trying to crack down on the number of things a person can buy for innocuous purposes that prove to be incredibly dangerous."

"Such as the flammable face cream," Tommy nodded.

"Precisely."

Herbert placed three sturdy white mugs on the tabletop. They had clearly had their handles broken on more than one occasion, and it was questionable whether the repairs Herbert had made to them would actually prevent them from falling to pieces in the middle of being used.

"That is wonderful news, Herbert," Tommy smiled at him. "I am glad to hear you are doing so well."

"I am glad to know that I am making a difference. Preventing dangerous products from being sold to the unwitting and causing terrible accidents is such an important task. It is a small drop in the ocean, but I hope that one day all products will have to be tested by men like myself, before being allowed on the market for general sale."

Clara was on the cusp of mentioning that it would also be nice if women could be included in such work, seeing as a lot of the most dangerous products were sold to them, but she refrained, deciding it had only been a slip of the tongue on Herbert's part.

"Now, to this matter of the suspect contract," Herbert looked at them keenly. "I haven't had a good handwriting case in a while. So, I am excited about this one."

"Excited is perhaps not the best word considering the lady whose signature has been forged is now deceased," Tommy rebuked him mildly.

"I apologise. That did sound rather vulgar under the circumstances. I suppose I get carried away, seeing the task of identifying the handwriting as a separate matter to the situation it came about from."

Herbert was only mildly embarrassed by his slip. Clara came to his rescue.

"It is easily done. I find myself having a similar problem when I get caught up in the minutiae of a mystery, forgetting that I am dealing with actual people's lives."

"Obsession is essential for the expert, I find," Herbert blushed. "We are a unique breed, with a tendency to forget everything but the task in hand."

"But that same obsession results in making the world a better place," Clara reminded him gently. "Without experts prepared to focus on things such as the loop of a J and the arch of an M, we would be a lot worse off."

Herbert was flattered and his blush deepened to include his ears. To spare him any further unease, Tommy produced the contract they had stolen from Stevenson and showed it to him. Herbert turned immediately to the signature that was his sole interest in the paperwork.

"Violet Starling!" he read the name and looked at them aghast. "Someone forged her signature?"

"I didn't realise you were up to speed on the movie stars of today," Tommy remarked.

"I might spend a lot of hours in this laboratory, Tommy, but I do leave the house at times," Herbert cheerfully corrected him. "I go to the pictures quite a lot too. Violet is one of my favourite actresses. She was delightful in that movie, *Queen of the Aztecs*. Woefully inaccurate from an historical perspective, of course, but charming nonetheless."

Clara had the impression Herbert had no idea Violet was dead. The news had been kept as quiet as possible, but in certain circles it was being whispered about. The police had somehow managed to prevent the press running the story as yet, but there were still rumours circulating around the town, and Herbert moved in the right circles to hear those rumours.

"Violet has..." Clara found the words drying up on her lips.

How was she supposed to tell the happily smiling Herbert that the actress he admired was dead? Her body flung before a train by an assailant Clara was determined to locate.

"Violet is in a lot of trouble," Tommy interjected to save his sister. "This contract might be key to all of it. We are not sure. It is very suspicious, you see..."

"Tell me nothing about the situation," Herbert held up a hand to stop him. "I prefer to come to a matter like this knowing as little about the circumstances as possible. You can never be sure if knowing about the details of a case might influence your judgement."

It was a wise statement, so they both fell silent as Herbert produced a magnifying glass and studied the signature.

"Interesting," he murmured. "Do you have something for me to compare this with?"

Tommy produced the magazine, folded back to the page bearing Violet's picture and the printed facsimile of her autograph.

Herbert's face fell.

"This is not an ideal sample," he protested. "The printing process will have caused defects in the signature that could lead to a false conclusion."

"It was the best we could do," Clara apologised. "We have searched everywhere for an actual sample of Violet's handwriting without success."

Herbert frowned, taking the magazine, and holding the magnifying glass over it.

"Fortunately for you two, the forger was rather inexpert at his task."

Clara sat up straighter.

"It *is* a fake?"

Herbert did not answer but moved from examining the magazine signature back to the contract.

"Whoever doctored this contract did it in the crudest fashion imaginable. They were presumably in haste and thought no one would look too hard at what they were doing. I can see very faint traces of what I believe is a pencil mark beneath the ink. Wait a minute, I shall get my microscope."

Herbert bustled about the laboratory and found his microscope, bringing it back to the table he glanced at them.

"Do you mind if I cut out the signature from the contract so I can put it beneath the microscope?"

"Do what you have to," Clara told him.

Herbert snipped the signature out of the contract with a big pair of scissors, oblivious to the fact that behind him the kettle had started to whistle. Tommy rose and went to the stove to finish making the tea, leaving Herbert absorbed in his task.

Once the signature was under the microscope, Herbert played with the knobs and lenses to adjust the focus and magnification. It was not long before he had the result he was hoping for.

"There we go. You can see it very clearly now."

He moved aside and motioned for Clara to take his place. She looked down the eyepiece of the microscope. What she saw, when she did, was the first letter of the signature brought into sharp focus and so close to the lens she could barely see where the edge began. Beneath the line of the ink, she could see a second faint impression, as if someone had written with a sharp pencil on the paper first and then drawn over it. The pencil had left a mark in the paper which the ink had subsequently fallen into, and the imprint remained even after the forger had added the signature.

"He drew the signature first with a pencil!" Clara said, elated by this news.

"He did. You see, most forgers do not want to take the hours and hours of practice required to mimic a person's signature perfectly when writing it out. Instead, they try to cheat by drawing the signature. I would suggest that this was done with an even less sophisticated approach. As a child, did you ever trace a drawing that you had scrawled graphite pencil on the back to make a copy?"

"I used to do that all the time," Clara nodded. "It was a fun way to copy an image."

"I think what this forger did was find a genuine signature from Violet. It might even have been something from a magazine, like this. They then drew over the back with a graphite pencil, covering the design. Next, they placed that real signature on this blank contract and traced back over the letters. The result was a facsimile of Violet's signature traced in faint graphite onto the new contract.

"The problem with such a method is manifold. The tracing will have defects not found in the original from the process of making it and subsequently inking it in. The pencil will leave an impression where it was pressed through to achieve the copying and ultimately the finished signature will look forced, because it was drawn over in a manner that was not fluid like the original.

"Yet, despite all this, it is a method that can, and has, been overlooked and such forged signatures have been deemed genuine. If someone was not looking too closely at this contract, they would never realise what had occurred. As I say, it is a crude method, but it works more often than I would care to admit."

Clara looked at the contract before her and took a deep breath.

"Well, we guessed it was a fake, but this proves it. Time to confront Mr Stevenson again?"

Chapter Twenty-Three

They drank tea and chatted with Herbert for an hour before they finally said their farewells. Jones had waited in the car, despite being extended an invitation to join them. Clara always asked the chauffeur if he would like to accompany them, but he never agreed. He had decided his place was at the car and he would not leave it unless Clara's life was in danger.

Clara suspected he was protective of the car and believed that someone might try to cause it damage if he took his eye off it for a moment.

As they were driven back into Brighton, Clara considered their next move.

"I have changed my mind," she informed her brother. "Returning to Stevenson at once will achieve very little. The contract is fake, but it tells us nothing about who might have wished Violet harm."

Tommy thought this over and then agreed with her logic.

"Are we at a dead end, again?"

Clara was frowning, her face pulled into a waspish look of deep concentration.

"Who benefited from Violet dying?" she said aloud. "Let's think about that for a moment. Who gained from her death at this exact moment in time?"

"Well, not Mr Manx or his assistant. The former might have his career as a director ruined if he cannot salvage this film, and his assistant is tied to his fortunes. Unless it was a pure act of spite without a care for the consequences, we have to assume those two did not do this."

"A fair point. Manx is out of the picture because he would not benefit from Violet's death. Edwin might have detested her enough to do something stupid, but I really don't think that the case. Yes, he was near the cables when she was electrocuted but he did not have opportunity to harm her at other times."

"That leaves us with Stevenson, who had just faked a contract to have Violet tied to him for another five years. His fortunes are severely damaged by her death."

Clara nodded her head in agreement.

"On the other hand, he was one of the few people who could have had access to Violet's room after she took the overdose of sleeping powders, not to mention access to his own car."

"Where does that leave us?" Tommy asked.

Clara leaned back in her seat and thought about things for a while.

"There is one incident we have not looked into in detail. Violet's sleeping powder mishap. I wonder who the woman was who found her and saved her life?"

"The fly in the ointment for the murderer," Tommy concurred. "She destroyed that plan which was probably the best of the bunch."

"Once that failed, the murderer was forced to take increasingly drastic and risky measures, such as adding the gun to the prop box and hoping Violet would be shot. That could have gone terribly wrong, well, it nearly did, didn't it?"

"And the incident at the train station was a rash move. Yes, after the sleeping powders went wrong it was as if the murderer became desperate and stopped taking care to plan out his attacks as he had done before."

"Jones, could you take us to the green? I want to speak to Mr Manx again."

Jones obeyed, turning them from the route they were currently taking and back towards where the film crew had their tents.

The site was unsettlingly quiet when they arrived, the usual buzz of industry missing.

"Everyone is waiting to find out what is going to happen next," Clara murmured to her brother as they headed towards the tent where they usually found Manx. "No one knows if the movie will continue or not."

"There are a lot of people who are going to lose money and work because of Violet's death," Tommy observed. "Whoever did this, they really didn't care about the effect on everyone else."

"I have yet to meet a murderer who was not wholly selfish," Clara replied. "Why should this case be any different?"

They entered the tent and discovered that Manx was absent from his desk, but Edwin was present, tidying up some paperwork and looking as though his world had collapsed around him.

"Could we talk to you a moment?" Clara asked him.

Edwin cast her a vicious look, which she had entirely expected.

"I have nothing to say to you."

Clara paused, thinking about the best way to convince Edwin to help her.

"We want to resolve this as much as you do, Edwin. We want to find out who put you all in such a bad position. Do you not wish for that?"

"How can you find out anything?" Edwin snorted. "The girl threw herself beneath a train. She is responsible for all this! Mr Manx received a telegram from the studio summoning him to a telephone meeting at the *Grand Hotel*. We both anticipate he is about to be fired, and that is the end of my career. I doubt I shall ever return to the pictures after this disaster, no one will want to take a chance on the assistant to the director who lost the biggest star of the studio! My dreams are over!"

Edwin suddenly dropped the papers he was holding and covered his face with his hands. To Clara's amazement, he began to weep. She looked at her brother, who winced, uncomfortable with seeing a grown man crying.

Clara cleared her throat, trying to find the words to console Edwin and coming up with nothing. Finally, she stepped forward and placed a hand on his shoulder.

"We want to find the real culprit behind this, Edwin, and bring them to justice. I now know that Violet was thrown beneath the train that killed her. She was murdered."

Clara had no actual proof of this theory, but she was pretty convinced by it, nonetheless. Edwin grew quieter.

"Murdered? Are you going to accuse me again?"

"No, I do not believe you did this," Clara reassured him. "You have too much to lose and nothing to gain by Violet's death. I do not think you hated her enough to be prepared to destroy yourself in the process of destroying her."

Edwin took a shaky breath and lowered his hands.

"What do you want to ask me," he said solemnly.

"Who was the person who discovered Violet had taken the overdose of sleeping powders and raised the alarm?"

Edwin blinked as if he had expected a much harder question.

"That is simple. It was Miss Jamieson, Mr Hershel's secretary."

Clara almost breathed a sigh of relief at the knowledge that the person they needed to speak to was so easily available.

"Thank you, Edwin. I hope the studio does not fire Mr Manx for something that was largely out of his control."

Clara started to move away when Edwin caught up with what she had just said.

"What do you mean, largely?"

Clara glanced back.

"Violet raised her concerns, and no one listened. Maybe if they had she would not be dead. Think on that, Edwin."

With that, Clara and Tommy left the tent.

They had Jones return them to the hotel. Joshua was still recuperating in his suite, and it seemed logical he would know how they could get in touch with his agent. In fact, Joshua had no need to send them anywhere else, because when they arrived at his suite, they found that Mr Hershel and Miss Jamieson were already there.

They were working on a statement for the newspapers about MacKenzie's accident. Joshua was arguing over the wording, disliking that every variation they produced made him sound like a cowering fool who had panicked the instant he was shot. Clara's knock was a welcome reprieve from the debacle.

"Afternoon, Mrs O'Harris," Joshua greeted her warmly.

Clara had lost all track of time over the course of her investigation and had not realised the morning was long gone; it was now the early afternoon. It did explain, however, why she was feeling so hungry all of a sudden.

"Good afternoon, I believe you all know my brother, Mr Fitzgerald?" she addressed the room, not solely Joshua, who was trying to absorb all her attention.

He had taken her hand and kissed it when he greeted her, and she had struggled to subsequently extract her fingers from his grasp.

"I hopefully won't interrupt you for long, but I wondered if I could have a word with Miss Jamieson?"

The secretary looked surprised and worried by the request.

"It is nothing to be concerned about, I merely have a couple of questions concerning the discovery of Miss Starling after her accident with the sleeping powders," Clara elaborated to put the woman at ease.

"Oh," Miss Jamieson said, rising from her seat. "I suppose I could spare a few minutes. Mr Hershel?"

"Go ahead," Hershel nodded at her. "We could do with a break from this, anyway."

Joshua looked aggrieved that Clara was leaving, and he was not to be the centre of attention, but he said nothing. They moved out into the hallway, which was as good a place as any to discuss the matter.

"What do you want to know?" Miss Jamieson asked.

"Could you describe everything that happened that night relating to your discovery of Violet?" Clara asked.

Miss Jamieson gave herself a moment to think about that night so long ago, then she took a breath and began.

"I was at the hotel with Mr Hershel and Mr MacKenzie. It was getting late, but Mr MacKenzie was agitated about the script for the following day and would not let the matter rest. In the end, we had to summon the film's director to make emergency alterations to the script, otherwise MacKenzie refused to perform."

"Sounds quite drastic," Tommy remarked.

Miss Jamieson refrained from rolling her eyes, but her expression said exactly what she thought of the overpaid actor and his foibles.

"These things happen. Mr MacKenzie felt he did not have enough lines for the particular scene. He hates when his co-star has more to say than he does. Really, it is just one of those things. You get used to such drama in this business. Anyway, the end result was a script rewrite, and the new pages had to be sent to Violet that night so she could memorise them for the next day. I was the one told to take the revised script up to her room.

"I headed to her suite and had to explain myself to that big oaf Stevenson hires to keep everyone away from Violet. Honestly, it was a nightmare trying to convince him I just wanted to drop off a new script. He acted as if I was going to do something to cause her harm or…"

"Or attempt to steal her from Mr Stevenson?" Tommy filled in the gap as Miss Jamieson hesitated.

Miss Jamieson pulled a face at him.

"She would have been better off with us, but that is beside the point. I was tired, and all I wanted to do was drop off the new script. I argued with the man and, eventually, Stevenson appeared from his room to see what was happening. He looked exhausted too and was clearly not pleased about my presence. He tried to take the script from me, saying he would give it to Violet himself. I refused, because I had been tasked with seeing it into her hands and I was not going to be dissuaded. If I let him take it, I had no way of knowing when he would give it to her.

"We had something of a stand-off, I thought I might have to summon Mr Hershel, then suddenly Mr Stevenson agreed. He threw up his hands as if I had asked him to sign over his life, or something ridiculous, then said, 'on my own head be it.'"

"That was an odd phrase," Clara said.

"I thought perhaps Violet was prone to being in a temper in the evenings if her rest was disturbed. Anyway, I headed into her suite at last, and to her bed. I shook her to wake her, but she didn't rouse. At first, I wondered if she was drunk, but there was no sign of alcohol in the room. I became more alarmed and shook her harder. Stevenson came into the room then and just looked at me. I yelled that Violet was not responding, and he just said something dully about she had probably taken her sleeping powders.

"I was shaking her so hard now. I was scared because she seemed to be barely breathing, then her eyes flickered open, she gasped and was sick all over the bed sheets. Mr Stevenson pulled a face and left the room. I rang for help at that point, using the telephone in the room. Mr Stevenson's driver turned up, and at least he understood my anxiety, and he agreed we should take her immediately to the hospital."

"Did Mr Stevenson accompany you?"

Miss Jamieson shook her head.

"It was just me and Mario. We made it to the hospital and Violet seemed to be rousing a little. The doctors took her in and when I described what had happened, they decided to pump her stomach. After that, I came back to the hotel. There was nothing else I could do."

"Did you notice packets of sleeping powders near Violet's bed?" Clara asked.

Miss Jamieson shook her head, looking uncomfortable now.

"That was something that caused me some concern later, but I did not know who to speak to about it. You see, when I went into that room there was no sign of any sleeping powder packages. There was an empty glass beside the bed, but that was all. Later, I was told there were empty sleeping powder papers dotted across the bedside cabinet, and that was proof Violet had tried to take her own life. But I never saw them."

"What did you think about that?" Clara pressed her.

Miss Jamieson looked miserable.

"I was not sure what to think about it. It seemed to me, someone wanted to convince the world Violet had tried to overdose."

"Who wanted to convince the world of that?" Clara persisted.

Miss Jamieson took a deep breath, considering back to that time and all that had happened.

"I suppose, the main person who was trying to convince us all was Mr Stevenson. He was the one who kept insisting Violet had attempted to overdose. It seemed very important to him that we all believed that."

Miss Jamieson paused.

"What was so odd about it all, now I consider it, was that the person he most seemed to want to convince it was an overdose, was the one person who should know exactly what happened," she said. "He wanted Violet to believe she deliberately overdosed. I always found that odd."

Chapter Twenty-Four

"Mr Stevenson, yet again," Tommy remarked as they left Miss Jamieson contemplating their conversation. "But we have already determined that he would not have wanted Violet dead. Haven't we?"

Clara was hardly listening, she was running through ideas in her head, none of which were quite jamming with each other, but she was beginning to see the hint of a pattern.

"There is a key to this which we are missing," she said softly to herself.

"He had the new contract," Tommy was still on his own train of thought. "The contract meant Violet was worth more to him alive. Before she had signed it, there might have been some argument for him killing her out of spite, so that others could not have his star, but even that is farfetched."

"Where did Mario and the bodyguard go?" Clara spoke aloud, jogging Tommy from his thoughts. "Did Mr Stevenson suddenly let them go?"

"You want to talk to them," Tommy understood. "They could have vital information. Oh, but that would be a very good reason for Mr Stevenson not to keep them here. Better they were not around for someone like us to question them."

"Maybe," Clara replied. "If Mr Stevenson is guilty. But they are unlikely to have simply disappeared in the night. Where would they go, for a start? Even if he dismissed them from his service, they would then have to make a decision where to go next. That takes time and, in my experience, people prefer to think about such decisions rather than rushing off somewhere else and wasting money on a train fare."

"What would two men like them do to find new work?" Tommy thought about it. "Mario is technically a driver and would surely look for something similar, as for the other man, who knows where his talents lie."

"Much like Stevenson, they probably have no fixed address as they are always travelling around with Violet. They have nowhere to head to, no family to fall back on. What would two men like that who have experience in the movie industry, albeit limited, do to find new work?"

Tommy grinned at his sister as he realised what she was saying.

"They would go to the next nearest place full of film people, and that would be on the green."

"Perhaps not immediately, however, they may well choose to wait until the situation surrounding Violet's death is dealt with, and everyone knows what is to happen next. Then they can start looking for work again."

"They will be waiting somewhere, a cheap hotel or boarding house, for the right moment to seek out Mr Manx or any of the film crew who have authority to assign them work." They were in the foyer of the *Grand Hotel* by this point and were poised to leave, and head back to the green once more, when they spotted Mr Manx, himself, appearing from the hotel manager's office.

He looked rather grey in the face, as if he had just had a rather unpleasant experience.

"Edwin said he had been summoned to the hotel to have a telephone meeting with his superiors at the studio," Tommy recalled, whispering this to his sister. "I am going to say it did not go terribly well."

Clara moved hastily across the foyer to intercept Mr Manx before he could depart. He gave her a sharp scowl as he saw her approach but was too exhausted and upset by his meeting with the studio bosses to avoid her. All his usual vitriol had been knocked out of him, and he simply waited to accept his fate.

"Mr Manx, I hope everything is all right?"

"Hardly," Manx snarled gruffly. "What do you want?"

"A few more questions, I am afraid," Clara said, trying a different approach to the one she had used earlier to persuade him to talk to her. He looked as though a gentler touch might be more effective. "But before I ask them, what if I was to say to you that I believe Violet was murdered, and the person behind it was someone close to her. Someone you could not have stopped, and thus all responsibility for her death should not be laid on your shoulders?"

"Violet threw herself under a train. The studio says I was not taking sufficient care of her. I was pushing her too hard, apparently. They blame me."

"Violet was *pushed* under a train," Clara corrected. "Something outside of your control."

Manx looked too tired to comprehend what she was saying. He leaned against the counter in the foyer.

"I don't see how that changes anything," he shook his head. "Look, I need to get to work. The studio has given me a week to find a replacement to fill in for Violet's final scenes. I need to find someone who looks just like her so the audience will never know."

"An impossible task," Tommy had approached them. "Your audience is not so stupid as to fail to recognise their favourite actress and to know when it is not her."

"Well, you would be surprised," Manx pulled a face at him. "In any case, with clever lighting, and the right angles, I think we can pull it off. Anyway, it's the only solution I have. So, if you will excuse me..."

"We are looking for the two men who were working for Mr Stevenson," Clara quickly interjected before he could escape her. "Have you seen them?"

"Mario and Clarence?" Manx blinked, slowly coming back to what she was saying. "What about them?"

"We need to ask them a few questions," Clara added. "Were you aware that Violet's contract with Mr Stevenson was nearly at an end?"

Manx rubbed wearily at his face.

"Yes, I knew it was coming to its end. The studio was keeping a keen eye on who might take over her management, they had a couple of recommendations and were trying to make sure Violet took their advice."

"Did you also know that Stevenson forged Violet's signature on a new contract, binding him to her for another five years?"

Manx clearly did not know this, the look on his face said it all.

"That fiend! The studio will hear of this, and he will never be allowed to work in the movie business again! He was old news anyway. He did not have the connections or knowledge that an up-and-coming star like Violet needed. She needed a professional company, not a single man whose biggest star prior to Violet was a ventriloquist who could make a large range of bird calls."

"Stevenson was desperate for her to sign a new contract with him, otherwise his career would be over," Tommy elaborated. "We think that might have something to do with her death."

"Stevenson would not benefit from her demise," Manx stated the obvious.

"No," Clara agreed. "But he would benefit from Violet being so anxious about her wellbeing that she felt he was the only person she could trust. If Stevenson played these accidents right, then Violet might run to him rather than away from him, seeing the man as her protector."

"Not sure Violet was that stupid," Manx huffed.

"Part of the problem, I fear," Clara said sadly. "Violet was not stupid. She saw through Stevenson."

"What does this all have to do with me?" Manx now demanded. "I have a new actress to hire."

"I am sorry to have delayed you, but I need to speak to Mario and Clarence, do you know where I can find them?"

Manx was not entirely paying attention to her. The news that Stevenson had forged a contract between himself, and Violet was worrying, and Manx did not fancy being the one to inform the studio of the situation. Such underhand tactics could not be tolerated, and Stevenson would face their wrath, but Manx was worried he might find himself suffering as collateral damage in the process.

"Mr Manx?"

"What?"

"Where can I find Mario and Clarence?"

Manx's familiar anger was returning, and he glowered at Clara.

"Mario, I have no idea, but you will find Clarence working at the props tent. We decided to hire some extra security after two fellows broke into the place the other night. Some backdrops were damaged and needed to be repaired. We can't have stuff like that happening and holding us back. Now, will you leave me alone?"

Mr Manx stormed off, shoving at the doors of the hotel rather than waiting for the doorman to open them for him.

"Two fellows?" Clara quoted him.

"We damaged nothing, I swear," Tommy responded. "Maybe someone else broke in?"

"Whatever the case, there is still time in the day. Let's go to the green and find Clarence."

It was only a short drive back to the green, but the sky was growing grey and dark as an early dusk drew on with the promise of rain. Clara pulled the collar of her coat a little higher about her neck, wishing she had brought a scarf. Jones deposited them at the entrance to the green and they headed immediately to the props tent, which was farthest from the entrance.

The tents were still quiet, compared to the hub of activity they had been before. A few lanterns had been hung up at convenient points to allow people to see as they moved about between the large canvas structures. Clara could hear someone feverishly typing at a typewriter, whether it was Manx or someone else she could not say.

They dodged puddles and finally found their way to the props tent. The interior smelt like fresh paint and sawdust. There was no sign of any of the usual workmen as they entered.

"They have a spot at the back walled off as a tearoom," Tommy explained starting to lead his sister around the various aisles of props.

They had not gone far, when someone loomed out of the shadows of a large rack of wigs and stood in front of them.

"You are not meant to be in here."

Tommy immediately recognised the man who had formerly worked for Stevenson and had threatened him in a similar fashion only the other day.

"You must be Clarence," he declared. "We have been looking all over for you."

The man was a mountain, the sort of individual who seems to have been carved from stone rather than who grew from a child. He was an unbecoming fellow, with a cloudy left eye, and a nose that had been broken so often it was now a bulbous smear across his face rather than a definitive shape. He had a thick jaw and appeared to lack a neck, though that was largely because of his powerful shoulders and the cut of his suit. He was not a man anyone wanted to get on the wrong side of in a fight, which made it even more remarkable that in the past more than one person had been prepared to take the chance and ended up breaking his nose.

Clarence frowned at them, folding his arms across his chest, and looking as if he might just pick them both up and toss them outside.

"Why do you want to speak to me?" he growled.

"It is about Violet," Clara hastened to explain. "You were in her company a great deal, and you might have vital insight into some of the things that happened to her over these last few weeks."

Clarence hesitated; for just a moment Clara thought she saw a hint of emotion on his burly features. Could it be Violet had worked her magic on him too, and he had cared about her?

"Violet is dead, and nothing can bring her back."

"That's true," Clara agreed with him. "But we can find who killed her, and make sure they face justice, which is just as important."

"Killed her?" Clarence frowned.

"Violet was thrown under that train. She did not jump. We have witnesses to the matter," that was stretching the truth dramatically, but Clara needed Clarence on her side and talking with her.

He was beginning to be convinced about speaking with her. He swayed from foot to foot as he made a decision.

"All right, I will talk to you. What do you want to know?"

Clara sighed with relief. She had feared for a moment that Clarence would refuse to have anything to do with them. Worse, if he was somehow involved in Stevenson's scheme to harm Violet, then he might have turned them away and reported their conversation to his former employer. Thankfully, that did not appear to be the case.

"Where you present at all the accidents that could have harmed Violet?"

Clarence frowned at her question. She had not anticipated that would be a difficult one for him.

"Were you present when she was electrocuted."

Clarence nodded his head.

"I was at the back of the set, just standing around."

"What did you see?" Clara pressed him.

"Not much. I wasn't watching the filming. I heard a cry and smelt this odd burning smell."

Clara feared he was not going to be able to offer her much more than that.

"What about when she was in the car and the brakes failed?"

"I wasn't there," Clarence shook his head.

"All right, then what about the night she took those sleeping powders?"

Clarence's face drooped with sadness as his memory went back to that occasion.

"I helped to rush Violet to the hospital. I never thought she would do something like that."

Again, this was not very helpful.

"You went into her room when Miss Jamieson discovered her?" Tommy asked, trying to get something from the man.

"Yes. Miss Jamieson had made a fuss about seeing Violet, and I had tried to stop her because I had orders from Mr Stevenson that Violet was not to be disturbed. But Miss Jamieson was persistent and, eventually, I had to let her in. She had only been in the room a moment, when she started to shriek that something was the matter with Violet. I darted in behind her and saw that Violet was lying very still on the bed. Miss Jamieson said she thought she might have taken something. Mr Stevenson appeared too, saying that she had probably just taken her sleeping powder and was not responding.

"Miss Jamieson insisted I take Violet to the hospital, and I did with the aid of Mario. When we got there, the doctors had already been alerted to our arrival, and they took Violet inside straight away. I later heard they pumped her stomach and that she would have died from an overdose of sleeping powders."

"Did you see any packets of sleeping powders scattered on her bedside cabinet?" Clara asked.

"No," Clarence shook his head. "There was just an empty glass of water."

"And after this happened, I take it Mr Stevenson has been keeping hold of the sleeping powders?" Tommy asked.

"No," Clarence said, looking as though it was a peculiar suggestion.

"Did you think it was odd that Stevenson seemed so unconcerned about Violet?" Clara pressed him.

Clarence thought about this for a few moments.

"I suppose I never really considered it. I was so busy making sure that Violet was all right and safely at the hospital."

They were getting no further forward. Clara had just one last question for the man.

"Can you tell us where Mario is staying?"

"Yes, he's at Miss Milner's boarding house. We both are. He still has not found any new work."

"Weren't you surprised how quickly Mr Stevenson dismissed you from his employment when he learned Violet was dead?" Tommy asked before they departed.

Clarence shrugged his shoulders.

"I was there to watch over Violet. If Violet was dead, then what was the point of me?"

That was that. Clarence had not given any deep thought to his employer's dismissal of him. Presumably, it was not the first time he had found himself suddenly unemployed.

"Thank you, Clarence," Clara smiled at him.

They headed back to the car, still finding themselves with more questions than answers.

"Stevenson seems to have been very nonchalant about his starlet's near-death experience. He didn't even remove the sleeping powders from her."

"Why would he, if he knew her overdose was not her doing?"

"You really think he was responsible? But then, wouldn't he have been more concerned about her being taken to the hospital promptly?"

"I think that very much depends on what his intentions were and whether he wanted Violet dead or not."

Chapter Twenty-Five

Jones dropped Tommy at his house before driving Clara home. She was looking forward to an evening by the fire, a chance to regroup her thoughts and try to make head or tail of this whole affair. There always came a point in a case when you had to stop and assess all the information you had gathered, trying to sort it into some kind of order.

Stevenson now was her primary suspect for the murder of Violet, but the real question was what was his motive? Everything pointed to him being worse off with her dead, and the new contract suggested he had made every attempt he could to retain her as his star. What could he possibly gain from her death?

O'Harris joined her in his private study, where she was cosy before the fire going through her reams of notes.

"You look busy."

"Not so busy I cannot pause to speak to you."

Clara popped up from her armchair and kissed him.

"How was your day?"

"I suspect it was rather mundane compared to yours," O'Harris motioned to all the scraps of paper Clara had laid out on the floor before her chair.

"I am at that point in a case when nothing quite makes sense, but a pattern is beginning to emerge," Clara explained. "I feel as though I can see everything aligning but I don't know the 'why' behind the connections."

O'Harris sat down in the chair opposite hers and took a look at the notes on the floor.

"What is this about a forged contract?"

Clara handed him over the contract they had stolen from Mr Stevenson's room.

"We are not meant to have that," she said with a smirk.

Clara was never meek about her antics as a detective, even if they were on occasion illegal.

O'Harris read through the contract for a few lines.

"Stevenson forged a new contract to tie Violet Starling to him for the foreseeable future."

"He did," Clara nodded her head. "It was a ghastly thing to do. Violet was on the cusp of being free of him and he did this to her."

"How does that link to her death?"

"I am beginning to think that Stevenson was plotting to do away with Violet out of spite because she would not sign a new contract with him, and he did not want her signing a contract with anyone else."

"That does not explain the accidents that befell her after he had created this fake contract," O'Harris reminded her.

"I know, that is where my theory falls apart. Why would Stevenson kill her after he had achieved what he wanted?

O'Harris began to slowly flick through the contract while Clara continued staring at her notes on the floor. Every once in a while, she would pick up a scrap of paper and move it to a new spot, adjusting the order in a manner she hoped would illuminate the situation further.

"Have you actually read this contract?" O'Harris asked her.

"Not really, only skimmed through it."

"Maybe you should read this part."

O'Harris handed over the contract to her, pointing to a specific page and a specific line. Clara took the document and carefully read through it. As she did, the puzzle pieces slowly began to fall into place, and she could hardly believe the true evil of the man who had created this document.

"Rather explains a few things, doesn't it?" O'Harris said when she had read through the section he had indicated.

Clara looked back at the papers on the floor. She began picking them up and rearranging them once again.

"The timing of the new contract, the way it falls just after Violet's supposed overdose, and how calm Stevenson was about the whole affair. Well, maybe he was right to be calm, if he knew that what Violet had taken would not kill her but merely render her unresponsive and give the appearance that she had taken an overdose. He was setting the scene for us, building a story we could all believe, and which would lead to one inevitable conclusion.

"Violet's death beneath a train," O'Harris concluded. "A man like Stevenson is cunning, he wasn't going to overplay his hand. He arranged things so that no one would question that Violet had been suicidal."

"If Violet had not come to me that first morning and laid out her fears before me, no one would have given it another thought. This is ghastly. We need to summon Inspector Park-Coombs, and as many people as we can find. We have to confront Stevenson and have this matter out in the open."

"What are you going to do about the fact you stole that contract?" O'Harris reminded her.

"I am rather hoping the inspector will be gracious enough to overlook my slightly illegal gathering of evidence, especially when it will ensure a killer is brought to justice."

Clara winced as she considered what she had done.

"He will forgive me, won't he?"

"Don't ask me. I don't go around stealing evidence."

"I shall just have to hope for the best," Clara decided. "Everyone must be gathered at the *Grand Hotel*. Stevenson cannot escape us, but with such limited proof of his crime, we are going to need to be clever and have him play into our hands."

"This is quite exciting," O'Harris rubbed his hands together keenly. "Sounds a lot more interesting than the paperwork I have spent all day working on."

"I better ring Tommy," Clara smiled at her husband. "He won't want to miss this."

Within an hour, they were all gathered in the ballroom of the *Grand Hotel,* where the unfortunate shooting of Mr MacKenzie had occurred. Present were Joshua, Mr Hershel, Miss Jamieson, Mr Manx, Edwin Cleethorpes, Mr Ferguson from the props department, and Clarence and Mario. The latter had been brought along by Clarence, after Clara had insisted he should be present.

Inspector Park-Coombs surveyed the gathering of people while they waited for the arrival of the main star of their party.

"You really have this all worked out?" Park-Coombs asked Clara as he glanced at his pocket watch.

He had sent two constables upstairs to collect Stevenson, with instructions that they were not to allow him to escape.

"I am certain on the matter," Clara promised him.

She had already conducted a circuit of the room to see if there was any sign of Gilbert hanging about hoping to overhear some secrets. She had tried to avoid involving the newspaperman, but Gilbert had a way of discovering things. Tommy had joked that it must be to do with the size of his ears, they probably amplified all conversations around him and gave the man an advantage. While Clara was not opposed to Gilbert eventually having the full story about this crime, and being the first to write about it, she would prefer if he were not present at this particular meeting. Gilbert was liable to say something that would only infuriate Mr Stevenson and leave them worse off.

Mr Manx was looking impatient as they waited for their primary player to appear.

"I have things to do," he declared to no one in particular. "This business is keeping me from my work."

Edwin was looking slightly sick, as if the events of the day had left him nauseated. He said nothing as his employer ranted about being kept at the hotel for pointless games by a woman.

Inspector Park-Coombs finally had enough of his whining and went over to have a quiet word. Clara had no clue what he said to him, but Manx fell immediately quiet and was most amenable after that.

"What is going to happen when Mr Stevenson appears?" Mr Hershel asked.

"I am going to explain to you how everything that has happened in the last few days was the culmination of a very clever plan to convince the world that Violet Starling did not take her own life."

Mr Hershel opened his mouth and stared at Clara, amazed by her statement.

"I beg your pardon?"

"It is best explained when Mr Stevenson is present, which, hopefully, will not be much longer.

As she spoke, they all heard a loud voice complaining about his evening being interrupted. No one had to be told that this was Mr Stevenson throwing a fit because he was being escorted by two police constables downstairs against his will. There was a look of glee on Park-Coombs' face as he heard the man swearing that took Clara by surprise. She had not realised how much he detested the man, though he *had* spent considerable time with him the other day, and an extended acquaintance with Mr Stevenson was bound to result in making a person antagonistic towards him.

Stevenson finally appeared in the room. He glanced around at everyone present, and his face pulled into an even deeper scowl. It did not take him long to spy Clara and to throw the full force of his rage in her direction.

"What are you up to now?" he demanded of her.

"I am merely exposing the truth," Clara replied.

It was at that moment that Stevenson saw she had the forged contact in her hand.

"Thief! Inspector, she stole that from my room! Arrest her at once for theft!"

Park-Coombs languidly looked over to Clara and the paper she held in her hand. Then he glanced back to Stevenson.

"Can you prove she stole it, Sir?"

"Prove it? What on earth do you mean? She took that from my room!"

"So you say, Sir, but I really have no evidence for such behaviour. Mrs O'Harris perhaps came across the contract quite by chance."

"What? This is preposterous!" Stevenson glanced around him at the faces in the room. "So, you are all against me?"

He turned around to make an attempt to storm off, however, his path was blocked by the two constables. He clenched his fists, and was about to protest, when Clara spoke.

"You really will want to stick around and hear what I have to say, Mr Stevenson. I have worked out why you wished harm upon Violet Starling."

Clarence and Mario both startled at this statement. Mario suddenly stiffened and looked as though he might go over to his former employer and knock his lights out.

"Is this true?" he demanded.

"Of course not, Mario! The woman thinks she can make these stupid claims against me and upset everyone, but it is all nonsense."

Mario did not look convinced, but he was not prepared to assault Stevenson in front of the police.

"Could someone please explain this to me?" Manx demanded. "I am sick and tired of all these games and have a lot of work to attend to."

"Very well, Mr Manx," Clara smiled at him. "The story is quite simple when you get to the heart of it, but Stevenson did a very good job of putting in a lot of false leads to throw off a person looking for the pattern in the events that befell Violet. Rather like a movie, it had plenty of twists and turns to keep the audience guessing.

"It all begins and ends with this contract."

Clara held the paper up so they could all see it.

"My initial interest in this contract was because it seemed so suspicious to me. Violet had stated she wanted to get away from

Stevenson, yet she signed a new contract with him, tying her to him for five years. That seemed unlikely unless Stevenson had found a way to pressure her into staying with him. What could have happened?

"As it turned out, the solution was far simpler than that. Stevenson forged Violet's signature on the bottom of this document. It is an exceptionally crude forgery, but it would have worked, nonetheless. With this contract signed, he could prove to the world that Violet had agreed to work with him for another five years, securing his future fortune, as he was to receive quite a hefty cut from the money she earned from her performances."

"The contract surely means that Violet was worth more to him alive than dead?" Manx grumbled aloud, thinking this was all a load of nonsense.

"You are right, at first glance it would seem that this provides Mr Stevenson with the perfect alibi. He would not have wished to kill a person who was of such value to him."

"There you go!" Stevenson threw up his hands. "I am innocent, the contract proves it. Now, will you all just leave me alone."

"Not so fast, Mr Stevenson," Clara interrupted him. "I said at *first glance* the contract appears to give you every reason to ensure Violet's safety. But upon closer examination, what I actually discovered was a motive for murder."

Stevenson grimaced at her, his confidence ebbing as he saw the look in Clara's eyes.

"There is nothing in that contract other than standard clauses," he said.

"I beg to differ, there is one very particular article that seems remarkably different from a regular contract," Clara turned over the first page of the contract. "I refer specifically to clause 12., which states exactly what would happen in the event of Violet's untimely demise."

Chapter Twenty-Six

"All contracts have death clauses in them," Stevenson huffed, unimpressed by Clara's statement. "It is standard in the industry, ask Mr Hershel if you doubt me."

"He has a point. Such clauses are necessary to stipulate what would occur after the death of the person in question," Mr Hershel reluctantly agreed. "It has to be stipulated where any outstanding payments would go, and also it ensures the manager does not sustain unexpected and potentially disastrous costs himself."

"Perhaps you could describe to me such a standard clause?" Clara asked Mr Hershel.

The man looked uneasy, glancing at Stevenson and sensing something was amiss with all this.

"Well, for instance, the clause I have in my contract with Mr MacKenzie states that should he die while in the process of making a film, I shall not incur any losses as a result and will retain my percentage from any fee he was due for his performance, while the rest goes to individuals he has nominated in a will. I do not retain any rights to future royalties, but I am allowed to take a certain amount from any final fees over my percentage, to cover me for any costs I might find myself facing because of his unanticipated demise."

"That seems a very sound and logical contractual agreement, a way to cover you from being left in a difficult position due to unforeseen circumstances," Clara agreed with him. "Does Mr MacKenzie have any life insurance on him?"

"What?" Mr Hershel looked confused. "No, he doesn't. At least nothing that would relate to me. If he has personal life insurance that is quite up to him."

"I have none," MacKenzie said loudly. "I am a bachelor and therefore I have no one who would benefit from such a thing. My money is willed to various theatrical charities for when I ultimately pass on, which shall not be for many a year."

Clara nodded her head to demonstrate she understood.

"Then it seems to me that the clause Mr Stevenson has in his new contract with Violet is somewhat exceptional, perhaps I might read it aloud?"

"What is all this nonsense about?" Stevenson barked at her. "Violet knew all the terms of the contract. She signed it after all. Why are we going through this ridiculous performance?"

"I doubt Violet knew every detail of this contract, because I doubt you ever gave her the chance to read it," Clara countered, staring at him sternly. "You forged her name, tying her to a particularly deadly contract, which set the stage for her final performance, the one you had been orchestrating from the moment you realised Violet would do all she could to escape you. Without Violet you had nothing, but you could only hold on to her for so long and even with a new contract, if Violet chose to argue it was fake, then there were certain powerful agencies wanting her as their client, who would gladly assist her to prove her case. You could not afford that to happen, so you laid out a convoluted and quite remarkable plan."

"No doubt you are going to explain to me how I was so exceptionally clever," Stevenson taunted her.

"I am," Clara smiled in reply. "Firstly, let's go back to clause 12., in this contract. It relates to what might occur if Violet died suddenly during the course of this contract. It states – *should Violet Starling predecease the ending of this contract, either via accident, illness or personal harm, the entire royalties both current and future from her performances up until the date of her death shall go to her representative, Mr Stevenson. In addition, any outstanding fees for her performances prior to the date of her death shall also go to her representative, Mr Stevenson.*

"This clause also requires the said Violet Starling to undertake to pay a certain amount of her fees each month to a life insurance policy, the beneficiary of which shall be Mr Stevenson. This policy shall cover all eventualities, aside from death by one's own hand. Violet Starling shall also name Mr Stevenson as an executor of her estate and supply him with the following amounts from her estates to cover his efforts to oversee the distribution and disposal of her estate.

"There then follows a list of percentages from various elements of Violet's finances that would see Mr Stevenson in a very favourable light. I do not have access to the insurance document, so I cannot see precisely what you would receive upon Violet's death, but I would imagine it is a healthy sum of money."

"It is just a clause in a contract," Stevenson shrugged. "There is nothing illegal about it."

"You do not consider it excessive?" Mr Hershel asked him in surprise. "I have never heard of such an extensive death clause, nor the amounts you clearly intend to collect from Violet's estate."

"I am not going to be out of pocket because my starlet dies," Stevenson huffed. "If you were not so coy, Mr Hershel, you would see how ridiculous your own clause is and how limited. I put everything into making Violet a star and I intended to get my money's worth out of the situation."

"Spoken like the true cold-hearted fellow that you are," Tommy snarled at him.

Stevenson was unmoved. His confidence had returned to him, and he was done with their accusations.

"You have not told me anything I did not already know. Aside from the slim possibility that I might have forged that contract, which you would have to prove in a court of law, I see no reason to continue this performance."

Stevenson turned towards the double doors of the ballroom and was nearly at them when Clara spoke.

"I haven't finished, Mr Stevenson."

"You do not appear to have anything left."

"I have a lot left. The contract was just the final piece of the puzzle, the element that explained to me why you did what you did."

"And what did I do?" Stevenson turned and looked at her smugly.

"You plotted Violet's death from the moment you realised she was going to leave you. The forged contract would never hold her for long, but if she was dead, who would there be to protest the matter? You arranged for a series of seeming accidents which would result in her death and leave you with a healthy payout.

"The first was the electrocution incident while on set. I should say that was the cleverest of them all, as it really did look like a simple accident, and no one believed Violet when she said she had obeyed the instructions from the prop department about which cable to touch.

"There was a red cord tied around the correct cable for her to pull on, but you moved that cord when you came over and stood behind her while Edwin was showing her the script changes that had been made. Perhaps you just took a chance, because you could not have planned for Edwin to speak to Violet and make it reasonable for you to head over and see what the changes were as her representative. There were certain arrangements in Violet's old contract that you had to uphold, including her not being touched by Mr MacKenzie during a scene.

"Whether it was a chance opportunity, or you had some other plan of how you would change the cord, the result was the same. You made sure that Violet would touch the electrified cable. It could have killed her, but unfortunately for you it did not, and so you had to consider another option."

"I don't see how you can prove I did anything," Stevenson still had that smug grin on his face. "I believe the cord was on the correct cable when the prop men went to look at it a couple of days after the accident."

"Yes, you had been careful to move it back. Easily done when everyone was busy worrying about Violet. You simply slipped into the studio and moved the cord."

"Again, prove it," Stevenson demanded.

Clara ignored him and carried on.

"The electrocution would have been a perfect way to dispose of Violet, but it failed to do the trick. You had to think of a new way of destroying her. Therefore, you tampered with the brakes of your own car. This was rather cunning, because if anyone realised the brakes and been tampered with, you could claim you were meant to be in the car that morning, not Violet, and so it would seem that someone had been after you and Violet had simply been an unfortunate innocent casualty.

"That plan failed as well because you overestimated the amount of brake fluid that was required to leak out for the brakes to fail, and they stopped working sooner than you had wished, allowing Mario time to bring the car safely to a halt."

Mario, stood beside Clarence, clenched his fists together as he heard what Clara was saying and took a pace towards Stevenson, looking as though he was ready to kill him.

"We both could have died that day!" he said to his former employer.

Stevenson was unmoved and did not seem afraid. He was too arrogant to be troubled by any of this.

"How would any of this help me? Violet was still under her old contract," Stevenson remarked with mild amusement.

"Another thing that was not true," Clara told him. "This contract is dated just prior to the first accident, and it stipulates on the first page that the terms in this contract override any previous contracts. The second you had forged this, Violet's life was in peril."

Stevenson still did not react.

"You are forgetting that Violet did not die in either of those unfortunate accidents. So, why are you badgering me about them?"

"What about her attempted suicide?" Miss Jamieson spoke up. "That could not have been caused by Mr Stevenson, because the contract stipulated the insurance would only pay out if Violet died by any means *other* than her own hand."

"A good point, Miss Jamieson, and that brings us to another of Mr Stevenson's cunning plans, this one I will add, was rather convoluted and somewhat risky, but I imagine he was starting to get desperate. Violet's old contract was nearly expired and sooner or later he would have to reveal to Violet the forged one. At which point, he could not guarantee she would not go immediately to one of the other agencies wishing to represent her and ask them to do something about the fraud. As soon as they were alerted to the matter, Mr Stevenson was in trouble. Even if Violet subsequently died, it is likely the studios would want to investigate the contract, especially if there was a reputable agency pressing them to look into the matter.

"That brings us to the sleeping powder incident, which at first looked like a suicide attempt. Violet insisted over and over she would not have attempted suicide, and Miss Jamieson can confirm that when she found Violet there was no sign of the sleeping powder papers that were subsequently dotted all over her bedside table, and convinced people Violet had intended to harm herself. That part is key.

"Very few people would have had access to Violet's room in the short window of time between her being removed to the hospital and others gathering to find out what had gone on. This means the perpetrator had to be on hand to stage the scene ready for when his witnesses gathered. As Mario and Clarence were busy taking Violet to the hospital, that leaves only one person with ready access to the room. Mr Stevenson."

Stevenson had not lost his smile.

"You really are entertaining me, Mrs O'Harris, perhaps you would care to clarify one point for me?"

"Just one?" Clara narrowed her eyes at him.

He ignored her.

"Tell me, why I would have staged Violet's suicide when it would have served me no purpose? Her life insurance would have been void."

"When did I saw you were staging a suicide?" Clara met his gaze, her own smile now on her lips.

Chapter Twenty-Seven

"Everything in Violet's room on the night she overdosed appeared to signal she was planning to kill herself. That was exactly what Stevenson wanted," Clara began.

Miss Jamieson suddenly put up her hand.

"Yes?"

"I interrupted his plan, didn't I?" she said. "I saved Violet's life."

"You did," Clara smiled at her. "If you had not been sent with script changes to Violet's room that evening, she would have perished, the unwitting victim of a poisoning, which was exactly what Stevenson desired."

"You talk yourself into circles," Stevenson snorted, amused at her statement. "If I wanted Violet's money, a suicide was of no use to me. Why stage one?"

"Because you were not staging a suicide," Clara met his eyes. "You were staging a murder that looked like a suicide, to throw people off the scent of you as a suspect, and to secure your fortune."

Stevenson roared with laughter at her statement.

"Please, let Mrs O'Harris finish," Mr Hershel protested.

"Fine, fine," Stevenson rocked with his own laughter. "This is truly entertaining."

Clara waited a moment to make sure he had his full attention on her and then she began.

"Violet's demise was now becoming a priority with your previous failed attempts. Violet was clever and she realised what had happened to her already were not simply accidents. She became afraid, and that meant she was becoming more cautious. She was also constantly telling people she was the victim of someone who wished her harm. All you needed was one of those people to take her seriously and you would have a problem.

"How to get rid of Violet in a way that did not cast suspicion on you, when she was being increasingly careful about her habits and where she went? She was always surrounded by people, and Mario was taking an increased interest in her wellbeing. No doubt he was regularly checking the car before he drove it, to ensure nothing else was tampered with, which put a motoring accident out of the question.

"Running out of options for killing Violet on set, you chose to act in a place where she felt safest, her own suite. I do not know what you used, but you doctored one of her sleeping powders with a substance that would have poisoned her. The plan was to wait until morning when Violet would be dead. She would not appear downstairs for filming, and you would have gone to her room to fetch her. On arrival, you would have found her dead.

"Next, you would have summoned help, probably calling for Mario or Clarence and making a sufficient fuss for an ambulance, that the entire hotel would have been alerted to what had occurred. Now, here is where things become clever.

"Violet's death would have required a post-mortem to explain what had caused her sudden demise. You were banking on that, because when the post-mortem was done it would reveal a poison in her system that would not have come from the sleeping powders, and the police would have realised there was foul play involved. This was perfect for you, as it tied in with the previous attempts on her life.

"The police would run around trying to find the killer, but without success. You would do exactly as you did with me and protest that without Violet your career was at an end, and it was terrible she was gone. No one would have given it a thought, not without seeing the new contract and realising just how much you actually benefited from her demise.

"With luck on your side, the investigation would come to an end without finding the actual killer. With Violet murdered, her life insurance would have remained valid, and you could have quietly claimed it at a suitable time in the future, when no one was paying you any close attention. Thus, you would have accomplished your goal.

"However, when Miss Jamieson arrived early and spoiled your plans you had to think fast. Violet was likely to survive with her timely intervention and she might come to realise that the only person who could have tampered with her sleeping powders and made her so unwell was you. In any effort to cover your tracks, and to make sure no one believed Violet when she claimed she had been poisoned, you staged the scene to look like she had overdosed. You scattered the sleeping powder package on her bedside cabinet and, sadly, it did not take a lot of persuasion to convince people to ignore her protests when she denied trying to take her own life.

"Even Violet could not comprehend what had happened, which meant you were still in a position to kill her when the next opportunity presented itself."

"Gosh, you have such a vivid imagination. Mr Manx ought to hire you to write a film for him," Stevenson chortled. "The trouble is, Mrs O'Harris, none of this can be proved. You are throwing out ideas, waiting to see if one sticks. Do you expect me to confess to any of this? I think not, the best you can achieve is proving that I faked that contract, *if* it is a fake. Because I shall claim it is the genuine article, and nothing will shake me from that."

The room became silent as his words hung in the air.

"Is he correct?" Mario asked Clara, not taking his eyes off Stevenson. "Can you prove any of this?"

"I can't," Clara admitted. "But that brings us to more recent events, and I think I can prove that Stevenson was the one who planted the gun in the prop box and went out of his way to try to get MacKenzie to shoot Violet."

"What?" MacKenzie spluttered in the background.

"This should be good," Stevenson chuckled, enjoying himself. "Go ahead, Mrs O'Harris."

Clara took a deep breath and began.

"The gun that was found in the prop box on the day of the rehearsal was not from the prop department. All their guns were accounted for. Someone added the gun to the prop box with the intention of seeing it used as a murder weapon. Now, Miss Jamieson brought that box over from the green the evening before, didn't you Miss Jamieson?"

Miss Jamieson became flustered at finding herself at the centre of attention suddenly.

"I did, but I had nothing to do with the gun. I barely looked in the box."

"You left it sitting in your car until the time of the rehearsal?"

"Yes," Miss Jamieson looked worried. "Was that wrong?"

"Perfectly harmless," Clara replied. "The car was locked at all times, unfortunately, which meant the gun could not have been planted while it was inside the car. The box was then brought into this very ballroom by Miss Jamieson in time for the rehearsal."

Miss Jamieson glanced around the room.

"I knew nothing about a gun, I swear."

"No one is blaming you, Miss Jamieson, "Mr Hershel took her hand and patted it in a consoling fashion.

"I am sorry to have upset you," Clara added. "I am merely painting the scene, Miss Jamieson, I do not believe you had anything to do with the gun incident aside from being an innocent player in the sorry saga.

"When the box arrived in the ballroom, carried by Miss Jamieson, it did not contain a gun. It was full of the regular props that had been ordered for the rehearsal. Could you tell me where you placed it, Miss Jamieson?"

Miss Jamieson moved hesitantly forward and pointed to one of the tables at the side of the room.

"Nowhere near any of the doors, or a window, meaning the gun could not have been tossed in from someone passing by. It had to have been brought into the room by someone who was attending the rehearsal, and that limits our suspects," Clara continued. "More to the point, it was Mr Stevenson who found the gun. I wonder how often Stevenson rummages through the rehearsal props' box? Seems an unlikely thing for him to do. The props were there for the actors, and if anyone was to lay them out, it would be an assistant like Miss Jamieson."

"Yes, normally I lay out all the props on the table," Miss Jamieson concurred. "But Mr Stevenson walked into the ballroom that morning and went straight to the box."

"I can explain that easily," Stevenson said, raising an eyebrow in amusement at Clara. "Violet had stipulated to me that she never wanted to do a scene with Mr MacKenzie where he touched her. In fact, she would refuse to do a movie with him if such a thing were required."

"How absurd!" MacKenzie snapped, becoming belligerent at this statement.

Stevenson ignored him.

"I had looked at the script, and there were limited stage directions, but one stated there was a struggle between the pair in this particular scene. Now, originally it was intended for MacKenzie to grab Violet, which would go against the stipulation I had in her contract. As per my promise to her, I went and looked through the prop box to come up with a fresh idea as to how the scene could play out, without requiring MacKenzie to touch her. That is all."

"That makes no sense," Mr Hershel interjected. "Why go looking in the prop box for ideas? You had no reason to suppose there was anything in there that could be used to change the way the scene played out."

"I was looking for inspiration," Stevenson replied to him angrily. "The gun proved to be inspiration."

"The gun you placed in the box when you pretended to rummage through it. The gun that you told MacKenzie to point at Violet and shoot, telling him he need not hold back as it could not hurt anyone."

"He did say that!" MacKenzie startled as he heard what Clara was saying. "He wanted me to point at Violet and pull the trigger as part of the scene. He said it would seem more dramatic than the original staging, which called for me to catch her by the throat and throttle her."

"In that scene, Violet was meant to appear to die. That was how the script was arranged," Manx now spoke. "That was going to be the twist. It looked like she was killed, but a few scenes later she would reappear, alive and well."

"None of this is proof I did anything," Stevenson glowered at them all. "I am pretty sick and tired…"

"We have been trying to trace the origins of the gun," Inspector Park-Coombs said calmly.

His quiet voice and plain statement caused everyone to pause. For the first time, Stevenson looked unsure of himself, but he recovered quickly.

"You can trace guns?" he said, nonchalantly.

"Yes, sometimes. You see, manufacturers put these little numbers on a gun so you can trace it to a particular shipment and when it was made and sold," Park-Coombs responded. "I have contacts in the military, who assisted me with tracing the history of this particular weapon. It was sold as part of a shipment of pistols to an army colonel just before the war, who subsequently issued these guns to men in his regiment. This was at a time in the war when troops were not always as well-equipped with weaponry as their regimental commanders would like. Taking a look at the regimental records for that period, my contacts were able to confirm that a gun from the shipment with this serial number, was issued to a private by the name of H. Stevenson in 1916. He was discharged from the army a short time later, due to chronic dysentery that had led to kidney problems. He never returned his gun, as he should have done. I am pretty confident that private was you, Mr Stevenson."

"So, you are now claiming I am a thief too?"

"If I was to chase down every man who brought his service pistol back from the front, I would have no time for anything else," Park-Coombs snorted. "But it does mean I can trace that gun and make a case for it being in your hands all this time."

Stevenson started to open his mouth to protest, but the words failed to come out.

"You were getting desperate," Clara said to him quietly. "And that made you reckless. You never thought someone would take an interest in the gun. You assumed they would believe it had come from the props department and had been accidentally loaded with actual ammunition. There were holes in this plan, big gaping holes, but you were prepared to take a chance because time was running out. Violet's old contract was about to expire, and she would come to you and tell you she was leaving. You would then have to show her the forged contract. As I said before, you could not predict how Violet would react, and you feared she would immediately inform the studio, or a rival agency that hoped to represent her, about the forged contract and then you would find yourself in legal trouble.

"You had no choice but to act rashly, and you were so close to succeeding, if only Violet had not improvised in that rehearsal and grabbed at the gun to point it at MacKenzie. We shall never know why she acted that way, but presumably she was caught up in the moment, and when she pulled the trigger, everyone discovered the gun was loaded."

"If I knew the gun was loaded, why didn't I stop her from shooting her co-star," Stevenson countered.

"Because that would have revealed your plan. Besides, everything happened so fast, you probably didn't have time. Once MacKenzie was down, you had to simply act as if you were as shocked as everyone else."

"Preposterous," Stevenson yelled, but his voice no longer sounded so sure.

"Now everything was falling apart," Clara went on. "Violet fled the hotel, and you were at the end of your tether. But you were arrested, so we know you could not have pushed her under that train. You must have had an accomplice who was willing to assist you for a cut of the insurance payout. I assume it was either Mario or Clarence."

"Hang on!" Clarence snapped. "You cannot accuse us of anything."

"Someone pushed Violet under that train," Clara continued. "I know it was not a suicide attempt. I have been to the station and spoken to witnesses. The whole way it occurred, it had to have been that someone pushed her."

"Hold on, Clara," Park-Coombs glanced at her. "There is something you should know."

Stevenson noticed the temporary distraction of the inspector and took advantage. He suddenly ran towards the double doors of the ballroom, and the two constables were slow to intervene. He made it to the double doors and flung them back, ready to make his getaway, when he came to a sharp and unexpected halt.

Everyone stared at the doorway in astonishment at what they now saw. Clara's surprise turned to annoyance, which she directed at the inspector.

"That was what I was about to tell you," Park-Coombs shrugged at her. "You see, Violet Starling isn't actually dead."

Violet Starling was standing in the doorway of the ballroom, a smile on her face as she looked at Stevenson. He could merely gape in astonishment, too amazed to do anything. The police constables grabbed his arms and pulled them behind his back.

"You weren't expecting me, were you," Violet smirked at him.

"She used my plot twist," Manx said, the words stuttering from his lips. "It worked so beautifully. I never saw it coming. She used my plot twist!"

"Violet!" Stevenson snarled at her. "Can't you ever stay dead?"

"I guess not," Violet stepped into the room. "Now, I think it is time I took up the story."

Chapter Twenty-Eight

"On the day of the shooting, I was so upset I raced out of this hotel intending to disappear and never come back. I wanted to be free of all the terror that was haunting me. I was living my life as if at any moment I would be murdered, and it was hideous. But as I ran down the road, something changed inside me. I didn't want to just give up and allow the person who was doing this to me to succeed. In that moment, I decided to head to the police station and explain everything to them.

"I am sorry, Clara, that I did not trust you to resolve all this for me. I suppose I should have gone to you, but when I realised Stevenson would not allow anyone to be near me who was not hired by him, I saw that you would not be able to truly assist me. I had to have help from someone who could overrule Stevenson.

"I was most fortunate that Inspector Park-Coombs was prepared to listen to my entire story and took me seriously. He had just returned from having arrested Stevenson and so he knew the sort of man he was. I had been asked to wait for him in his office, so I never saw the arrival of my manager, and he never saw me.

"When I told the inspector I had gone to you, Clara, and you believed me, he was convinced I was telling the truth, and agreed we had to do something. In a matter of moments, we had come up with the idea of me staging my own death on the train tracks, to allow me some peace, and to be free of the death threats while you could continue to investigate the matter."

Clara frowned, her gaze going from Violet to Park-Coombs.

"Why did you not tell me all this?"

"That is my responsibility," Park-Coombs replied. "I advised Violet that we should say nothing to you. I felt you would work better if you believed she was dead. We needed the situation to be utterly convincing so that the killer would not come looking for Violet and keeping the truth from you seemed a logical solution."

Clara did not know what to say. She felt hurt as well as embarrassed that she had not realised Violet had staged her train accident.

"I should have guessed," Clara said. "Violet had returned to her hotel suite at some point and collected all her personal items, including the sleeping powders."

"I had someone sent over to collect those things when we were searching Violet's room for 'clues' as to her death," Park-Coombs confessed. "I even had involved in the scheme, so that he could confirm when Violet fell on the train tracks that she was dead."

"He was the doctor who happened to be in the station waiting room at the time Violet perished," Clara said, feeling a fool for not seeing the truth. "How dare you not tell me!"

"I would apologise Clara, but I honestly felt it was for the best and I would do the same again in a heartbeat," Park-Coombs replied to her. "It gave you such a good opportunity to dig into this affair and look what you came up with! All I had was that gun and no idea why

Stevenson would wish to hurt Miss Starling."

"Even I did not know why he would try such a thing," Violet added. "I could not fathom why the man who I entrusted my safety to would act in such a way. I knew nothing about the new contract, which I state unequivocally is a fake."

Stevenson winced at her statement. His arrogance had faltered at the sight of her and, knowing the game was up, his bravado flagged.

"You fitted all the pieces together Clara, without that, we would never have realised how convoluted and cunning a scheme this was," Park-Coombs tried to appease Clara.

Clara was not in a forgiving mood. She folded her arms across her chest and scowled at the floor.

"Take Mr Stevenson away on charges of attempted murder and fraud," Park-Coombs said to the constables.

Violet walked further into the room, straight past her former manager who still managed to scowl at her. Violet was not intimidated this time. She had her freedom, and she had people who could truly protect her. Stevenson no longer scared her, and she smiled at him as he was led away.

Mr Manx hurried forward before anyone else could intercept Violet.

"It is a miracle! The movie is saved!"

Violet chuckled as he clasped at her. Suddenly, everyone was descending on her, embracing her and saying how glad they were to see her alive. Clara stepped back from the scene; after a moment, she quietly left the ballroom. Tommy followed her and they left the hotel in silence.

Clara's pride had been hurt, and she was angry with herself as much as she was angry with Park-Coombs. The inspector's failure to trust her, implied that she must have done something in their history together, to make him suppose she could not be relied upon and that stung.

She did not want to congratulate Violet on her successful performance or tell her how relieved she was she was alive.

She had shed tears over that woman! She had beaten herself up with guilt she had failed her, and all this time Violet had been alive!

Clara was so furious she did not dare to speak for fear of the words that might spill out of her mouth. All she wanted to do was head home and forget all about Violet and the inspector's betrayal.

She did not say a word to Tommy as she hastened to the car. He was sensible enough not to speak to her in return. They both felt used, and it was a very disagreeable feeling.

"I think you are taking it too much to heart," Annie said as she poured them out a cup of tea.

They had all returned to Tommy's house to collect their thoughts and consider what had happened. Jones had been reluctantly persuaded to abandon the car and come indoors for a cup of tea. As usual, he was silent as he was served; if he had an opinion on the sudden reappearance of Violet, he was not about to voice it.

"The inspector demonstrated that we could not be trusted," Clara said sulkily.

"He did what was necessary," Annie replied. "He wanted you to behave as if Violet was dead and, therefore, it was easiest to keep you out of their plan to fake her death."

"We should have guessed," Tommy spoke. He was more upset that neither of them had realised that Violet could be alive, than that the inspector had misled them. "The train accident was all wrong to fit in with your theory, Clara. Stevenson needed Violet's death to appear either as if it were an accident or someone had harmed her, not suicide. But the train incident was always labelled as a suicide."

"And it was the one incident that Stevenson could not have been present for," Clara groaned, feeling despondent that she had not noticed sooner the incongruities of that last incident. "It was all wrong when we looked at the pattern, but I was prepared to assume he had an accomplice rather than suppose Violet could be somehow involved in that final act." There was a knock on the door as they sat around moping. Annie looked at them to see if either were going to move, when they did not, she got to her feet to answer the door.

"Try to cheer up," she told them as she departed. "At least that poor woman is not dead."

"Hardly consolation for being so fooled," Clara said sharply, then immediately regretted her words and looked abashed. "That sounded different when I was thinking it."

"I know what you are saying, it is not about being callous, it is just that we feel awfully stupid," Tommy sighed. "How did we not see this?"

"You were not intended to see it," Inspector Park-Coombs appeared at the kitchen doorway. "I thought you might have hung around to see the outcome of your case."

"We saw Stevenson being arrested, what more was there?" Clara scowled at him.

"You really are going to hold this against me? Hardly fair, Clara, there have been plenty of occasions when you have carefully avoided revealing certain truths to me."

"That is different," Clara protested. "I never actively lied to you."

"A fair point," Park-Coombs rubbed at his moustache. "I suppose there is little I can say that will help you to understand why I felt it was necessary. I believed that Violet's life was in peril, but to draw out the killer we needed to convince everyone she had already died. It was a risk, no doubt, and perhaps not my best plan, but I rather fancied that if you thought the killer had achieved their ends, you would redouble your efforts to identify them, and in that regard, I was absolutely correct. You excelled yourself, Clara, you did more than I could have done because you were unfettered by the protocols I have to abide by. I am truly proud of you."

"Flattery will not earn my forgiveness," Clara grumbled, though she was mellowing at his words. "I just cannot believe you did not trust me to tell me what you were up to."

"It was a simple matter of the fewer people who knew the truth the better," Park-Coombs shrugged. "In hindsight, that was perhaps rather unfair on you."

Clara sighed to herself.

"What charges will Stevenson face?" she asked.

"Attempted murder will be the main one, we have the evidence you have kindly supplied, though it is more circumstantial than I would have liked. We have the forging of the contract as a back-up if we can't nail him for trying to kill Violet. That being said, I do not think Violet has anything to fear from the man now he has been caught. He will never work in showbusiness again. This whole scandal has seen to that."

"Violet is finally free of him," Tommy allowed a smile onto his lips. "She can sign with another management agency and hopefully progress her career in a way that suits her."

"Most importantly, she is no longer looking over her shoulder for fear someone is going to hurt her," Park-Coombs added. "Violet wanted to come here and explain the matter to you herself, but Mr Manx rather took hold of her and said they had to get back to filming after the delays they had suffered. She asked if I could deliver this invitation to you both."

Park-Coombs held out a handwritten note. Tommy was nearest him and took it from his hand.

"What does it say?" Clara asked quietly.

"Violet would like us to attend the filming session tomorrow. She wants to apologise for misleading us and hopes having front row seats to her performance will go some way to make up for what she did."

Tommy's eyes had lit up, and though he was cautious not to allow his excitement to enter his voice, Clara knew her brother all too well.

"Of course we shall attend," Clara smiled at him. "It is not Violet I am really angry with, after all."

Clara's glance went to Park-Coombs.

"Will you ever forgive me?" the inspector asked, though he did not sound terribly concerned if she didn't.

"I suppose I must," Clara told him. "But do not ever do something like that again."

Park-Coombs nodded his head at her with a slight smile.

"I assure you I will not. Well, I must get off, I have an irate theatrical agent to interview, and a long report to write out."

The inspector gave them another nod and doffed his hat as he departed again.

"Being present on a movie set!" Tommy said in elation as soon as they heard the front door shutting.

"You are no doubt more excited than I am," Clara frowned. "I fancy it will be a lot of waiting around."

She glanced at Jones who was sitting solemnly as always and proving impossible to read. Sometimes Clara wondered if he had been like that before the war, or if his time serving with Captain O'Harris had changed him, and led to this man who could almost act like a statue at times.

"Jones, would you like to come along? You were as much a part of this investigation as we were."

"I merely drove you places," Jones said, showing a rare touch of surprise at her question.

"Without you driving us places, we should have never achieved what we did, and had we needed someone to back us up against Stevenson, you would most certainly have done so. I therefore think it only fair you should accompany us to the film set, if you wish to, of course." Tommy nudged the driver.

"What do you say, old man?"

Jones still looked amazed at what they were saying but a smile slowly crept onto his face.

"I would like that very much."

The following day, they arrived at the film set looking forward to seeing how the 'magic' occurred behind the scenes. At the last minute, Clara had extended an invitation to Oliver as well, feeling that his role in assisting Tommy deserved some compensation too, especially as he was the unfortunate victim of an assault with a cosh in the process.

Oliver's interest in movies was focused on the camera equipment itself and no sooner had they arrived at the set (which was in one of the larger country houses on the outskirts of Brighton) he had drifted away to ask about the various lenses, film reels and other technical elements of the process.

Clara and Tommy found a quiet spot at the back of the room to watch the proceedings. Tommy was chattering fast about what would occur, using the limited knowledge he had scrimped from various film magazines the night before. Clara only had half an ear on what he was saying. She was waiting for Violet to arrive.

It was almost ten when the starlet appeared through a side door. She glanced around the room, clearly looking for someone, when she saw Clara and Tommy she stopped and smiled.

"Oh, you came! I am so glad!"

She walked towards them and embraced Clara, kissing her cheek, before extending a hand to Tommy to shake.

"I was worried I had deeply upset you when you left yesterday."

"You did rather upset us," Clara was never one to sugarcoat the truth. "But we are over it. The important thing is that you are alive and well."

"I really do feel so alive Clara!" Violet said in elation. "After all that happened, I thought I had fallen out of love with acting, but I was wrong, it was just the stress and pressure I was under. With Stevenson out of my life and I can now feel free to enjoy my acting again."

"For that I am truly grateful," Clara hugged her again. "You deserve to have a beautiful life Violet, one you can enjoy every moment of."

"Thank you," Violet sighed.

From behind them Manx was calling for his actress. She excused herself and went to greet him. Clara and Tommy settled down to watch the scene.

"I bought a copy of the *Brighton Gazette* before we left this morning," Tommy whispered to his sister as the set grew quiet around them.

"I saw you had the paper, is there anything in it about what happened?"

"Gilbert has gone to town this time. Written an extensive piece and made sure everyone knows he was the star of the show by finding that fake contract. He makes it sound as though he solved the case single handedly."

"You sound surprised by that," Clara smirked. "Gilbert is hopelessly self-absorbed, but I really do not care for publicity, so he can have this one."

"Oh, he mentions us a couple of times. Just in passing, as if we were bit players in the whole affair."

Clara was amused.

"Gilbert never changes, not even after he nearly gets his head taken off by Stevenson."

"Irrepressible is our Gilbert," Tommy agreed.

Someone called out for quiet on the set and everyone obeyed. The corner Clara and Tommy were sitting in seemed to get darker as the big stage lights were powered up and trained on Violet and Joshua MacKenzie. The world seemed to shrink as everyone focused all their attention on the two people ahead of them about to enact a scene from the movie.

Clara found a smile creeping onto her lips as she watched Violet begin to act. She could not be angry with the woman, nor could she really be angry with Park-Coombs, who had only done what he had thought best and – when she considered it – she would have probably done something similar if the circumstances had been reversed.

She settled back into her seat and watched on, only feeling a momentary pang of unease when a prop gun was produced. Thankfully, this one was unloaded.

Clara could not say she was a fan of this movie business, but she could appreciate its appeal, and she was very glad she had saved the nation's favourite starlet from an unhappy fate.

As Clara watched the performance unfold, she started to find herself enjoying the process and feeling relieved that a frightened woman had been brave enough to seek her out for help on that cold morning, just a few days ago.

Enjoyed this Book?

You can make a difference

As an independent writer reviews of my books are hugely important to help my work reach a wider audience. If you haven't already, I would love it if you could take five minutes to review this book on .
the platform you purchased it from.
Thank you very much!

The Clara Fitzgerald Series

Have you read them all?

Memories of the Dead
The first mystery
Flight of Fancy
The second mystery
Murder in Mink
The third mystery
Carnival of Criminals
The fourth mystery
Mistletoe and Murder
The fifth mystery
The Poison Pen
The sixth mystery
Grave Suspicions of Murder
The seventh mystery

The Woman Died Thrice
The eighth mystery
Murder and Mascara
The ninth mystery
The Green Jade Dragon
The tenth mystery
The Monster at the Window
The eleventh mystery
Murder on the Mary Jane
The twelfth mystery
The Missing Wife
The thirteenth mystery
The Traitor's Bones
The fourteenth mystery
The Fossil Murder
The fifteenth mystery
Mr Lynch's Prophecy
The sixteenth mystery
Death at the Pantomime
The seventeenth mystery
The Cowboy's Crime
The eighteenth mystery
The Trouble with Tortoises
The nineteenth mystery
The Valentine Murder
The twentieth mystery
A Body Out of Time
The twenty-first mystery
The Dog Show Affair
The twenty-second mystery

The Unlucky Wedding Guest
The twenty-third mystery
Worse Things Happen at Sea
The twenty-fourth mystery
A Diet of Death
The twenty-fifth mystery
Brilliant Chang Returns
The twenty-sixth mystery
Storm in a Teacup
The twenty-seventh mystery
The Dog Theft Mystery
The twenty-eighth mystery
The Day the Zeppelin Came
The twenty-ninth mystery
The Mystery of Mallory
The thirtieth mystery
Death at the Sun Club
The thirty-first mystery
The Disappearance of Emily Potter
The thirty-second mystery
Bright Young Dead Things
The thirty-third mystery
The Price of Honour
The thirty-fourth mystery
Murder on the Silver Screen
The thirty-fifth mystery

The Gentleman Detective

Also by Evelyn James

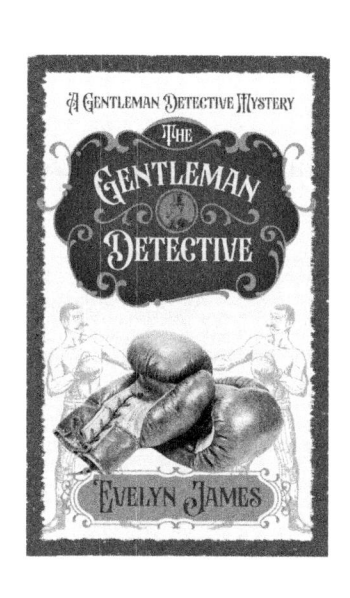

The Gentleman Detective

Norwich 1898.

Colonel Bainbridge is wondering if it is time to hang up his magnifying glass when a pugilist dies unexpectedly, and an innocent man is accused of his murder.

Distracted by trying to save a friend from the noose, Bainbridge finds himself investigating the murky world of street fighting and match fixing.

Can he determine who really killed the boxer Simon One-Foot or will a innocent man end up swinging for a crime he could not have committed?

The Gentleman Detective is the first novel in a brand new series from the creator of the Clara Fitzgerald Mysteries, Evelyn James.

Start your investigation with Colonel Bainbridge today!

Available on Amazon

About the Author

Evelyn James (aka Sophie Jackson) began her writing career in 2003 working in traditional publishing before embracing the world of ebooks and self-publishing. She has written over 80 books, available on a variety of platforms, both fiction and non-fiction.

You can find out more about Sophie's various titles at her website
www.sophie-jackson.com
or connect through social media on Facebook
www.facebook.com/SophieJacksonAuthor
and if you fancy sending an email do so at
sophiejackson.author@gmail.com

Copyright © 2025 by Evelyn James

No form of generative AI was used in the creation of this work

All rights reserved.

The moral right of Evelyn James to be identified as the author of this work has been asserted by her in accordance with the Copyright, Designs and Patents Act 1988.

All the characters in this book are fictitious, and any resemblance to actual persons living or dead is purely coincidental.

No part of this publication may be reproduced, stored in a retrieval system or transmitted in any form or by any means, without the prior permission in writing of the publisher, nor to be otherwise circulated in any form of binding or cover other than that in which it is published without a similar condition, including this condition, being imposed on the subsequent purchaser.

No part of this book may be used or reproduced in any manner for the purpose of training artificial intelligence technologies or systems.
Evelyn James is a pen name for Sophie Jackson.

To contact about licensing or permission rights email sophiejackson.author@gmail.com

Image Credit: Garashchuk (licensed through Shutterstock)

Printed in Great Britain
by Amazon